# STELLA GIBBONS

Stella Gibbons was born in London in 1902. She went to the North London Collegiate School and studied journalism at University College, London. She then spent ten years working for various newspapers, including the *Evening Standard*. Stella Gibbons is the author of twenty-seven novels, three volumes of short stories, and four volumes of poetry. Her first publication was a book of poems, *The Mountain Beast* (1930), and her first novel *Cold Comfort Farm* (1932) won the Femina Vie Heureuse Prize for 1933. Among her works are *Christmas at Cold Comfort Farm* (1940), *Westwood* (1946), *Conference at Cold Comfort Farm* (1959) and *Starlight* (1967). She was elected a Fellow of the Royal Society of Literature in 1950. In 1933 she married the actor and singer Allan Webb. They had one daughter.

Stella Gibbons died in 1989.

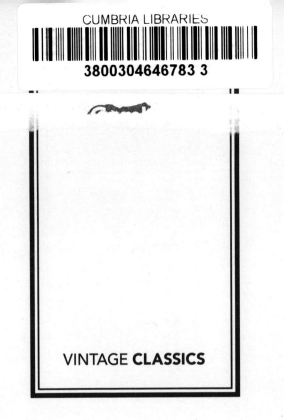

VINTAGE **CLASSICS**

STELLA GIBBONS

# Pure Juliet

VINTAGE

1 3 5 7 9 10 8 6 4 2

Vintage
20 Vauxhall Bridge Road,
London SW1V 2SA

Vintage Classics is part of the Penguin Random House group of
companies whose addresses can be found at
global.penguinrandomhouse.com

Penguin
Random House
UK

First published in Great Britain by Vintage Classics in 2016

www.vintage-books.co.uk

A CIP catalogue record for this book is
available from the British Library

ISBN 9781784870270

Typeset in India by Thomson Digital Pvt Ltd, Noida, Delhi

Printed and bound by Clays Ltd, St Ives plc

Penguin Random House is committed to a sustainable future for our
business, our readers and our planet. This book is made from Forest
Stewardship Council® certified paper.

MIX
Paper from
responsible sources
FSC® C018179

For Rosemary Steiner

'Yet once in a while the miracle seems to occur; an effect of great splendour is produced without visible cause. There will be a sort of immaculate conception, and a mind of great power and originality will develop, where heredity and environment would lead one least to expect it, engendering in itself, apparently without any fertilizing contact, a violent impulse towards some science, some art, which it pursues with unaccountable love.'

Margaret Lane, in an essay on
'The Boyhood of Fabre'

*'La demarche scientifique . . . est une patiente recherche, une minutieuse comparaison d'un petit nombre de facteurs, dont le savant essaie les rapports profonds, cachés sons des apparences superficielles.'*
Pierre Gaxotte, de l'Académie française

'Theory is grey, but green-gold is the tree of life.'
Johann Wolfgang von Goethe

# BOOK ONE

# 1

'I'll be *more* than glad to see the back of *that* one.'

Miss Roberts jerked her head towards a solitary figure moving swiftly across the otherwise deserted playground of Hawley Road Comprehensive School.

'Why 'specially her? She's extra bright, and doesn't muck about in class. I hardly notice her.'

'She gives me the creeps.'

'God knows there are enough things here to give anyone the creeps. Thank Him we shan't be seeing any of them for six weeks. Come on.'

Mrs Arrowby flung a bright scarf about her neck, shook back a shock of ragged hair, snatched up a case heavy with books, and stood impatiently while Miss Roberts hauled up her jeans and adjusted her linen jacket. The women teachers' cloakroom was empty now but for these two.

'Get your skates on, Mary. I can't wait to get out of this place,' Mrs Arrowby said.

It was the end of July, but not the end of summer. Roofs and houses baked in the late, blazing light that filled the horizon and, beyond the silent expanse of playground, home-going traffic was beginning to roar.

'She gone?'

Miss Roberts opened the cloakroom door a little wider and took a longish look. 'Of course she's gone. You are jittery, aren't you? Halfway home by now . . . Where does she live, by the way?'

'Oh somewhere on one of those new estates between here and the Archway – I don't remember . . . We're off, Peters, bye-bye until September,' she called to the school caretaker, who was approaching with keys swinging from a finger.

'Bye-bye. Enjoy your hols. And if you can't be good, be careful.'

'Saucy old . . .' The sentence was lost in a wave to the man as the two young women left the building and began to cross the playground.

They spoke no more. The exhaustion of the school year fell upon them, together with the unnatural silence that had invaded the shabby building with the departure of the twelve hundred adolescents who, every day, had tramped through its corridors, sending their ugly fresh voices ringing about its great rooms. The shadows of one or two plane trees, their trunks deeply scarred with initials in spite of the wire fences surrounding them, drifted over the two women as they passed beneath.

'Well, you won't have to get the creeps over Slater next term,' said Mrs Arrowby, as they reached the gates.

'She hasn't left!'

'She has, though,' Mrs Arrowby nodded. 'No university entrance exams for her.'

'What – after all those bloody A levels?' Miss Roberts marched on. 'I thought she'd be a cert.'

'No. We did write to the father, of course, pointing out how bright she is and so on – blah blah blah. And the Head got a letter back, quite well written and spelled, I heard, just saying Julie was going out to work like any other girl and no thank you.'

'What did *she* say?'

'I never asked her. Come on, we'll miss our train.'

They began to walk fast, and their footsteps died away under larger trees, covered in the swart green of late summer, until they were lost in the crowds of the high street.

The person described as giving Miss Roberts the creeps proceeded at a swift pace ahead of the two teachers. She was noticeable for this unusual quickness of movement; for her hair, which was so fair as to look silver in certain lights; and for the expression in her eyes, small and so full of light that their colour was hard to name. These eyes remained fixed steadily ahead of her, looking unseeingly down the long, ugly, crammed street, with an inward gaze. Her sallow face was expressionless. She was thinking. A forehead too high and her lack of colour, added to a breast almost as flat as a boy's, made her unattractive. But it was another quality, difficult to define, that had given Miss Roberts the creeps.

She was carelessly dressed in that global uniform of the young, a shabby T-shirt and denim jeans; and she carried a case full of books. A cigarette stuck out between her thin lips, and as she smoked one down, she paused to light another.

Presently she turned aside, and left the crowded high street, following quieter and ever more ruinous roads in process of demolition, until she reached a block of new council flats. The lowest storey was sunk below pavement level behind a tiny garden and a wall some six feet high – a sign of the times (vandals might hesitate to jump down into a place whence a sudden leap back was not possible).

Juliet Slater glanced down at the garden as she passed: grass was clipped and smooth; beds were weeded and bearing the dahlias, Japanese chrysanthemums and late geraniums as if autumn had come early. Ivy and passionflower twined up a plastic trellis beside shut French windows curtained in snowy nylon.

A look of interest came into her eyes as she glanced down into the little wells of greenery. She turned, and went up a railed ramp leading to the front doors at the back of the row, secured at night by massive locked gates.

She rang the bell of the fifth door, and soft chimes sounded inside.

In a moment, slow footsteps were audible.

'Hullo, Julie,' said the woman who stood there, drowsily. 'Didn't expect you yet. I was having a kip. I knew there'd be a bit of a party, seeing it's the last day . . .'

'There was. I came away, couldn't stick it.'

She pushed past her mother. Mrs Slater put out a hand uncertainly, then withdrew it as Juliet went down the narrow passage, glancing as she went into a brightly coloured living-room, where a budgerigar perched on top of an armchair screamed and fluttered.

'He wants his drink, bless him.' Mrs Slater was slowly following. 'I'll just get it . . . D'you want your tea, love? I've got some pork luncheon – too hot for cooking.'

'I don't mind, Mum. If it's ready.'

Juliet's voice came from her own room, a slip of a place furnished with a narrow, gaily covered bed, a wardrobe and chest of drawers painted pale blue and, in front of the window, a bare, square table that looked too large for the room. Juliet set down her case of books, called an impatient answer to a distant question from her mother, then glanced at the alarm clock ticking on the chest of drawers. It was just five o'clock.

She drew in a breath, not deep, not agitated, yet as if some inner pressure had forced it to come, then stealthily moved across the room and noiselessly locked the door.

'Mum?' she called.

A pause, then the heavy footsteps. 'Oh Julie – you're locked in. You are a funny girl, I wanted a bit of a chat – alone all day – what is it?'

'I need more fags.'

'Can't I come in?'

'I'm changin' me clothes.'

Their voices sounded flat in the bright, comfortable little place, Mrs Slater's soft and slurred, Juliet's thin and high.

'Shan't be a tick. You have the tea ready.'

She had pulled a suitcase from under the bed, and was rapidly putting into it the clothes she took from the chest of drawers; when the case was full and shut, she noiselessly unlocked the door. She could hear the sounds made by her mother moving about the kitchen, and water running, and plates being clashed, and a humming of 'I Could Have Danced All Night'.

Rapidly, she opened the case of books and took out some volumes dealing with physics, mathematics and other scientific disciplines, and all bearing the label of Hawley Road Comprehensive School. She crammed them into a plastic carrier.

She set suitcase and bag down beside the door.

'Ready, Julie.'

'Righto.'

Her mother, coming slowly into the living-room some moments later carrying the teapot, found her standing by the cage stroking the bird's blue and yellow back with a touch as light as one of the glowing feathers, while it perched on her finger.

'Bertie,' she was saying, in a lowered tone, 'Bertie-boy.'

'Get him his drink, will you, Julie? And you might fill up his seed bin, too; my feet are awful today, it's this heat.' She sank into one of the armchairs, and began opening a packet of cigarettes. 'You don't want to go round to Mawser's just as your tea's ready, you have one of these.' She held out the packet.

'You know I like my own . . . I'll get his drink . . . and then I won't be five minutes.'

She went out with the two little containers and came back with both freshly filled, and arranged them carefully in the cage to which the bird had retreated.

'Bye-bye, Julie, bye-bye,' came a tiny elf's voice from the cage.

'Oh . . .' Juliet paused at the door. 'Bye-bye, Bertie-boy. Now you be good.'

'Bye-bye, Julie. Bertie love Julie. Bye-bye.'

Mrs Slater's lids were drooping.

Juliet almost ran down the passage, snatched up case and bag, and a second later her mother saw her pass the living-room; saw, too, with humble pleasure, that she wore a cap Mrs Slater had knitted for her. In the dusk of the little narrow passage, the suitcase and bag, which Juliet carried on her far side, were not visible.

The front door shut sharply. Mrs Slater sighed, inhaled smoke, and settled herself more comfortably. Perhaps Julie would tell her something about the school party over tea. Not that she ever talked much, Julie. Mrs Slater's thoughts began to play discontentedly about her daughter, named after Julie Andrews in *My Fair Lady*, in memory of that one, never-forgotten evening out with Dad a few days before their wedding. She had so hoped that their daughter would grow up to look like the star.

Clever she *was*, an unusually clever child, them at all her schools had said – and what use was that, her and her cleverness? Didn't care how she looked, except for brushing her hair, nice hair, Julie had, though not much of a looker, as George said right out. And them at the school wanting her to put up for the university! Did they think George was a millionaire? There he *had* put his foot down: she'd leave at seventeen and find a job like everybody else, bright or not. As for boys, they might be elephants, thought Mrs Slater resentfully, for all the notice Julie took of them or they of her.

Come to that, if they *had* been elephants, Julie might have noticed them; Julie liked animals, as much as she liked anything, and this *boys and elephants* was an old joke between herself and her mother, and the only one.

Oh, she was a funny girl. Sometimes she made you feel she wasn't all there – nor you there with her neither, come to that.

Mrs Slater lit another cigarette.

'Bertie,' she said softly, looking towards the bird where he sat preening himself and chirruping in the fading light, 'who's Mum's boy, then? Bertie-bird . . .'

## 2

Juliet walked the length of Ava Street, then turned onto a highway crammed with traffic. From here, the road went steadily upwards.

Having paused to buy two packets of cigarettes at a small stationer's, she scrambled on to a bus, and alighted at a cross-roads just beyond the summit of the great hill, where most of the traffic passed on its way under a notice saying TO THE NORTH, and another road, less wide and busy, led away under its own legend: TO ST ALBERICS, HERTFORD, STAVENHAM.

Here, on a corner where the cars set out on their longer journey, she took her stand. The last of the light caught her hair; she was, for once, conspicuous, and it was an advantage.

It was not yet dark. The sun's falling rays were hidden behind little, old low houses, but every hint of grey, of dun, of brown was brushed with their softness; the massive trees along the verges drooped in dusty near-blackness above the moving ruby lights of the cars.

Juliet studied her prey carefully. Not a lorry: that meant dangers about which she knew, but never thought. Not elderly men driving alone, who looked too angry, exhausted and

11

intent to bother with her. Here came something that would do – a middle-aged couple looking mildly worried and driving carefully.

Out went Juliet's arm, as the woman's eye strayed to her glittering hair. There was the briefest of consultations between the pair, and the car slowed down.

'Goin' anywhere near St Alberics?' she called shrilly, putting out the third cigarette since her vigil began.

'Passing through it,' the man called back, with an unexpectedly kind smile. 'Only hurry up – this is a bad place to stop.'

Juliet darted across the few feet of road and settled herself and her case and bag along the back seat. She slammed the door.

'Here, young lady, steady on.'

'Sorry – I'm not used to cars.'

The woman turned, and smiled. So young! And that lovely hair. Had she a family? Was she running away? Oh, the perils of this world for the young, the beloved, the rebellious young.

'And what's your name and where are you off to?' the driver asked in a tone more of the politeness of the road than of curiosity.

'Sandra Smith, and I'm goin' to stay with my auntie. Lives just outside St Alberics.'

'Well, I hope you have this lovely weather for your holiday. Break up today, did you? I noticed the children coming out as we passed through London,' the woman said. When did she not notice children? Everywhere, and always.

'Left,' said Juliet; almost snapped the word.

'Oh – I expect you're sorry to leave school and all your friends. I know I was.'

Juliet nearly answered: Haven't got any friends, but her instinct for secrecy intervened, and she satisfied her questioner with a 'Yes', as regretful-sounding as she could make it. And the second expected, and undesired, question, *And what are you going to do now?* did not follow.

The woman smiled again, and turned to watch the rapidly darkening landscape going by.

There was no more conversation. They had entered a motorway; their pace had increased, and there began to be a dream-like quality about their flight beside other dark shapes, following scores of ruby will-o'-the-wisps. In the orange glare of the lamps the general ugliness was not veiled, but emphasized.

Juliet noticed nothing; she was thinking.

They turned aside at length, down a narrowing road where a softer light shone on a sign and its arrow: ST ALBERICS. STAVENHAM.

Another half hour, and the car stopped in the brightly lit high street of a country town whose shops were small imitations of those in Oxford Street. Here and there, the three-hundred-year-old face of a cottage showed its forlorn and gentle beauty to the chemical glow of the lamps.

The driver turned, smiling, and said, 'All right for you? Where does your aunt live?'

'Oh, not far, 'bout five minutes' walk.' Juliet was gathering up case and carrier.

'Because, if it's not far, we could—'

'Yes, do be careful, my dear,' from the woman.

'I'll be all right; there's plenty of people about.' Juliet was out and on the pavement. Indeed at that moment, a bus-load, scattering in different directions, alighted at a coach station where other passengers were waiting. The scene was neither lonely nor desolate.

'Cheerio.'

The pair smiled and waved; the car moved off, grew smaller, turned a corner, and was gone.

Juliet had already left behind the shop windows, where fashion models postured, and was walking quickly onwards.

She turned aside at the far end of the high street, down a narrow road without shops and with only occasional dim lamps on old-fashioned iron standards. It was lined on either side by ancient cottages. One had a turquoise-blue door; some others had additions to make them acceptably contemporary, but Ragnall Street was unmistakably in a small country town: narrow, ill-lit, silent, and filled with air scented by leaves and grass in hidden fields.

Juliet's pace quickened. A man on a bicycle passed, calling 'Goodnight!' A woman hurried by with a heavy shopping bag and entered a cottage that had a light glowing behind its flowery curtains; children's voices greeted her as she opened the front door. The sky, lucid blue and as yet starless, was gradually becoming the most noticeable part of the scene. The sky, and the silence.

The last cottage was left behind, its garden glimmering with white dahlias. Fields stretched away, behind low hedges of thorn, into the twilight; the great elms typical of Hertfordshire were just distinguishable as darker masses against the darkening blue.

Juliet was crossing a stone bridge, humped and ancient, with hidden water running quietly beneath, when a car came past, too quickly, headlights glaring; she pressed herself against the stone parapet just in time. Then the sky and the silence, as the brutal noise died away, resumed their power, and she turned down a lane, with a signpost that said, she knew, TO LEETE. And suddenly a high brick wall was beside her, some fifteen feet tall, ending in iron gates intricately wrought in a design of grapes and vine leaves and, in the centre, a group of initials.

She stopped and pressed a bell set at the side door inserted in the brickwork.

Then she put down her luggage, seated herself on the grass verge, and prepared to wait.

## 3

It was dark, but a grain moon was rising, huge and warm-tinted above the elms. Through a thin place in the thorn hedge she could see swathes of mist covering the meadows. There were far-off sounds, and the sudden sweeps of distant headlights in the darkness, but all around her was stillness and silence. She glanced impatiently at the door.

Now there were voices, approaching and raised in argument, though she could not make out what they were saying.

The door jerked open suddenly, and she stood up. A light came on above the gates, revealing a figure known to her, in the familiar black dress which was too short and showed stout legs in pale stockings. A cross old face, a pompadour of white curls.

Behind this person hovered the brown, smiling face of a man above a white jacket.

'So it's you, is it. Trust you to get here when dinner's over—'

'Hullo, Sarah.' Juliet began to pick up her baggage. But the man darted forward.

'I take for you.' And she let him have them, even giving him a brief smile.

'Mrs Bason, to you,' said Sarah, in a voice meant to be dignified but betrayed by age at the conclusion of her sentence into a squeak.

'Mrs Bason – sorry.'

'How do you look when you're glad? Come on, hurry up, she's been all on edge ever since your letter come.'

The old woman turned, grumbling under her breath, the man shut the door behind them, and they went along a wide, curving path leading up to a large house with lit windows.

'When did it come?' Juliet asked, knowing that Sarah was less irritable if a flow of unnecessary detailed talk was kept going.

'This morning. Posted day before yesterday, wasn't it? These posts, they get worse and worse. If I'd thought when I was your age I'd live to see the day when it took forty-eight hours for a letter to get from London to Leete, and seven pence to pay at that, and herrings at ten shillings the pound—'

'Yes, awful,' Juliet muttered.

As they approached the house, whose door stood open revealing a dimly lit hall, a group of faces could be seen peering out into the dusk, and gabbling in Spanish became audible. There was waving of hands, to which Juliet responded slackly, and the group, consisting of a young man and three girls, moved forward to meet her.

But Sarah, assuming an authoritative manner, said sharply, 'That'll do now, off you go,' and they disappeared, without haste and smiling over their shoulders, in the direction of a door covered in green baize at the end of the hall.

The older man shut the front door.

Sarah turned to Juliet.

'She's in the drawing-room. Best go in. She's bound to ask if you want something – I'll see about it. Always on the go, I am. On a blessed tray, I s'pose.'

'That'll do nicely,' Juliet quoted, showing teeth white and small between her pallid lips: it was not a smile of sweetness.

Juliet crossed towards a door on the left. It was of dark wood, like the panelled walls. The hall had a pseudo-antique appearance; its many old portraits lacked distinction, and the long oriental carpets had the hard colours of modern work rather than the silky dimness of the real thing.

Sarah had disappeared.

Juliet gently opened the door, there was a pause, then a soft old voice exclaimed: 'Why, it's my girl! Darling! I was getting so worried!' and Juliet went forward into the room.

A long face, irresistibly suggesting that of a sheep, below silver hair, smiled at her from a wheelchair drawn up to an electric fire. The room was stiflingly hot, in spite of the summer heat outside; the occupant of the chair's skeletal arms were bared to the elbow by a long dress of blue silk.

Juliet went up to her, sank to her knees beside the chair and, putting her arms round the thin old body, lifted her face passively to receive kiss after lingering kiss, while she shut her senses against the odour of verbena toilet water and eighty-year-old flesh.

'You're really here! I can't believe it, let me look at you – that lovely, lovely hair – how long is it since you were here, my darling?'

'Easter, Auntie.'

'I couldn't believe it when I got your letter – how can your mother bear to part with you?'

Juliet sat back on her heels.

'Five of us, Auntie, and no dad. 'T'isn't easy for her.'

'Yes. Yes. Oh that was a day blessed by God, when I saw the sun shining on your hair . . .' She leant forward, with difficulty, to lift a tress in her knotted fingers. 'My girl! Here at last. My lovely, lovely . . . *daughter*.'

The last word came out reverently, as if she spoke of something sacred.

'What have I done,' she went on, quaveringly, 'that God should be so good to me?'

She paused to wipe her eyes, while Juliet, moving no closer, made vague sounds that might have been intended for comfort.

'Ah, here's Sarah – and Rosa with your supper, dear – we can't call it dinner, it's only something light, but you must be hungry. I told Sarah to save some chicken, the nicest part. Now you eat it up, my darling, while I watch you.'

Sarah, looking more than sour, prowled in silence finding small unnecessary things to do while the plump, pretty Rosa set down a tray on a low table, smiling shyly at Juliet. With the air of one being at home, Juliet got up and fetched a tuffet covered in rose-red brocade, and arranged it beside the wheelchair.

Chicken and salad, with fruit and a glass of orange juice, were set out appetizingly, and, settling herself on the tuffet, Juliet began to eat, while the sheep-face watched with an expression of the purest, foolish delight.

'Time for your bed, Miss Addy,' Sarah said. 'Close on nine.'

'I know that, Sarah, thank you,' the old lady said sharply. 'I'm staying up.'

'Upset yourself – you know what Dr Masters said.'

'It won't hurt for once. I'm so happy, and this is a special occasion.'

'Please yourself.'

Sarah was going out of the room when her employer said, in a different voice: 'Sarah!'

'Yes, Miss Addy?' turning sulkily.

'Ask Antonio to bring up a magnum of champagne – and eight glasses. We're going to celebrate.'

'Champagne! There's none chilled, and it'll kill you, this time of night.'

'In half an hour, Sarah, please. And tell the other servants they are to be my guests.'

Sarah stalked out. Her hands were at her sides, but her expression raised them in the position of those of the old steward in Hogarth's painting.

Juliet had not watched any of this tiny drama, nor noticed the deliberate use of the expression 'other servants'; she was eating.

In a moment the old lady said: 'And so you passed all your examinations, darling?'

Juliet, with her mouth full, nodded.

'A levels, they call them now, don't they? I'm sure my clever girl did well, didn't she? And was she nervous?'

'Course not.' Juliet gulped orange juice.

'Were you – top, would it be – in any of the subjects? What were they?'

The faded eyes, behind the spectacles of the strongest power available, fixed themselves greedily on the young face, as if passionate to draw from it information about a world, ideas,

habits, of which their owner was ignorant. Behind the glare
of curiosity there was a hint, too, of piteousness: *I am so old*,
said the look. *And helpless. And helpless, for all my five servants
and my faithful Sarah. Helpless.*

'Oh' – Juliet used her tongue to dislodge a fragment of
lettuce – 'mathematics, physics, chemistry – that kind of subject.
I got five As.'

'And did you expect to – is that exceptional, dear? Five As?
You must forgive your old auntie, she isn't "brainy", like you.
You know, at my school, the North London Collegiate, only
the cleverest girls studied science. That was more than sixty
years ago . . .'

Juliet pushed the tray aside and drew her knees up to her
chin and circled them with her arms, in her first gesture that
evening suggesting youthfulness. She wanted a cigarette, but
decided against asking; there would be a fuss, probably a
lecture.

'Five As is good,' she said. '*Very* good, they said at the school.'

'But didn't you find those scientific subjects very dry, dear?
And such hard work, all those figures . . . I never was any
good at arithmetic. I used to cry over my sums. Wasn't I a
silly-billy?'

'Course they aren't dry – they're ever so interesting. Easy,
too. Only . . .'

Juliet paused, and her gaze moved away from the eager old
face into some other world. Her own face became expressionless.

'Are you thinking about – him, darling?' the old lady said
softly, in a moment.

'Who?' The thoughts, whatever they had been, vanished
beneath Juliet's eyes, like some unknown species of fish

darting down into fathoms of icy water. 'Who do you mean – him?'

'Silly Auntie thought perhaps there might be some young man – some boy, don't they say nowadays? – that her girlie was . . . very fond of.'

'Chr—! Course not, Auntie. I don't like boys, they're always making a row. Me and Mum, we have a joke about that, see, 'cos she says I take as much notice of boys as if they was elephants, and I say, if they *was* elephants, I'd take a bit more notice.'

She smiled. Her little teeth flashed: the too-white teeth of the child fed on the wrong food.

The old lady was looking bewildered. 'Do you like elephants so much, then, dear?'

'Not all that. But better than what I do boys.'

'"Better than I *do* boys," Juliet. Not "what I do".' Her voice was gentle as ever, but authoritative.

'Better than I *do* boys.'

'You see, my darling' – lifting a tress of silver-gold hair – 'you're such a lovely girl . . . and I want my girlie to talk as prettily as she looks. You don't mind my telling you about these little faults?'

'Course not, Auntie.' Juliet was staring down at her shabby jogging shoes. They were dirty, and the side of one of them was split.

A procession entered, with Sarah, looking disapproving, at its head. She was followed by the white-coated servant, carrying a silver bucket from which peered the head of the magnum. A young man was negligently flourishing a grubby white cloth to wipe up spilt drops; he had found a red plastic carnation somewhere and stuck it in his buttonhole. Three pretty young women were carrying glasses.

Their employer clapped her hands feebly. Her face had suddenly gone pale from exhaustion, but seemed to be shining from inward joy.

The white-coated servant set down the bucket on the table, copying the demeanour of an English butler seen on television, and, beckoning imperiously to the girls, took two glasses (which needed polishing) and handed them cere-moniously, one to the old lady and one to Juliet. He gestured that a glass should be given to Sarah, who grimly waved it away.

The champagne was opened with a satisfactorily loud pop, and the cork flew off somewhere into one of the dim corners of the hall amid much ducking and many screeches. The wine, never lacking glamour for some ingenuous hearts, slid hissing into the shallow glasses. The servants, in response to beck-oning from the old lady, drew near to her wheelchair and stood in a circle about it. She reached out and took Juliet's hand in her own.

'Goodness, childie!' she exclaimed in a startled tone. 'How cold you are! Do you feel quite well?'

'Course, Auntie.'

'Well – so long as you feel all right.'

She looked straight at Sarah, who was standing with folded arms outside the circle.

'To Miss Juliet,' she said, raising her glass together with her weak, ancient voice, 'who's going to be my dear adopted daughter for a – a – whole . . . wonderful . . . year . . . to Miss Juliet.'

'To Miss Juliet!' came the cheerful echo in five young voices, sending for a moment a ripple of human gaiety through the large old house standing in its great gardens under the wide country sky.

Their glasses glowed like topaz in the lamplight. The eyes of the young man, dark under the perfect bow of his brows and shaded by heavy lashes, wandered speculatively, as he sipped, over Juliet's meagre body. *She was nearly seventeen, wasn't she? Well then, let her get what girls of seventeen must get. It would be difficult, of course. The more fun for that.*

'I'm so *tired.*' The old lady suddenly set down her glass. 'Sarah, take me up. Goodnight Antonio, Maria, Rosa, Pilar, Rosario. Goodnight, my girlie,' patting Juliet's arm. 'You'll come up and say nighty-night to old Auntie when she's in beddy-byes, won't you? Goodnight, then. Goodnight to you all.'

'There's a good half of that magnum left,' Sarah observed. 'More'n half, I'd say.'

'Oh never *mind*, Sarah – let them have it. I said it was a celebration.'

The senior servant – Antonio – who had been unobtrusively hastening the departure of his retinue in case this fact should be noted, turned at the door with a flashing smile as he heard the permission, then disappeared.

Only young Rosario had lingered, on pretext of looking for the champagne cork.

Juliet had seated herself on the tuffet which had been established as her own place since her first visit four years ago, and was lifting her almost untouched glass to her lips.

He circled about until he stood above her, looking down with his bold, usually successful, smile. 'You come and sit with us in our room, Juliet?' he said softly in the broken English that, in a man's voice, is irresistible to some women. 'When *she* in bed? We laugh and perhaps sing – you come?'

She did not look up at him, but uttered in a quiet but clear voice a phrase of the harshest vulgarity which told him to go away.

He stared down at the fair, lowered head with the eyes of a hurt dog. It was less the insult than the shock of hearing those words, which he had heard in the backstreets of Stevenham, from the lips of a creature who seemed to him, though not beautiful, of a stubborn virginity, and therefore the better worth conquering.

He turned away and followed his family out of the room.

Juliet, slowly sipping champagne, did not look towards the staircase, visible through the door which Rosario, in his wounded pride, had deliberately left open.

The wheelchair stood at the foot of the stairs, and a figure was crawling upwards, with one swollen hand grasping at the banister; the elegant, floating blue dress gave the final grotesqueness to the hardly human, bent shape. Sarah hovered above it; the sound of her grumbling, affectionate voice came to Juliet through the silence. She leant forward and turned out the fire.

She drank off the champagne and glanced at the ornate French clock, set with gilt symbolical figures of Peace and Plenty. Ten. She could count on four hours of reading before she felt the need for sleep.

The air had been overheated for too long for any cooling to be noticeable, but the heat was no longer coming at her in waves. There was not a sound in the long, coldly lit room, nor from the blue night outside where hung the great stars and planets of late summer, low, and stilly burning.

Gradually Juliet's face became as calm, as still, as those circlers in the depths, with the same look of remoteness. She sat as if charmed.

'Here, Miss Pennecuick wants you to go up.'

It was Sarah, standing over her, morose and pale.

Juliet did not move for some seconds. Slowly her eyelids lifted and she looked at the old retainer in silence, and smiled. It was well that Sarah thought a smile from Juliet, any smile, suitable in any circumstance, and did not observe its quality.

Juliet's mother knew the smile well; she had seen it when Julie came out of her bedroom at the request of well-meaning visitors. Mrs Slater had never allowed herself to think consciously about it, because it frightened her.

Sarah, mollified by a gossip and an affectionate goodnight from her mistress, was feeling penitent. She stooped with difficulty and switched the logs on again.

'Freezing in here . . . have a bit o' warmth. Up you go.'

Miss Pennecuick, piteous in nylon and lace, was sitting up in another stifling room.

'Ah, there you are, my pet. Come and sit by old Auntie.' She patted the coverlet of fine embroidered lawn, and Juliet obeyed.

There followed twenty minutes of explanation as to why Miss Pennecuick preferred to climb the stairs unseen by anyone but Sarah. 'When I was young like you, darling, Auntie was pretty. And then this old arthritis came along and took all my prettiness away . . . It hurts me, dear. Perhaps you'll understand, one day . . . that's why I don't want you to see me unless I'm nicely dressed, or all covered up as I am now. Wipe my eyes, love – as if you were my own dear daughter . . . hanky under the pillow, dear.'

Juliet, with a delicacy of touch learnt from using geometrical instruments, mopped Miss Pennecuick's tears as carefully as if her heart were full of love.

'Hadn't you better settle down, Auntie?'

'Yes, darling. I am rather tired, it's the excitement. Dr Masters said . . . Give me that little book, yes, the one with the red cover.' *Daily Light*, inset with a gilt cross, and worn with many years of use.

Juliet put it into the knotted, slow-moving hands.

'Find the date for me, dear. You see, it has texts from the Bible, all on the same theme, for every day in the year . . . so comforting. Juliet, do you ever think about God?' Again, that change to a quality like authority in the old voice. Then her head sank back. 'No . . . I'm too tired tonight,' feebly. 'We'll talk about it tomorrow. And another thing . . . make sure the servants say *Miss* Juliet. Goodnight, my lovely girl, my baby.'

The lightest pressure of her lips on the hot, old-smelling skin, a darting smile, and Juliet was away.

The bed in Juliet's room was spread with a white honey-comb quilt, the carpet and walls were respectively tan and beige; the chest of drawers matched the light oak frame of the bed, and was decorated by small carvings that served as handles.

Juliet switched on the bedside lamp under its shade of cream silk. At the window, she drew aside the heavy curtains drawn an hour ago by Pilar, then opened the casement and leant out.

Darkness made visible by the great moon, elms seeming to float as a deeper blackness against the colourless sky, sweet exhausted scents of dying flowers and leaves.

*Damn, no table,* she thought.

She drew in her head, shut the window, drew the curtains again, and began to unpack; the putting away of her few, Marks & Spencer clothes was soon finished. Then she sat down on the bed and looked about her.

There had not been an artist or a rebel in the Pennecuick family for a hundred and forty years, but that is a long time to be middle class and very rich, and their investments, derived from coal and later from the rents of valuable land, had inevitably, on one or two occasions, been spent on the products of fashion.

Here was one of them, hanging on the wall: at once mysterious and decorative, the shape of the Möbius ring had caught, first the eye of some artist, and then the eye of a Pennecuick with money to burn.

Juliet was familiar with the print; it was the first detail in the room that she had noticed on her original visit to Hightower some four years ago; and suddenly, as she studied the arcane shape, she experienced a sense of *safety*.

She was here: she had done it; she had escaped from noise and continual interruptions and her parents and the dirty fools at the comprehensive; she had left them all behind for a whole year.

The thought of dirt sent her springing up. She snatched thick towels from a heated rail, and almost ran along to a bathroom at the end of the passage. And soon she was lying relaxed under the water; her body congruous in its chaste modelling with the old-fashioned furnishings of the room, and her hair floating about her like the myriad lines of some geometric problem – not to be solved by an earthly brain, and belonging to a sphere other than this.

# 4

'Mum?'

'So it's you, is it? Where you been all night? Anyone else, I'd say you was off with some boy.'

'Well I wasn't – and if you was all that worried you could have phoned the Elephant House at the zoo.'

But the feeble old joke brought no response except: 'Where *are* you, Julie?'

'With the old lady – you know – Miss Pennecuick. I am staying off – for a year, anyway.'

'A year! I thought you was telling me you was getting a job?'

'I'm not getting a job. I'm staying here. She wants me – kind of an adopted daughter, like.'

'Well I'm sure I hope she'll find you a better daughter than what I've done . . . what you goin' to do with yourself all day? She got a car?'

'Read. Work things out, go on a bit further than me A levels. I don't know. S'pose so. She's rich.'

'You are a funny girl. You beat me, honestly you do . . . As for a job, me and your dad can manage without anythink from you, thank you. I can always go out and do a bit, if we run short, though he won't like it. Rich, is she? Nice for you. What'll she buy you? Books, I s'pose – clothes'd be wasted on you.'

'I dunno – bye, Mum. I'll phone you again next week, same time. Mrs B's number.'

'Julie – here, don't cut off—'

But the line had gone dead. In the little living-room of her neighbour, Mrs Barnett, where the telephone was, Mrs Slater slowly put back the receiver. Her slack, rosy face became doleful. Now there would be lies to think up to tell Mrs Barnett about the phone calls, and George creating when he woke up . . . there was always something. And no Julie coming in round four o'clock . . . better than nothing, when you hadn't spoken to a soul all day but the milkman or them in the shops. There was always something.

Juliet came out of the telephone box on Church Corner, Leete, which hardly deserved the name of village: a shop, a group of sturdy flint cottages, and an exquisite fourteenth-century church locked and falling into ruin. The telephone booth had been given a recent going-over by delinquents from St Alberics, and was hardly usable, and she hoped that it would soon be repaired; she did not want to use the telephone at Hightower. The servants might know more English than they admitted to, and she did not want them speculating about those four siblings and dead father.

She set off at her swift pace between hedges of thorn dense with green leaves, along the few miles to St Alberics. It was about three in the afternoon, and the lanes and surrounding meadows were silent in the summer hush. The road to tiny

Leete ended in its miniature green and a maze of pot-holed lanes leading to grazing land; few cars went exploring there. The occasional enthusiast who had heard of St Helena's drove down into the secret little place, only to be disappointed by the church's shut, ancient door, and shocked by black gaps in the windows once filled by dim blue and violet glass.

Juliet had had from Miss Pennecuick that morning, during two hours of fondling and chatter, an inspection of her split shoe; and the suggestion that she should go that afternoon into St Alberics (fumbling extraction of a five-pound note from a handsome leather handbag) and buy another pair: 'a prettier one, this time love, to please old Auntie'.

Juliet had not yet faced the question of how five pounds was to buy 'a prettier one', which would cost at least fifteen pounds; now she was looking, without interest, at the shops in St Alberics high street. She was walking with her usual fleet step, thinking about a problem which she had been studying at three o'clock that morning, when a man's voice, deep and musical, said somewhere above her head:

'Good afternoon, Juliet.'

She stopped, startled and angry. 'Who the hell are you?'

'I'm sorry, I didn't mean to frighten you—'

'Who's frightened? How j'oo know my name?'

'I've heard my great-aunt speak of you lots of times, and only one girl she knows could have that hair.' He looked at it admiringly. 'I'm on my way to see her now: shall we walk up together?'

'Who are you, anyway?' She did not move, but stood staring up at him.

*Oh God,* he thought, *eyes like a mermaid's or a fay's. Oh God.*

'Frank Pennecuick. Hasn't she ever spoken of me?'

'Yes – come to think of it,' Juliet admitted grudgingly. 'You been abroad.'

'Yes, all over South America, looking for grasses to eat' – expecting a laugh and some comment.

She uttered neither.

They had paused in the middle of the high street, which, although it was late afternoon, was crowded with inhabitants who appeared never to stop shopping. Frank and Juliet, motionless and apparently gossiping, were attracting irritated glances as people walked round them.

'Let's get on – we're holding up the consumers,' he said, and they fell into step. Juliet did not, after her first angry stare, glance at him again.

She had seen a face she thought of as 'kind of wet'; brown, above old brownish clothes, with a shabby rucksack on narrow shoulders. Brown, too, were the large eyes that had smiled down into her own. He was about thirty, and too thin for his height.

In a moment, she stopped. 'I got to get some shoes. She— Auntie give me a fiver.'

'Can't I come in and assist?'

'S'pose so – I can't get the sort she wants me to get for a fiver, anyway.'

She turned towards a shop where racks stood outside, laden with single shoes priced at between two and three pounds and made of canvas and plastic. She unhesitatingly picked one out, marched up to an assistant who was loudly laughing with a young man who was attempting to label boxes, and said: 'I'll have these. Three quid, aren't they?' She handed over the notes. 'Don't wrap 'em up, I'll wear 'em.'

She sat down and slipped off her own broken-soled pair, her head bent so that her hair showered down.

Regarding the hair as a personal affront, the girl assistant undulated to the till. 'Two-fifty,' without turning her head.

'These'll do – no, better have a smaller size. These slip about.'

The assistant, whose feet were large, banged about among the boxes until she knocked down a pile of them.

Frank Pennecuick, too, studied that hair. He had last week got back from a three-year stay abroad, trying to forget the pain of an excruciating love affair with just such another dryad (these were his type) with the same abundance of hair. But Ottolie's hair had been red. Also like silk, as thick, but pale red as the hair of some dragon's daughter. What had he done, that his aunt's protegée should turn out to be his type again? His fatal and fascinating, irresistible type?

And once more, he groaned in his heart, *Oh, God. All that to go through again?*

But he had observed the everyday miniature drama going on in the shop, and, desiring to get Juliet to himself as soon as possible, strode inside and said to the girl scrabbling irritably among the scattered boxes: 'I say – that's a bit of a disaster. Can I give you a hand?' in his most flirtatious tone, which gained much from the beauty of his voice.

'I'm looking for a Size 4,' said the assistant, instantly all sweetness.

'Here you are – no sooner sought than found.' Frank whisked up a box from the pile and held it out, smiling.

'Thanks ever so.' And she writhed away to Juliet, who was gazing, shoeless, out of the door.

In two minutes the smaller size was on (*Runs in her tights*, he noted. *That wasn't like any of the others*) and they were walking together down the high street.

'Is that the lot?'

'Pardon?'

'Any more shopping to do?'

'No, thank God.'

'Why? Don't you like it?' (*Oh, those 'walks' with Ottolie or Fiona or Deirdre, walks which had always ended, somehow, in the smartest shop in whatever town they were staying . . .*)

'Hate it.' Juliet was walking so fast that she was almost running.

'Good – so do I.'

They turned out of the high street into the quieter road leading to Leete.

He hesitated, then went on: 'I may be coming to live near here. At Wanby. It's about four miles from St Alberics. Do you know it?'

A shake of her head. She was walking through the pools of last night's rain, heedless of the new shoes. Her manner was not encouraging.

'I'm hoping Great-Aunt's doctor, Dr Masters, will sell me two meadows he owns there, with a couple of old sheds. It's as much "miles from anywhere" as a place can be in this terrible modern England' – a glance at her; no reaction – 'and if I get permission, I can make the kind of home there that I want.'

'You're lucky.'

'Why? Haven't you got the kind of home you want – with Great-Aunt?'

'Sooner be by myself,' she said.

With Frank's obsession with fays and water-sprites, went a passion for what was delicate and beautiful; in fact, obsession and passion fed upon one another, and it was not possible, it *really* was not possible, for him to experience the dawn of a satisfyingly painful love for a girl who showed no sign of interest in anything he said, splashed in new shoes through puddles, and looked – let him confront the fact – but for her hair, unhealthy and plain.

'You lived in London before you came to my great-aunt, didn't you?'

A nod.

'And there are five of you . . . you, and two sisters and two brothers?'

'Yes . . . s'pose Auntie told you. And me dad's dead.' Her eyes (*Bright with anger, surely?*) were turned full on him.

'In her letters, yes. She's very fond of you, Juliet, you're the daughter she's always wanted. And when I telephoned her this morning to say I was back in England and coming to stay with her—'

'You comin' to stay?' Unflattering dismay in the thin voice. (*Ah, the languorous note in the voice of Ottolie . . .*)

He laughed. 'Don't sound so horrified. I shan't be in much, I'll spend half my time over at Wanby, arranging things with Dr Masters and seeing the council . . . damn, I meant to buy a bicycle . . . Never mind, tomorrow will have to do. When I telephoned this morning, Great-Aunt told me that you had come to stay for a year. What—'

'Won't you get a car?' she interrupted.

*Ha, a crack in the armour! Disappointing.*

'No, I hate the filthy things, for what they're making of England. I wish every car in the world were at the bottom of the Pacific.'

'You can get away in them,' she said.

They had turned down the narrow, winding lane leading direct to Leete, where fields, of so dark a brown as to look purple, stretched away on either side behind hedges of withering thorn.

'Away from what?'

But he knew.

'People,' was the muttered answer.

'People! What's the matter with people?'

'Always on at you.'

'Not always. I—' He turned to her, swept by one of the impulses he usually came to regret. 'I – I won't be, Juliet, I promise you.'

'You won't get the chance,' she grinned, and set one foot firmly down in a puddle. 'Damn, now that's gone up me tights.'

This silenced Frank. The immodesty of his past loves had been sensuous, and carefully calculated to stimulate, in a satisfying way. But this – this suggested a fifteen-year-old boy on his way back from the rugger field. And the legs covered by the torn tights were thin and shapeless. Frank, to his surprise, found himself thinking: *Poor little beast.* The very way she splashed through the puddles was like a heedless boy.

Why? She had youth, lovely hair, apparently unshakeable self-confidence and a rich patroness. Why should he think of her as a poor little beast?

He decided to persevere.

'How did you meet Great-Aunt Addy? Something about squirrels, wasn't it?'

She gave him a cautious sideways look, and now he felt suspicion. Why should she look cautious? But, if she lied to him, he could always check with Great-Aunt. Unless she was lying to Aunt Addy as well. His suspicion increased. He was fond of his aunt, and would see to it that she was neither deceived nor hurt; the latter was the more important.

'Oh – four years ago, it was,' Juliet now said. 'She came up to this hospital near where I live, see, 'cos they got some machine there what's good for her illness, o'ny one in England, it is, and one of them at the hospital had her out for a breath of air in one of them wheelchairs – when she was a bit better, that was – and I was comin' home from school through the park. She was feeding the squirrels and I'd got a few nuts, so I stopped too. And we got natterin'. 'Bout the squirrels. That's how it was.'

It was the longest speech she had made for days.

He had no conception how long, nor what an effort it had been for Juliet, who had, very early in life, discovered that talking used up energy that could be more usefully employed; also, that silence was a weapon.

He said: 'What a coincidence.'

She whirled round on him, stopping full in her swift walk, fixed him with eyes that, for one startling second, seemed to be darting flashes, and snapped loudly: 'What?'

'What?' He stared, but before he could speak she said again, louder:

'What j'oo say? About coincidence?'

Frank was irritated; he was used to softness, teasing, mystery, and remote sweetness in the female friend.

'I meant that it was an extraordinary coincidence that there should be that *one* hospital in England with that machine, and she should go *there*, and that *you* should be coming home through just *that* park and you should meet . . . And here you are. The whole thing due to a series of coincidences. That's all I meant.'

Juliet's nose was raspberry pink, and what he could see of her legs were spattered with mud, and the sun had gone in, so that her hair looked dull. She stood, staring at him.

'Don't be cross, Juliet,' he said gently. 'I didn't mean to upset you.'

'Who's upset?' She began to walk on. 'Yes, it is a – coincidence. Funny. I . . . I been thinking how funny it is, these four years.' Her voice died away, and there was a long pause.

'And then – who wrote first?' he pursued at last.

'Auntie. She took a fancy to me, like, and asked for me address and we used to meet every day, after that, and she asked me would I send her a line how I was getting on. Goin' in for me O levels, I was.'

'And you'll be here for a year? Whose idea was that?'

'You naturally nosy or just nosy with me?'

It was the first hint of girlish sauciness that he had had from her, and he was oddly relieved. He laughed.

'Both, I think. Go on, tell me.'

'*She* wanted to adop' me. Course, Mum wants me to get a job and help the others get on, so she wasn't having that. A year, Mum says, I could come for.'

'And then?'

She shrugged. They had paused at the door in the wall surrounding Hightower.

'There's the others to think about.'

'Are they bright, too? How old are they?'

'Fifteen, John is – Sandra's twelve – I dunno, can't remember exactly, seems like there's ten of 'em sometimes, the row they make. I don't think about them, most of the time. They'll get on.' She pressed the bell savagely.

The door opened after the usual delay, and there, all apron and eyelashes, was Rosario.

'Good morning,' smiled Frank. 'Are you Antonio?'

'No, sir. Rosario. Madame tells us you are coming. Welcome, Mister Frank. Hullo, Juliet.'

'*She* says you're to say "Miss". She hears you, you'll get a strip torn off of you,' Juliet said over her shoulder.

'Why should I say "Mees" to you? Antonio say you come from the oppressed masses.'

# 5

It occurred to Juliet, as she sat, weeks later at the large table she had persuaded Miss Pennecuick to instal in her room, that Dad drove what she thought of as 'his train' every other day through St Alberics station.

But he doesn't know I'm only a couple of miles away, she thought with satisfaction, and drifted off into the meditation from which the far-off sound of a passing diesel had aroused her.

She had not feared that her father would inform the police about his missing daughter. How could you call anyone missing when they phoned their mum once a week? Also, such an action would have meant the interruption of his habits – those habits which he preferred over wife, daughter and home.

These habits consisted of his work: the alternation of days spent driving the train between St Pancras and Standish far up in the Midlands, with stops at every commuter station on the way; his silent fellowship with mates known for twenty years; the homeward journey, after his arrival at the London terminus, by the 214 bus to his own neighbourhood; a pause to pick up the late-night *Evening News* at Mawser's on the corner; the hour spent in the Duke of Gloucester over a couple of pints;

then the short trudge through the dimly lit streets; his key in the door – boots off – the greasy, ample tea, and the paper and television until bedtime.

When he was on the night shift the routine was even more compelling, because there was in it an element with which years of experience had not made quite familiar: darkness; faces less known than those seen by day; fewer people about; long periods, in fact, of complete solitude, especially on the walk back to his home. Pallid light flowed along the damp pavements. There lay the humped shape of his wife in the double bed; he growled a greeting as he got in beside her, and then there were hours of heavy sleep, through daylight and noises in the street outside.

Very strong in George Slater were self-will, grudgingness and obstinacy; but stronger than anything else was his feeling for this pattern that he relished with a hardly conscious enjoyment. He would put up with anything rather than 'put himself out'. His daughter knew this.

*As for Mum, if she had a cup of tea and Mrs Next Door to yak-yak with, she was not going to create, neither.* The telephone calls had already settled into routine questions about Julie's health, and warning repetitions about Dad not wanting to see her unless she got a job like everyone else.

For a year, she was safe.

She stared across into the yellowing elms at the end of the lawn, and the faintest glint of pleasure came into her eyes. Then her gaze passed over the solid oak surface of the table; there was more than enough room for books and yet more books, geometric instruments, pencils, everything. She liked this table better than any object in Hightower; its squareness and firmness and proportion satisfied some quality in her nature.

Every morning after breakfast, she ran up to her room and seated herself at it.

Miss Pennecuick was always at her most frail in the mornings, and ate her slight repast in bed, while Frank had usually been out on his own affairs for an hour when Juliet came into the dining-room. Sarah was usually hovering about; if Juliet had listened, she would have heard mutterings about Mr Frank killing himself eating that rubbishy hay stuff, enough to murder anyone. But she did not listen. She was not interested.

Once seated at her table, she forgot everything but the shapes and theories haunting her brain.

She leant back easily in a comfortable chair, sometimes with a book in her lap, sometimes with one open on the table. But always she remained motionless, her narrow breast hardly seeming to lift and fall, and her eyes fixed upon the pages she was studying.

The hours between breakfast and twelve passed like a quarter. They would have been tantalisingly short had she not already been at her table since five each morning, her face splashed with cold water to awaken her thoroughly from light sleep, her hair drawn up into a knot to keep it out of her eyes.

Those were mornings of a hazy light, silence and mist that, to another kind of imagination, would have seemed sad or lonely. Juliet did not notice the stillness until the first birds broke it with their thin greeting. Then she would lift her head, and listen, and a faint look of pleasure would come into eyes reddened by lack of sleep.

Frank was not often in to lunch, but when he was, he observed Juliet closely.

She gobbled. But he did not put this down to what he thought of as working-class habits, nor yet to appreciation of better food than she was accustomed to, nor to simple greed.

Juliet gobbled partly because she was not interested in eating, and partly because, like himself, she was eager to get out of the dark overheated house into the leafy way that led to Leete, and thence to even narrower footpaths and silent meadows.

He had spent his morning inspecting, measuring, talking, calculating, bargaining. How had she spent hers, in her room looking out over the great elms?

And what did she think about, while she 'fleeted' (*like swift Camilla*) over frosty ruts, her hair bundled under a badly knitted woollen cap (Frank was a severe critic of handicrafts; all his own skills of that kind were admirable) and her hands in the pockets of a tough, elegant cape chosen and bought for her by Great-Aunt Addy? Its sandy hue, Juliet's own choice, was unfortunate with her colouring (*Ah, the misty aquamarine and lilac tints favoured by Ottolie – and, for that matter, by Deirdre and Fiona . . .*)

What did she think about? Nothing, he was dismally certain, that a mermaid or a fairy might.

No: of Juliet the song for the Edwardian musical comedy *Our Miss Gibbs* was true – '*Mary is a girl and not a fairy*' – and he was beginning to feel that she was not even a girl.

He could not cease, in spite of the many activities crowding his days, from studying her.

'Dearie, must you eat so fast? Auntie doesn't like to see her girlie gobbling away like a little piggy-wiggy. It isn't pretty.'

\*

Rosario threatened to become a nuisance.

Juliet had known Antonio, eldest of the five servants, since her first visit there some four years ago, and had seen the gradual infiltration into the household of his younger siblings: Maria, Pilar, Rosa and, finally, Rosario.

Quick-witted, content under the benevolent rule of their mistress, tactful with the privileged Sarah, and fully appreciating the shops, excursions, cinemas, discos and pick-ups to be had in nearby St Alberics, none of the family wanted to leave their English place. Antonio's diplomatic skills were much admired, and they took his advice – as the eldest, the knowing one, who had whisked them out of a poor, dirty, hungry life in a small Spanish town, into all this.

All five had a childlike enjoyment in mere living: they groaned, they wept. An hour of sunlight produced a mental state of playing the guitar with a rose over one ear.

Their English equivalents would have been bored by the isolation, and contemptuous of St Alberics imitation of London pleasures, envious of Sarah, and spitefully inquisitive about Juliet. The Spaniards laughed over every small frustration, and Antonio added to the gaiety by encouraging the bringing into the house of bottles of wine by sheepish admirers of either sex, occasionally administering a rebuke should spirits be introduced.

Their widowed mother cheerfully and boastfully wasted the generous share of their wages sent to her every week back in Spain.

But Rosario . . . *He is not quite broken in, that one,* thought his elder brother, having seen him give a light pull, in passing, at Juliet's hair. *That is a very peculiar girl. Her voice is of the backstreets, it isn't like the Senora's. Her clothes are torn. She cares nothing for boys, only for books. It is not natural. Rosario must leave her alone, because the Senora dotes upon her. We do not want troubles.*

He administered a short lecture to his brother. 'We are very well placed here. Good money, no hard work, plenty of free time, a little town near with girls and wine shops. Why, we live like Onassis—'

'I like to pull her hair. She hates me – me! You know how all the girls were crazy for me at home.'

'So you say, and I know you've been very successful, little one. But this is different. She is not pretty—'

'Holy Maria, no! No bosom at all. I have more, myself.'

'Then leave her alone. The next time I catch you pulling her hair, I hit you really hard.'

Rosario looked sulky and said nothing.

But it was not Antonio who hit him really hard.

Juliet was sitting on her tuffet one day, just before the lunch hour, and Rosario, gliding around the table adding finishing touches, squatted down when he came up to her, stooped his dark curls so that they almost brushed her cheek, and whispered, 'Silver hair. I pull it really hard – *feel*, Juliet!'

And he pulled.

She did not look up, but struck out so violently, with a shoving movement, that he lost his balance on the highly polished floor, and fell flat on his back, uttering a roar of rage.

At this moment the door was slowly opened by Sarah, and Miss Pennecuick crept in. Both paused, exclaiming and aghast.

'Rosario! What's the matter? Are you hurt, my poor boy?' Much rubbing of the curls was going on. 'Juliet, what happened?'

Juliet smiled, and said, 'Morning, Auntie.'

'Come on, now, get up, you aren't dead,' Sarah said roughly, as he continued to lie there and shout in Spanish.

'Did he slip on the floor?'

'What on earth's going on?' demanded Frank, coming in at that minute.

'Rosario fell down—'

'There's nothing the matter with him—'

'Here, let's see if any bones are broken—'

But even as Frank advanced upon him, Rosario scrambled up, bowed fiercely to the elder ladies, and marched out, shutting the door with a slam that shook the room.

Frank raised his eyebrows.

Juliet got up to kiss Miss Pennecuick's cheek; then sat down again.

'Now you come out of that book, Miss, show a bit of sympathy for once – poor young fellow, that floor's hard, as my knees know to their cost. You be in to lunch, Mr Frank?'

'Yes please, Sarah.'

'It's a nice bit of roast lamb – but I expect you've brought your own grass and stuff?'

'No, I could manage a nice bit of roast lamb, for once' – cheerfully.

He sat in an armchair opposite to Juliet, noticing that red burned in her cheeks, though she was apparently interested only in her book.

'Well, Aunt Addy, I've got some good news—'

'Oh have you, dear boy? Well done – let's hear it. Juliet,' gently, 'it isn't nice to read when other people are talking – put your book away, dear.'

'Sorry, Auntie.' The book obediently dropped at the side of the tuffet; the red deepened, as Juliet fixed her gaze on Miss Pennecuick's face.

'Yes, I really think everything's arranged at last. I'm going to get the necessary papers signed next Monday.'

'Then you'll be in by Christmas. How delightful. We must have a party – and talking of parties, Clemence and Dolly are coming for the weekend.'

At this point the luncheon gong sounded, and they went in.

'I already see lots of Clem in Wanby,' Frank said, as he drew his great-aunt's chair for her, and she laughed and pinched his cheek.

Here Sarah, who was sourly handing vegetables, said loudly, 'Dr Masters ought to see that boy, Miss Addy. He's got a bump on the back of his head the size of an egg. Some people ought to be ashamed of themselves,' fixing Juliet with a glare.

Juliet, gobbling, did not look up.

'Well, Sarah, I did ask you to tell Pilar not to polish the floors so highly.'

'You like the floors well polished, Miss Addy, and besides it wasn't the floor. She pushed him.'

'Pilar? His own sister?'

'No, Miss Addy. Her,' indicating Juliet with a jerk of the head.

'Did you, Juliet dear? Surely not – what happened? Tell old Auntie – she promises not to be cross with her girlie.'

'I expect he pulled her hair,' Frank said. 'I've seen him at it more than once.'

'Did he, Juliet?'

A nod.

'And did you push him?'

'Yes. As hard as I could.' She gulped some water.

'Well . . .' Miss Pennecuick said helplessly, while Sarah's voice cut in: 'Comes of wearing it all over the place, instead of done up decent. What does she expect?'

'It served him damn well right,' Frank said calmly, 'and if he does it again, you do it again, Juliet. That will do, Sarah, thank you,' with a smile.

Sarah crept out of the room.

'I – I really don't know what to say . . .' Miss Pennecuick leant back feebly, pushing away her plate. 'Sarah can be so tiresome – she's faithfulness itself, of course, and she's been with me so long, nearly fifty years, but it makes it so difficult sometimes, she gets jealous, I don't know how it is, *you* can always manage things—'

'I'm a man,' and he laughed.

Juliet continued to eat.

'I'm so pleased and relieved, dear boy, that you're coming to live at Wanby. Now if only you would settle down with that sweet girl—'

'What sweet girl, Aunt?'

'Now you know perfectly well who I mean—'

'I assure you I haven't the faintest idea . . . are you ready for pud?' and he rang the bell.

It was true; he had not the faintest idea. For he did not think of his great friend, Clemence Massey, as a sweet girl.

Once or twice during the consumption of the pud, Juliet looked at Frank with a long stare. He had stood up for her. Not as that old fool of an auntie would have, but sensibly. If someone at the Comp hit you or pulled your hair, you hit or pulled back. Only common sense, that was, only natural.

For the first time since their meeting in St Alberics high street, she thought about Frank Pennecuick. Bolting pudding, because she had forgotten Auntie's gentle reproof, she let him invade her mind.

An unfamiliar feeling came upon her when she looked at his long brown face. She wondered if she could talk to him about that part of her mind which was suffering confusion. For what she was beginning to feel towards him, without knowing its nature, was trust.

At the Comp, the mathematics master had been permanently irritable and exhausted, and the one thing that he had always made starkly plain was the fact that no individual could have more than three minutes, preferably two, of his time.

Juliet wanted an hour, perhaps half a day; she did not know how long because she did not know exactly what she wanted to talk about. It was something to do with maths . . . and why certain things happened . . . and if there was an answer . . .

She had a vague, yet strong, idea that 'coincidence' was the word that expressed her fascination, interest, whatever it was.

But what, exactly, was coincidence?

She knew about reference books; she had been, one Saturday afternoon, to the public library and, having asked the girl assistant for a 'dictionary', and being asked what kind, had answered that she did not know.

'Well, what do you want to look up, dear?'

'Some word . . . coincidence.'

The assistant was tactful as well as kind. She went herself to fetch the *Pocket Oxford*, and gave it to this dwarfish enquirer with a smile.

How eagerly Juliet had turned the pages! She did not know what revelation she was expecting – perhaps some other long words which would explain the lure, the fascination that, for her, surrounded this particular word and its associations. She read: 'Coincide: fill the same portion of space or time; occur simultaneously.' Her eyes hurried on, that wasn't exactly what . . . ah . . . 'Coincidence: notable concurrence of events suggestive of but not having causal connection.'

She could not quite . . . quite . . . the words were so long, and most of them she had never heard of.

Then the page before her eyes drifted away, and there came upon her a double inner sensation: as of immense size and microscopic smallness; both together; not feelings; not pictures, though images of stars were in the hugeness; the experience was unlike anything she had ever felt in her life . . . or was it?

A memory floated up from somewhere within herself. She had had this sensation before. She could feel the damp warmth of her cot blankets enclosing her baby body . . .

'Find what you wanted, dear?'

She looked up into the young assistant's smiling face.

'Yes. Wasn't sure how to spell it.' And she was off.

*Funny her eyes looked*, the girl thought, looking doubtfully after her.

The experience of double-size – as Juliet came to think of it – haunted her from that day, although she reluctantly came to believe that there would never be any explanation of it in the mathematical terms which she had at first expected. She must just 'take it for granted', as she put it.

But that other sentence – *why* should there be no 'causal connection'? (She went to another library to look up those two words, not relishing the elder-sisterly attentions of the young assistant.)

Why?

And she began to turn the question over in her mind, to approach it mathematically, because mathematics was the only subject in which any difficulties she encountered were worked through, or leapt over, by her brain – without effort, and with enjoyment.

*Examples is what's needed*, she thought; *lots of them, like they give you in the textbooks*. And, from the age of fourteen, she had begun to collect coincidences, laboriously writing them down in a notebook in her squared, state-educated hand, numbering each carefully, and adding after each one the comment 'Pure' or 'Only half' ('Pure' in the sense of absolute coincidence: one in which *apparently* no 'causal connection' could be found.)

And gradually, as the noisy, dull months went by, lit only by this interest within her mind, she came to what she called to herself *me ambition – to find some reason that explains why these things happen seemingly without cause.*

To work on this ambition she needed solitude and time: uninterrupted, endless time. That was why she had run away to Hightower. 'It's quieter there,' she would say to herself, in the weeks before she walked out of her home on that last day of the summer term. 'I'll get a bit of peace there, p'raps.'

It was not quite as peaceful and quiet as she had hoped. *Auntie was for ever on at you. But Frank, he let you alone. All right, he was.* And he had stuck up for her against that Rosario. She might talk to Frank, perhaps; about coincidence. Not about her ambition: that was a secret.

But she did not get away on her walk at once, because there was that business of having coffee in the drawing-room, as usual.

'How is that poor boy's head?' Miss Pennecuick enquired of Maria, whose task it was to bring in the tray.

'He suffers much,' was the simple and disconcerting reply, as cups and jugs were deftly arranged.

'Oh dear! You don't think . . . perhaps . . . the doctor?'

'It is in his feelings he suffers.' On a more sombre note: 'He is a loving boy, Rosario, our mother say he is.'

'Yes, thank you, Maria. Coffee looks good, as usual,' said Frank, and he sent her away smiling.

'Dear boy! Are you going to join us?' Miss Pennecuick paused, holding a frail red and gold cup in one shaking hand.

'Good heavens, no, Aunt dear. Absolute poison. Like me to do that?' And her cup was whisked away and half full of the poison before she could wipe off two tears of gratitude and love.

'Aren't you having something else, dear?'

'I'll wait until tea. I've got a new herb brew I'd like you to sample,' smiling.

'No wonder you're too thin. Clemence may be here by tea-time – I'll get her to lecture you.'

'Clem knows it wouldn't have any effect, so she never tries.'

'It would have an effect if you were married.'

But the mutter was not heard by Frank, who had turned to Juliet.

'Going for a walk? Mind if I come?'

She hesitated.

'I won't talk,' he added, and the unfamiliar feeling of trust came upon her once more.

'All right. I'll get me things,' and she rushed out of the room. 'Frank?'

'What, Aunt?' turning, as Sarah wheeled in the chair.

'You – you aren't . . . ?'

Sarah began to bustle with cushions, listening intently.

Miss Pennecuick indicated her, and made helpless gestures. 'Getting – fond,' she mouthed at him.

'Not a bit. I give you my solemn word.'

He stood straight before her, looking, for once, grave and without the playful expression that usually made his face attractive. And as he said the words, he felt, with a little surprise, how true they were. Not one glimmer of romantic feeling had he for Juliet Slater.

# 6

When Frank went through the hall with Juliet he saw Rosa and Pilar, singing softly as they polished and dusted. Telling himself that he was rejoicing aesthetically in the sight of rounded bosoms and smooth skins, he said, 'Surely those girls don't work all day?'

'Fit it in when they like, seems. That old Sarah, she does try to make a kind of timetable, but Auntie don't mind, so they do as they please.'

'Doesn't mind, dear.'

She just glanced at him; no coquettishness, no consciousness. '"Doesn't mind"', obediently.

'Do you mind my correcting your grammar . . . and . . . calling you "dear"?'

She looked up at him and smiled, not her usual dutiful grin. Then she shook her head, and he opened the front door and they went out into the quiet golden afternoon.

'That house is too dark and hot,' he said.

'I know. I'm always gaspin' for a bit of air.'

'But it isn't depressing. The girls wouldn't sing, if it were. That's Aunt Addie, of course; she's full of love and kindness, and it gets through the house.'

'Bit too full of it, if you ask me. Gets you down.'

'Aren't you fond of her, Juliet? She loves you so much and she's been very kind to you.'

'S'pose so.'

Withdrawal, and the usual shrug.

But this afternoon he was not going to be put off by Juliet's reserve; he meant to find out *what she was*. When they got back to Hightower, Clem and that old monster, her mother, would be there, and there would be fewer opportunities.

'You don't like people, do you?' he asked.

'They're always on at you,' sullenly.

'That's partly because you're young. They're always on at me, too, in a different way, because my views on life aren't like theirs. We'll turn down here, I want to show you my meadows.'

'Where you're goin' to live?'

'Yes.'

It was the usual Hertfordshire lane, a narrow passage, pot-holed with puddles reflecting the fading gold of the sky, hedges of ancient thorn where purple-red berries glowed, with shining ivy; humble pebbles large and small embedded in the mud, and scattering over all, like another light, the song now near, now far, of a robin. *English earth, as it might be remembered in the future by human exiles on another planet,* he thought.

He glanced at her and caught a listening expression on her face.

'That's a robin,' he said.

'I know. Used to feed one in that park where I met Auntie. Got quite tame, he did. Never would come onto me hand, though. Hours, I reckon I wasted on him, stoopin' down holdin' out bits of bread.'

'They weren't wasted.'

'What d'you mean? He never came.'

'But you looked at him. You got to know the look of him exactly. That "red" isn't true red, it's a kind of orange – you'd realized that, hadn't you?'

After a little pause she nodded. The robin, drawn inevitably by the presence of man, was fluttering after them down the lane, and in a moment Frank stooped, picked up a length of stick and began to imitate the action of someone digging. Juliet stood still. The robin hopped nearer, skittered away, came back again, and alighted on a branch within three feet of the moving arm.

Frank began softly to repeat aloud the legend of the Crucifixion and the gift of the red breast, and Juliet listened, expressionless, her eyes fixed upon the tiny, breathing cluster of bone and feather that seemed, with tilted head and brilliant eye, to be listening too. But before the story was ended, the bird suddenly flung away into the air, dived heedlessly into a bank covered in ivy, and vanished.

'Is it true?' she asked in a moment, as they walked on, Frank smiling at the dramatic exit.

'Oh Juliet, what a question! How can anyone possibly tell whether something that's supposed to have happened two thousand years ago is true? Do you mind, if it isn't?'

'What's the point, if it isn't?'

'There isn't a "point". It's just a beautiful and moving legend connected with – another beautiful and moving legend. If it were true—' He paused, and she glanced at him questioningly.

Talk with her was so difficult. Every sentence, almost every word, had to be pondered. *Dammit, it's like chatting with a dolphin*, he thought.

'If it were true,' he said slowly at last, 'I think it would be . . . overwhelming.'

A long pause. They had reached the end of the lane leading to Leete, and come out upon the wider one that would bring them to Wanby.

'I don't see that,' she said at last, dodging a car with a miserable-looking driver.

'Well . . . the contrast between the – the creaturely innocence of the bird, and what was happening on the cross – from a Christian point of view, I'm speaking now – and (our imaginations have to make an almost impossible leap to conceive this) if the feathers of the countless succeeding millions of robins were dyed red by a shock inherited from that one bird – it would . . . would imply more concern on the part of the Star Maker with the smallest of this creation than . . . than most people are able or prepared to accept.' The sentence faded ineptly.

'You religious then?'

Her tone was touched with contempt and distaste. He had been expecting such a reaction.

'In a way, I suppose – yes.'

'On about religion at the Comp, they were – that was another thing,' she muttered. 'Got me down.'

And, wondering whether he had said enough for one afternoon, he said no more.

But now he knew what he felt towards her: a teacher's impulse. He wanted to fill the vast gaps in her mind with rich facts. Not what he thought of as the colourless facts of mathematics and other branches of science, but the nourishing facts that feed the senses; and, above all, to make her feel the beauty of Nature, which the old world before science came used to spell with the capital letter, bestowing femininity and deity on – on an abstraction? Yes, an abstraction that took a million forms.

Wanby was a village so pretty, so well kept, that passing motorists were apt to pause, with murmurs of admiration, looking around for somewhere providing luncheons.

There were none. So far as the grosser appetites were concerned, Wanby was fairy gold, a hollow mockery and a Barmecide feast.

For that same sour-reputationed nobleman, who owned the land where Hightower stood amidst its four acres, also owned Wanby, and all attempts to obtain licences for cafés or restaurants had been dismissed with urbane indifference. Nor did the occassional cottager display the consoling word *Teas* in the picturesque window, for in Wanby there were no cottagers. Long ago the last of them had thankfully fled to council houses and flats in Stevenham or St Alberics, for like Edith Cavell in another situation, they had felt, strongly, that views and elm trees were *Not Enough*.

Their former homes were grouped about a triangular village green, shaded at its verges by sturdy elms, with a picturesque dry old well in its centre. The houses were not marred by pastel front doors; a chaste scheme of brown, black and white was strictly kept to, under the eye of the Wanby Amenities Committee; and there was not (let the imagination ponder this, and let it sink in full horror into the soul) . . . there was not a garage in the place. When a retired company director or superannuated admiral had trouble with his car, he had to telephone to Stevenham fifteen miles away, or perhaps to St Alberics, which was five. The one Wanby public house, the Two Doves, permitted no coaches and 'did' nothing more solid in the way of eatables than the superior kind of biscuit containing no fat and little sugar. There were those, bicycling sullenly through Wanby on their way home from the few working farms left in the district, who bitterly referred to it as a *bleeding museum*; but in ten minutes they could dismount outside the Green Man on the road to Stevenham, where the proprietors did 'do' lunches; ploughman's, greasy sausages and limp chips. Coaches were permitted, and one could be companionably sick in the yard. The Green Man's lights were visible, nay, even bursts of drunken song on Saturday evenings were audible, in autumn and winter, through leafless old thorn hedges surrounding Frank Pennecuick's two meadows.

Frank now led Juliet past the immaculate cottages, and down through a thick clump of elder, hazel and thorn, which in a few moments opened out onto meadows: green, empty, still, in the fading light.

'My house is in the other field, through the gate.'

When they were halfway across the meadow, she stopped, and stood as if listening.

'That isn't a robin?' she said questioningly.

'No, that's a blackbird – better than the nightingale I always think – in spite of—' He had been about to quote Arnold, but checked himself.

Only six months ago, 'Eternal passion! Eternal pain!' had run intolerably in his heart by night and by day. The line did not do so now. So much for 'eternal'! *Really*, he thought, *I am nearly thirty-two. Isn't it time I stopped being adolescent?*

'There 'e is!'

Her exclamation cut across the silence as the blackbird, after the habit of its kind, darted out of its bower, low and away above the grass, and Juliet's 'h' went with it.

Frank gave her a smile of approval and – yes, he felt that it was – affection as they walked on.

They went through the gate, which he carefully shut behind them, and then he turned and pointed across the second and larger meadow, with a group of fine oak trees at its far end, their sturdy branches black against the opal sky.

'There – that's my house,' he said.

'But it's cowsheds,' said Juliet flatly, after a stare.

'I know. But it won't be for long. See that board? "Abbot Bros – Conversions". And it's only one cowshed. There's a tiny cottage as well, two rooms up and two down, where the herdsman used to live – see,' pointing across the dim expanse of grass, 'that white thing. It's weatherboarded – I'm going to keep that – and in front of it there's been a vegetable garden. The rest of the meadow I'll plough up and grow wheat for my own bread.'

They were slowly approaching the group of low, shabby buildings. It was almost dark; the first quarter moon was rising through the oak boughs.

'Can we get inside?' she asked.

'Not tonight – it's too dark to see anything . . .'

'But there's electricity, isn't there?'

'No, I'm having oil lamps.'

'You won't half be living in a funny sort of way, won't you?'

'I'm expecting everyone will say so, yes. You see,' he turned away from his property, after a long, possessive gaze, 'I've got quite a lot of money for one chap, Juliet. My father left it to me and I've never known what sort of work I wanted to do until a couple of years ago. I do know now. My life's work is going to be for the Earth.'

'Don't know what you mean.'

'I can't explain it all now. We must hurry or we'll be late for dinner, and it's a very complicated subject.' He shut the gate behind them. 'But – very briefly – I want to increase the world's food supplies. I support a movement called the Association for the Investigation of Edible Grasses; and my ideal vision is of Man returning to a life lovingly linked with Nature.'

There was no response to this. It was now too dark to see her expression, but his words sounded to him inadequate, even foolish, spoken earnestly in the soft darkness. He also suspected that his companion had gone off into one of those reveries to which she was – a victim? Certainly she never seemed to try to resist them. The phrase *maddening brat* came, unexpectedly, into his mind.

'Look, we really *must* hurry,' he said sharply, as they came out onto Wanby village green.

She shot away from him, calling: 'All right – race you?' and was lost in the dimness.

But he had seen a car emerging slowly beside one of the pretty cottages, and set off running towards it, shouting, 'Clem! Hi! Clem!'

At the same moment Juliet returned out of the dusk. 'Thought you might get lost,' she said, grinning her unattractive grin.

'We're lucky – here's Miss Massey and her grandmother. They'll give us a lift.'

The car stopped, and a young woman's voice said enquiringly, 'Frank?'

'None other – and here's Juliet. You can save us from Sarah's scowls. In you get,' to Juliet, as the driver opened the door

next to herself. 'No, on second thoughts, you get in the back.
We've been looking at my house,' he added, as he settled himself
beside a pleasant-faced girl wearing a raincoat in a murderous
shade of blue. 'Oh, sorry, Dolly – this is Juliet Slater – Juliet,
this is Mrs Massey, a very old friend of Aunt Addy's. And this
is Miss Massey.'

'How do you do?' said a deep voice from a large shape seated
beside Juliet. It was swaddled in numerous shawls and rugs, on
the summit of which one of the new 'stableboy' flat caps could
be seen incongruously perching.

'Oh – hullo,' Juliet muttered, and the car moved off and
Clemence Massey, catching a glimpse of silvery hair and
youthful contours in the subdued light, thought despairingly,
*Oh God. Just his type.*

'*I* should have said "Hullo". I beg your pardon,' said the voice
next to Juliet, awfully; and Clemence and Frank exchanged a
glance with the corners of their lips lifting. Then no one said
any more, as they went onwards.

*And so young!* Clemence was thinking. *Oh, why does God or
Something make it so difficult for me to have the one thing I want?*

'And what did you think of Mr Pennecuick's dreadful little
shacks?' Mrs Massey demanded presently of Juliet. 'Doesn't
it seem *strange* to you that anyone should *wish* to live in such
a peculiar style? But I suppose, being young, you see nothing
peculiar about it?'

'We never went inside,' was all Juliet could think of to say.

'You haven't missed a thing,' said the deep voice triumphantly.

Clemence Massey was not a young woman of dramatic
temperament; one of her strongest traits was common sense.
But if anyone had quoted to her Thoreau's verdict on the mass

of mankind living lives of quiet desperaton, all her deepest longings would have cried: 'Yes, oh yes – that's me!'

She was twenty-seven.

Since early adolescence, her longing had been for a baby, a home, a husband: perhaps in that order. However, Nature had given her the type of ordinary, pleasant personality and appearance least likely – unless from an unusual stroke of luck – to attract men. And then, to add a stronger pain to the ever-present conviction that she was unlikely to marry, she had drifted gradually into love with her childhood friend Frank Pennecuick, the most unsuitable man possible.

A romantic, a solitary, an adolescent lover of girls who suggested mermaids or fairies, a conservationist. A Friend of the Earth. And, in many people's eyes, a crank; his very name rhymed with the contemptuous word.

They were 'best friends'. Frank had more than once said so. And sometimes she felt that it was not he whom she loved, but what he could give her: the baby (babies, rather, for Clemence wanted six) and the home.

She had also faced the fact that she wanted to change him. She wanted to see him put on a stone and a half in weight, eat 'proper' food, live more as other people did. And, in the unlikely event of his proposing to her, he was not going to like that aim at all.

So the days of quiet desperation marched on: ten o'clock until twelve at Dr Masters's surgery as his receptionist; the drive home from St Alberics to lunch with Grandmamma in the pretty cottage in immaculate Wanby; the afternoon back at her desk and telephone; the drive home to Wanby at the end of the day through winter sleets, long fading summer sunsets, flying autumn leaves, the aching evenings of promising springs.

But at least he was coming to live at Wanby. In those awful converted cowsheds. The whole of Wanby would be good-naturedly amused. But he was coming.

*And that mane of hair and that slender young body had come to live at Hightower, too, five miles away.*

The car stopped at the gate of Hightower and Frank rang the bell.

'I hope Sarah won't come down; it's got really cold,' Clemence remarked, aware that lowered spirits, rather than the chill autumn evening, had caused her to shiver.

'If Sarah likes to make a fool of herself that's her business. Juliet, you may help me out.'

Juliet, a romantic figure in her hooded cape, advanced upon the capped bundle, and spent the next minutes supporting one cold, squarish paw as it crept from the car, and then, under sharp instructions, rewinding scarves and shawls about it.

The light above the gate showed delicate features sunk in smooth flesh of that tint suggesting a tea-rose. Narrow dark-grey eyes sparkled out from a massive old face.

'Ha – Antonio – good,' Mrs Massey observed, as after nearly ten minutes, the gates swung open. 'Thank heaven for a man.'

'Really, Grandmamma,' Clemence said absently.

'Good evening, Antonio – how are you? And the pretty fiancée? And the naughty Surprise?' said her grandmother.

'Grandmamma, don't you want to go up by car?'

'Antonio will give me his arm.'

Antonio courteously assenting, the procession set off.

'Do you want to ride, Frank?'

'Good heavens, Clem, a hundred yards won't kill me—'

'I only thought – if you've been chasing about all day.' She guided the car within the gates, and braked.

'You know I can walk fifty miles without tiring,' and he turned back. 'Juliet! Buck up – we're late.'

*I know you're still thirteen, in some ways, and that's one of the reasons I . . . feel about you as I do,* Clemence thought, as she locked the car.

Frank waited impatiently until she had carefully done so, tested the result, and put the keys into her purse, then pulled her arm within his own, pulled in Juliet on the other side, and marched them both off.

'I cannot stand that stuff your grandmother uses,' he confided to his best friend; the scent of 'French Almond' was diffusing itself around the majestic progress of Mrs Massey and Antonio.

But Clemence felt too depressed for more than a wan smile. She already knew he disliked artificial scents; hadn't she given up her own timid use of 'April Violets'? Of course, he had not noticed.

'Can he really? Dear little *bambino*,' Mrs Massey was saying in response to Antonio's confidences concerning the individual whom she called, playfully, the Surprise. (Mrs Massey, who disliked small children more often than not, regarded the Surprise as a naughty joke; the child's hastily married parents had been full of shame, and had received a severe lecture from Father Beccio. Nor did Antonio relish the remarks of Senora Massey. He looked upon her as a rather disgraceful old woman.)

Now he nodded obediently. Yes, his little son could say 'Papa'. It was for the boy, and in a lesser degree for Anna, back in

Spain, that Antonio had bullied and argued and shouted his brother and sisters into coming to work in England. Now he would be glad when they reached the house.

Frank was aware of Juliet's arm held firmly within his own, and it was bony. Not attractively fragile, not limp and clinging. Just *bony*. And his next thought was: *Have to feed her up, poor little devil*. A thought he had decidedly never had about any of the others.

## 7

'Dolly, my dear!'

'Adelaide, how lovely to see you!'

The stout figure, having shed its coverings in the hall to reveal a smart black dress (worn over two black brocade petticoats and two bodices of light wool), marched across to the wheelchair, and a tea-rose cheek was pressed to one suggesting wrinkled leather.

'I kept dinner back half an hour – what detained you, dear?'

'Oh – something with the car – I don't know – Clemence is so clever with all that sort of thing.'

Mrs Massey settled herself with enjoyment close to the log fire, and her gaze just touched the drinks table. But—

'Wouldn't you like to go in at once, dear? You won't want a drink – you must be hungry.'

Miss Pennecuick began making helpless rising movements, and even as Mrs Massey thought *Oh, won't I?* Frank had an arm about his great-aunt, and was carefully leading her towards the dining-room.

'I'm longing to learn what you think of my little girl. Did I hear Frank say you picked them up in Wanby?'

'Yes – he'd been showing her those dreadful cowsheds.'

Mrs Massey, deprived of the preprandial short, noticed with satisfaction, as she took her place, that Addy had done her guests handsomely with the wines. But then, she always did. The weekend was going to be a shocking bore, with no company except that of Frank – *if only he would marry my poor girl!* – and the anaemic cockney chit, but at least the food and drink would be good.

And there would be the girl's background to investigate (Mrs Massey had thought her story fishy, from her first hearing of it) and she must find out if Frank were attracted to her; she was rather his type. Poor Clemmie. Yes, after all, there might be something to pass the time. And when she got them alone, she could always gossip with the servants.

She slowly made her way through the excellent dinner, her bright eyes moving curiously from face to face. *The chilly wind has flushed Clemence's cheeks unbecomingly and that shade of powder was wrong. Why, oh why, didn't she inherit some of my looks and charm?*

'How is Pamela?' began Miss Pennecuick, having slowly disposed of a fragment of plaice. She relied upon Dolly for news of mutual friends who were too old and frail to 'get about'.

'Dying,' said Dolly with disapproval, savouring her own plaice.

'Oh dear – how dreadful for Charlie—'

'Don't think he cares a button,' said Dolly, with relish. 'Can't wait to get her money.'

'How long does Edward give her?' (Edward was Dr Masters.)

'Oh good heavens, Addy, how should I know? This is very good Sauterne. Do you still go to Weston's in St Alberics?' Dolly held her glass up to the light.

'I believe so – Antonio attends to all that sort of thing. Have you any news of Betty?'

The news of Betty, extracted by a process which reminded Frank of a fisherman skilfully landing a fish reluctant to be caught, was not good. Neither was the news of Herbert and Marie, and not much could be said for Doris and Martin. He did not try to catch Clemence's eye; he knew she would find nothing amusing in the conversation. And when he turned for entertainment to Juliet, she was staring with parted lips up at the window.

He lifted his head to see what had caused that expression: Antonio had not drawn the curtains fully and between the folds shone the quarter moon. ' "Goddess excellently bright",' he quoted softly, thinking, with a return to the romantic mood which had fed and tortured him since adolescence, that Juliet's hair was exactly the moon colour.

'Pardon?' This came after a pause, as she seemed to realize that he had spoken. 'You say something?'

'Yes I did, and it was damn silly of me and I shan't make the same mistake again.' He did savage things to his table napkin.

Juliet showed no interest either in his romantic murmuring or in his subsequent temper, and it was with relief that he heard Clemence say firmly: 'Grandmamma, tell Aunt Addy about your latest battle with Mr Peppiat.'

'Oh yes, Dolly, I shall be so interested – but are you quite certain you want to leave dear little Wanby? So pretty – so idyllic.'

'Quite sure, thank you,' Mrs Massey snapped. 'If it wasn't for the sherry bottle, I should have cut my throat years ago, living there.'

Miss Pennecuick knew that her old friend loved to shock, and dutifully played up. 'Tell me about Peppiat, tiresome man. I remember his grandfather being just the same.'

'So do I, Addy.' Mrs Massey was for a moment annoyingly divided between a desire to appear both younger, and as old, as her friend. 'It's in the family, I suppose. Oh, he shillies and shallies, you know. Isn't sure whether he'll want the property for his son and daughter-in-law if they come back from Australia. And that goes on from week to week. It's maddening . . . and now he's talking about a higher rent.'

'*You* like Wanby, don't you, dear?' Miss Pennecuick turned to Clemence's quiet, attentive face.

'I'm perfectly happy there, Auntie. But I do realize it's pretty deadly for Grandmamma. There's nothing really *there*, you know . . .'

'Some of the finest elms in Hertfordshire.' A snap from Frank.

'I can't live on *elms*,' struck in Mrs Massey. 'At least in St Alberics there is a rep, and a public library, and the arts centre, and a few people under . . . a few interesting people.'

'Everybody,' Frank observed morosely, 'is interesting,' and a silence fell, devoted to eating. He did not hear Mrs Massey's mutter of 'Fiddlesticks'.

He fell to wondering, as he sipped apple juice of his own brewing, how Juliet felt at being waited on by servants. Probably she did not think about it at all; she was staring at the moon again.

He felt decided relief. He had finished with the elusive fairies who had held him, as in the net of Vivien the Sorceress, since he was sixteen.

Gradually, but surely, a love for the huge Earth and a longing and intention to devote himself to its welfare – and rescue – had replaced the mood of the knight palely loitering. (It will have been noted that Frank was a confirmed quoter, perhaps because his feelings were stronger than his capacity to express them.)

A mild conversation about the repairing of clocks and watches in the neighbourhood had begun. Antonio was sliding crystal plates, laden with something Portuguese and creamy, before each guest.

How nearly Frank had lost his freedom for ever! Three years ago, that pale red hair and siren's mouth had so enthralled him that he had proposed marriage. The greedy girl had accepted him, as a man rich enough and besotted enough to give her all the rubbish she wanted.

There had followed eighteen trial months, in which they tore one another to pieces.

He knew that most people would have said that he was the one who should give way – Ottolie's desires for a smart modern house, gadgets, a very large car, foreign travel, and four dinner parties a week were all natural; it was he, loving simplicity, solitude, silence and the company of one beloved other, who was the crank.

To be fair to her, she had tried. But in arguing with her, he had felt that she looked on him as actually mentally ailing. Who but one so afflicted could prefer a bunch of weeds to a great 'arrangement' of roses at one-fifty each?

He had been living, at the time of their affair, in a cottage rented from his friend Edmund Spencer, the poet, and – his reverie again remorsefully acknowledged it – Ottolie had praised the light given by the oil lamp, admired the clusters of wild roses in summer and what she called 'but-they're-only-leaves' in winter, even played at simple-life housekeeping.

But it had been hopeless.

There was nothing to do (she had said) in the evenings, but talk or read; and she had been a reader only of books dealing with some resurrected political or sexual scandal. Wonder she never experienced; mystery, in the true sense, passed her by. Personalities and money were the only things that interested her. At the end of the eighteen months he had told her, with agonising regret for the beauty and the false fairy spell he was discarding, that they must part.

Their first night absent from one another he had spent in tears; for his loss and for the waste, the bitter waste.

Ottolie, who was twenty-two and feeling that hols had started after a term of some sixteen years, gave a party that same night long remembered in the neighbourhood with pursed lips and waggings of the head.

What came to Frank's rescue was the simplest and humblest of growths on earth: grass. He had taken a degree in botany in his early twenties, and had kept up, in a casual way, his reading of journals devoted to that subject and to ecology; he grew gradually more interested in the questions relating to the cultivation of wild-growing grasses for food, and finally, chancing in a small seaside town in Essex upon a society of amateur enthusiasts calling itself the Association for the Investigation of Edible Grasses, he joined it, put some thousands of his money into housing it, engaged a small, well-paid, dedicated staff, established himself firmly as adviser and supplier of cash – and found that grass had purged the poison from his spirit.

'Like a dog or a cat,' he said to Edmund Spencer. 'I was ill, and I needed grass.'

Now the AIEG's membership was global, and rising into its second hundred thousand.

*Poor Clemence*, Mrs Massey would sometimes think. *First airy-fairy Ottolies, and now grass. Who but Frank Pennecuick could present such a combination of rivals?*

But he was very comfortably off, and one day soon he would inherit his great-aunt's fortune. He would do very nicely for dearest Clem, who would of course cure him of all that grass nonsense and make him live in a proper way, when once they were married. Mrs Massey encouraged the idea.

Mrs Massey drank strong and well-sugared coffee. Frank held a light for Juliet's cigarette.

'Juliet, baby, I wish you wouldn't smoke so much. It worries me,' said Miss Pennecuick plaintively. 'You know, the doctors say dreadful things can happen.'

Juliet used the weapon she had found the most useful for many years: silence. Her mother called it the sulks.

'I can put you onto a cigarette made from herbs, Juliet, that won't hurt you at all,' said Frank.

'Except making her sick, I should think,' said Mrs Massey. 'Give me one, Frank, will you? No, not your home-made horrors, an Embassy. Thanks—' as he held a match for her. 'Now tell me, how is *your* house going?' She puffed, in a self-conscious, Edwardian style.

'Well enough for me to sleep there next week – if that suits you, Great-Aunt?' turning to her.

'Of course, dear, you know you can come and go as you please, though I always love to have you here. But won't it be terribly damp?'

'Not in my sleeping bag.'

'And so isolated, Frank. It really worries me.'

'A mile from the M1,' smiling. 'This place is more isolated, really, you know.'

'Yes, but we have two strong young men on the premises—'

'And aren't I a strong young man?'

She laughed reluctantly. 'Of course, dear boy. But it really will be – it sounds – such a *peculiar* way to live, it isn't as though it were *necessary*,' delicately implying the healthy state of his income. 'The fact is, you have made yourself *unfit* to live as most people do.' (Here Mrs Massey nodded emphatically.)

His expression, which had been indulgent and amused, hardened.

'I've given that life a fair trial – some twelve years of it. It didn't work. Now I'm going to try living as I want to.'

'You'll be so *uncomfortable*.'

'Not half as uncomfortable as I would be living surrounded by hundreds of unnecessary objects, as most people do.' (He suppressed *as you do*; he was fond of his great-aunt.) 'In a hundred years most people will either want, or have, to live as I'm going to. Have to is more likely, at the rate things are going.'

Juliet was staring into space.

*He can't surely fall for such a mannerless, ungrateful brat,* Clemence thought; and then, *Oh yes he can – what about Fiona, and Deirdre, and Melisande and that awful Ottolie?*

Clemence was a gifted pianist, but with her duties as Dr Masters's receptionist, the supervision of housekeeping, and the demands of her grandmother, she got little enough time for the practise necessary to keep her technique at its best.

She loved her music, which seemed in some way to soothe those feelings which she was too sensible and sober to indulge freely, and when on the next evening Miss Pennecuick said, turning to her, 'Clemmie, give us some music, won't you, dear,' she went to the handsome old rosewood piano with a sensation of relief.

A long walk in the afternoon had brought colour to Juliet's cheeks, and made her a little less plain than usual. Frank had commented casually but favourably on the flush, and now Clemence felt inclined to dash into her stormiest Beethoven.

'Don't give us any of that dreadful modern stuff,' warned her grandmother, elegant in soft shades of brown, from the long sofa.

'Yes, something tuneful and pretty, dear,' from Miss Pennecuick, haggard in rose silk in the wheeled chair.

Clemence mentally dismissed Beethoven. *But I'm damned if I'm giving them the Spring Song,* she thought, as she gently lifted the piano's shining lid, inlaid with sprays of pale yellow and cedar-coloured flowers.

She settled herself on the stool, paused for a moment looking down at her large hands – so useful for a stretch – then struck out the first chill, simple notes of an air by Bach.

It wound and rippled on: to each listener suggesting vague pictures, or merely an agreeable sound. But Frank was looking at Juliet.

Her head, as he watched, had turned slowly towards the piano, and as the themes proceeded, growing ever more complex and interwoven, and giving an ever-increasing beauty to the simple opening theme, her gaze did not move from the player's hands. She was listening – listening as she had listened to the song of the robin.

It was the first time, except when she had looked at the robin, that she had shown attention to anything but her own unguessable thoughts.

The beautiful sounds ceased. Clemence allowed her hands to rest on the keys for a moment. Then she turned to her audience:

'That's only the first movement. Shall I go on?'

'Rather heavy, isn't it?' from Dolly.

'Very pretty, and thank you, dear, but what I'd really like is some Mendelssohn. I'm so fond of him,' said Miss Pennecuick.

Clemence found some Mendelssohn in the rosewood chest, and played on for another half hour. Juliet was again staring into the ferns: not listening, now, he thought. But she *had* been listening: listening more intently than most people do in a lifetime.

At ten, Sarah arrived to help her mistress to bed, and greeted Mrs Massey with a respectful near-sparkle.

Mrs Massey was her ideal of what a lady who was 'getting on' ought to be. *Nicely dressed and fond of a laugh, and no ailments. Quite cheered you up, to have her in the house. Not but what Miss Addie didn't dress nice,* Sarah mused.

Those remaining by the fire tactfully refrained from watching the piteous exit and, as the two disappeared, Mrs Massey turned determinedly on Juliet. (*Contributing nothing, but nothing, to the evening's entertainment, which, heaven knew, had been dull enough!*)

'Now,' she began, '*you* can tell us your plans. What are you – Seventeen? At seventeen' – two stout arms spread wide – 'I felt the *world* was at my feet!'

Juliet looked away from the self-important old face. Her own expression made Frank think of an animal being poked out of its hole by a stick.

As no one said anything, Mrs Massey retreated in excellent order by snapping, 'It wasn't, of course. But I *felt* that it was, and that's the important thing. What do *you* want to *do* – to *become* – to *be*?'

'Dunno.' Juliet looked at the floor.

'Don't know! But you must have *some* idea. What are your hobbies, interests, tastes? Do you like this "punk" music?'

'Nope,' decidedly.

'Well, that's something, I suppose . . . but how do you intend to earn a living? I had played in a Number One tour of *Our Miss Gibbs* when I was your age.'

'Had j'oo?' It might have been the original production of *Phèdre* for all the interest Juliet expressed.

'Plenty of time, Juliet,' Clemence put in. (Frank must be irritated to see the girl baited.) 'The important thing is to know *what* you want.'

'Maths and physics are all right,' Juliet said after a pause. 'I got A levels in all them subjects.'

' "Those subjects", dear,' from Frank.

'Those subjects.'

'Then why,' demanded Mrs Massey, 'didn't you go to a university? All those As and Os – so confusing – oh for the good old days when young people went to a university when their parents could afford it, and didn't when they couldn't.'

'Pardon?'

'Didn't when they couldn't. Afford it,' snapped Mrs Massey. She disliked having to repeat her pronouncements.

'My dad wouldn't have it. Set on me getting a job he is . . .'

Juliet's voice, already faint, died off into a mumble. But this time, one hand went slowly up to her mouth and two fingers stroked her lips, *As though* Frank thought, *to hush them into silence. So she's a liar, is she? I'd thought as much. We'll certainly have another walk.*

But no one else seemed to have noticed the slip.

'Don't see meself stuck in some factory all day,' Juliet went on smoothly, lighting a cigarette and shaking out the match with force.

Mrs Massey saw no reason why someone with that accent should not be stuck in a factory. But she never let herself appear disagreeable when she could avoid it; an amusing elderly tartness is one thing, an old woman's spite another. She said indulgently:

'But with all those levels or whatever they're called, surely you could get something better than a factory?'

Juliet shrugged.

'As a secretary?' Mrs Massey turned to Frank. '*Two thousand a year* girls are getting now; I saw an advertisement the other day. *Two thousand pounds* – why, my father brought us up, three of us, on five hundred – and very well he did it, too.'

'Wouldn't keep me in fags, that wouldn't.'

*What strange eyes Juliet has,* Clemence thought. *But all his girls are weirdies, in some way.* Then, suddenly, there came into her head the lines written of Newton – '*A mind for ever / Voyaging through strange seas of Thought, alone.*'

'If everybody won't think me rude,' she said, 'I'm off to bed; we've got to be up early tomorrow, you know, if I'm going to drop you at home, Grandmother.'

'Of course, dear,' said Mrs Massey briskly. 'I'll come up too. I make it a rule,' addressing the room, 'to be in bed by half-past ten . . . unless, of course, I'm at a party.'

Neither Frank nor Juliet registering surprise or admiration at this statement.

Clemence held out her hands to help her grandmother rise.

As she did so, she thought with gratitude of her grandmother's part in her own life: never allowing a situation to become embarrassing if she could steer it round the social rocks; so amusing; so comfortingly devoted to Clemence herself, and, yes, so silently understanding of the 'situation'. *How infinitely worse my life might be*, Clemence thought.

When Frank and Juliet were alone, and the voices of the others had died away, he felt stealing upon him a familiar, dreamy pleasure. It stole up, to a point: then, so to speak, it shook itself and was replaced by other feelings.

Outside, the great stars of late summer blazed in the clear darkness; the house in its wide garden was surrounded by fields dimly seen under the albescent moon.

The two were alone, and he knew that the romantic aspects of the situation were felt solely within his own imaginaton.

Juliet was smoking and staring at the floor. This evening's exchange of ordinary remarks with four other people was the closest she had ever come in her life to conversation.

At school, words had not got beyond snaps at her fellow scholars, answers in class and, on the occasion when her possible application for a university place had been discussed, a ten-minute shooting out of monosyllabic answers to the dutiful, mechanical probings of a headmaster too drained by exhaustion to feel more than a faint interest in the brilliance of her A level results.

She had made no friends.

In her home no one but a guest at their table (but there so seldom were any) could have known how few and how uncommunicative were the sentences exchanged between herself and her parents.

Demands for food or drink to be passed; comments grudgingly commendatory or sulkily complaining, about the cooking; an occasional announcement from Dad that he was 'off now' or from Mum that she was 'just going to pop out'. A 'Shocking, that's what I say it is,' about some scandal illuminated by the *Daily Mirror*. These had been the Slater versions of conversation, every day, every week, since Juliet had been a silent, swift-moving child old enough to understand words.

The mere unusualness, the mere gentleness, of the exchange between the guests at Hightower had compelled her attention. She was so accustomed after nearly seventeen years, to grunts and mispronounced sounds passing for communication that it was only when the rise and fall of agreeable voices – and Frank's was beautiful – had continued for some time that she had begun to notice it. She had liked it; *smashing*, she had thought.

'Smashing', and 'all right' were the only words of commendation she knew; and she had picked them up at the comprehensive as she might have done a germ.

'Oh!' She uttered a little scream and shook her fingers. 'Burnt meself – wasn't thinkin'.' She ground out the stub in the ashtray.

'But that's just what you were doing, Juliet. Thinking.' Frank leant forward. 'What about?'

The usual shrug. 'Oh – nothin' much.'

He studied her coolly. He felt, strongly, that there, sitting across the hearth from him – thin and angular, with glittering hair spread above the girlish, unbecoming dress chosen by Miss Pennecuick – was someone very *strange*. *Not quite human*, he thought suddenly, with satisfaction at having solved what had been puzzling him, *not quite human*. *Something vital to human beings is lacking*.

'That piano music she was playing,' Juliet said suddenly. 'Did she make it up, then?'

'Of course not, Juliet.'

He had to talk to her as if she were a child. But how else could he talk? He was generally sensitive to the vibrations given out by human beings, but never had he encountered any like those of Juliet. Immense force and – immense negativeness. Extraordinary.

'It was written by—'

'Do people write music, then? Like books?'

'Of course – do you really mean that you didn't know that?'

'The groups make it up,' on a note of defiance.

'Yes, but that's different. Didn't you notice that she, Miss Massey, had some sheet music on the piano while she was playing the other thing – the Mendelssohn?'

'Wasn't listenin' to that. That other what she was playing—'

'*Which* or *that*, she was playing.' He began to laugh, looking at her affectionately: 'Oh Juliet! You really are . . . did you like it?'

Silence for a moment. Then, in an expressionless voice, with a nod: 'Yes . . . It was like maths.'

'Some people see a connection between the two,' he said casually. 'People who are good at one are often good at the other.'

'I couldn't never play on the piano.' She shook her head. 'Maths – I'm all right with them.'

'What did the Mendelssohn make you think of?'

'Nothing – I told you, I wasn't listenin'.' She stood up quickly, and stretched. 'I'm off upstairs. Got some work to do. 'Night.'

She was half across the room.

'At this time of night? For heaven's sake?'

'Oh – just somethin' I'm tryin' to work out.'

She flashed a real smile at him, and was gone.

# 8

The presence in St Alberics of an ancient grammar school, which had so far successfully resisted attempts to turn it into a comprehensive, had encouraged the proprietors of the Pickwick, the Owl and the Waverley to establish their bookshop in the town. They had hoped for a regular flow of customers, drawn from a predominently middle-class background: schoolchildren in search of books to help with their homework and the two levels; old people who had retired to St Alberics to die. The Pickwick, the Owl, and the Waverley sold books. No book tokens; no cards of any kind – birthday, wedding or Christmas; no pencils, no pens, no rubbers, no pocket devices for adding up sums. Just books.

One morning late in November, Juliet darted in with a book in her hand and thrust it at Arthur Robinson, aged nineteen, in charge of the shop while the manageress went out for a coffee.

'Got anything about this?' she demanded.

If Juliet was a most unusual girl, Arthur Robinson was a not quite ordinary boy. He looked at *The Roots of Coincidence* by Arthur Koestler, which came from St Alberics public library.

'About coincidence, do you mean?'

A nod.

Arthur's spirits had lifted on seeing that hair come through the door. There was hardly any light in the low sky, and her head caught what there was, and glittered. But her face caused his heart to sink again – even puppy fat and trousers thrust into cowboy boots were better than a face like that. Reg Porter, who boasted that he could make the toughest chick, would have said: *Why the hell does a pretty girl like you want to read about coincidence? It's a coincidence you and me's here together, that's all that matters.*

Oh, Arthur could invent the dialogue all right (he was, like most young men in the British Isles, writing a novel). But he could not speak it. Besides, she might know she was not pretty and one couldn't (at least if one was A. Robinson) go around hurting girls' feelings.

'There's one by Sir Alister Hardy,' he said. 'That's about decoincidence, written together with that chap,' nodding towards the book she held.

She hesitated. 'All right if I look round?'

'My pleasure,' said Arthur, pleased with his reply.

He returned to his duties. One or two customers came in and were served. An unexpected-looking person went off, obviously gratified, with *The Lesbian Murders*, and someone else parted (gloomily, and with the air of one doing their duty) with £9.99p for *Anxiety and Lust*, by J. Benelheim in paperback.

Half an hour passed.

'Found anything?' he enquired, appearing round one of the tall, double-sided bookcases that were arranged about the shop. Unerringly, he had approached the one carrying titles on New Mathematics, Geometry, the New Physics, and similar works dealing with the sciences.

Her months at Hightower, eating nutritious food and enjoying plenty of solitude, had put flesh on Juliet's frame and removed the slight frown, caused by the perpetual straining after that solitude.

She would never, now, have the usual bloom of the late teens, but the aura of some kind of starvation that had hung about her had gone. And, although Miss Pennecuick worried about her darling's small appetite, every day thousands of cubic feet of pure air poured into her narrow lungs, thickening and reddening her seventeen-year-old blood.

'Come to the movies with me tonight?' blurted Arthur Robinson, affronted at being looked through, and wishing to emulate Reg Porter.

She laughed.

What he afterwards described in his novel as a 'bloody awful sensation' came down upon Arthur: a mixture of pain somewhere within himself (*It's because I wear glasses*) and an impulse to hit something.

But almost before the pain had time to grow, she said: 'Can't help laughing. Reminds me of elephants.'

'*Elephants?*'

The pain subsided. Was she a mental case?

'Yes . . . My mum, see, she says I'm more interested in elephants than what I am in boys, that was why I laughed. Kind of a joke, really.'

He smiled rather constrainedly.

'Well, how about it? It's *Star Wars* at the Odeon.'

'Don't know – I'm stayin' with my auntie, and she likes me in evenin's.'

'Oh, you don't want to take too much notice of her!' cried Arthur, with that confidence in giving advice bestowed by an, on the whole, contented temperament and an easy home life. 'Can't you get away without her knowing?'

Juliet considered. 'S'pose so . . . I know, I'll say I'm going over to Frank's.'

'Who's Frank?' Was this girl, interesting now to the novelist Arthur rather than to the Arthur who wanted to get level with Reg Porter, already booked?

'A friend. All right, what time?'

'Seven, it starts. Meet you outside, twenty-to? We'll have to queue.'

'All right . . . I must be off.' And she was round the shelf and at the door almost before he could cry:

'Here – what's your name?'

'Juliet Slater.' She did not turn round or ask what was his name, and now she had gone.

A solemn, luxuriantly haired male had been a silent observer of their exchange. Having purchased a copy of Freud's *The Future of an Illusion*, he marched home and wrote a short story with which he was pleased. It was about two young people, tormented by unremitting lust, who slept together in a 'grubby bed-sitter'. They were sadly disappointed by their encounter, which ruined both their lives. It got itself published in a little magazine, and in another realm, certain lesser angels, who should have known better, held their dazzling sides while they laughed.

Arthur arrived at the meeting place in his usual observant state of mind, mildly interested to see how Juliet Slater would 'turn out'.

This was far from his first date. Although no Reg Porter, he had pleased certain girls since his sixteenth birthday by his good manners and his lack of grabbing, and was going steady with Brenda Lewis, who lived just down his road.

True, there were female admirers of Reg Porter who described Arthur as wet; he did not like this, though he was still quietly determined to be what he was, rather than what others expected him to be. It was because he felt that it would give him more standing with Reg's girls (whom he both feared and found boring, yet wished to impress) that he had, on impulse, invited this unusual Juliet Slater to see *Star Wars*.

He had expected her to arrive late, and had timed the meeting with this possibility in mind, but at twenty-two minutes to seven there she was, caped and hooded, her thin face pink from the bitter wind and her eyes – gosh, they were smashing – glittering.

'Hi, there,' he said, advancing.

'Hi,' said Juliet.

Some unconscious calling of youth to youth had prompted her acceptance of Arthur's invitation. At home, she would have had to sit with Auntie, and she had also decided that some fieldwork, some looking out for coincidences in streets and shops and buses, might provide useful material.

Arthur had taken some trouble to get seats in the second most expensive part of the house, but he did not expect Juliet to comment on this and she did not; nor did she look about her with any interest until the audience began crowding in; then her gaze swept over them, and the expression of her eyes changed.

*Takes no more notice of me than if I was invisible*, Arthur thought resentfully. Either she *was* mental or she was the rudest girl he had ever met.

'Don't you like the movies?' he asked at last: the house was full now and an electronic overture, of a nature suitable to the film, was thundering forth.

'Only been once before, when I was a kid.'

She turned the light-filled eyes on him, and a shiver touched his spine: she certainly was a funny-peculiar girl.

'Bit unusual, isn't it? Most kids go through a stage of going a lot.'

'Went with my mum.' (*Oh. Yes, they had that 'joke' about the elephants. Probably a funny kind of mum, too.*) 'Took me for a treat, like, but I wasn't all that interested, so she never took me again.'

'Oh . . . I see . . . What are your . . . hobbies, then?'

By this time Reg Porter would have been in the full flow of a taunting, tantalizing dialogue, laden with hints and double meanings. But with this girl, Arthur's own modest imitation of Reg could not get started.

'Oh – readin', I read a lot.'

'Georgette Heyer, I suppose.'

She was Brenda's favourite author, together with the anony-mous presenters of the articles in *Over 21* and *Honey*. (Arthur's attempt to 'get her on to Jane Austen' had met with a bewil-dered, 'But, Artie, it's so dull.')

'Who's she?'

Arthur stared, and was pleased. Here was a chance for some mind-improving, an exercise which gave him satisfaction.

'Very popular romantic novelist. We sell about thirty a week of hers, in the shop. But I prefer Jane Austen.' (A part of him also 'preferred' Isaac Asimov, but he did not think it necessary to mention this.)

'We did about her at school, Jane Austen.'

'Where was your school?'

'Hawley Road Comprehensive – a dump, it was.'

'In London?'

Nod. 'I got five As,' she added suddenly, with that satisfaction she always felt when making the statement.

'Crikey – you must be bright,' commented Arthur respectfully; he had two. 'What subjects?'

'Oh – all science. The other stuff wasn't interestin'; I done – did – badly in them.'

'You must be very bright,' he said again (but mental people sometimes were).

'S'pose so . . .' a shrug, and at that moment the lights began to dim. The film had been showing for over ten minutes before it engaged Arthur's attention. He saw then that it was a marvellous construction, a miracle of technology. Millions of dollars had been expended upon devices, costumes, conflicts – and not one gleam of imagination, not one, decided Arthur, who was a reader, and proud of it. Watching, he was confirmed in his belief that *Books Are Better*.

He moved his hand slowly towards Juliet's, the position of which he had taken care to notice. It gleamed whiter than its actual tint in the immense glare from the screen. Brenda's hands were rosy and had dimples over the knuckles.

Gently he slid his own over it – gosh, it was cold! – not icy, just cool enough to be called cold, and faintly damp; not cosy at all.

She turned and looked at him.

'What's up?'

Arthur was considerably taken aback.

'Oh – nothing. Just thought we might hold hands.'

Juliet slid her hand away.

'Don't want to.'

'*Why?*' Arthur's whisper was conventionally urgent, concealing relief.

'Cause you aren't an elephant,' with a quick grin that warmed him towards her, in spite of the snub.

The conventions appeased, Arthur proceeded to enjoy the film by criticizing it, while his thoughts turned occasionally to Juliet. Any girl thanked you for the seats: even Brenda, his steady, did. No. This was the last time, he decided, that he dated Juliet Slater, who, had there been a prize for dropability, would have won by many a head.

But he had his manners, and would keep them until the end.

'Come for a coffee?' he asked, as the lights and sounds of the film died away, and there began a desperate scrambling among the audience to get out of the place while 'The Queen' was being pumped forth. 'We've got time. Your last bus is ten forty-five.'

'I don't mind.'

But he took her to the cheaper of the little town's two cafés; the evening had cost him quite enough already, and his job at the Pickwick, the Owl and the Waverley was not paid at full-time assistant's rate, as it was only temporary, a fill-up before he went into a small printing firm, owned by his uncle, in the town, where, he was warned (more frequently than he liked), he would start at the bottom and be expected to work his way up.

'I'm hungry,' she announced, as they sat down in the hot, noisy, brightly lit place.

'So'm I, but it'll have to be sandwiches – they take about twenty minutes doing a hamburger in this joint. We'd miss your bus.'

She gave her nod; and presently, when they were hastily eating and gulping a tepid brown fluid, she turned to take a prolonged stare round the room.

'Nuisance,' she said at last. 'I don't know . . .'

'What did you say?' For she had spoken with her mouth full.

'. . . don't know . . . see, I wish I knew if all these here kids' – for the café's clientele was largely under eighteen – 'if anything had happened to them like . . . a coincidence.'

Arthur, chewing hastily, stared at her. *It's like taking a talking animal out, or one of her blasted elephants,* he thought. Yet as her eyes fixed steadily upon his own, there was in them a light that never shone in those of any animal.

'You'd have to ask them, I suppose,' he said gently. (*Or a very small kid. She's like that too. But five A levels!*)

'Can't stick talkin' to people. 'Sides, take me all the week.'

How precious time was to her! He had noticed that: she darted everywhere, her walk was almost a run; she seemed to grudge the passing of every minute.

'You're crazy about coincidences, aren't you?' he said.

The light in her eyes seemed to dim. Here was the usual ignorance that had driven her to run away to Hightower.

Arthur observed the dimming.

'Here, if we want that bus we must run for it,' and in a few seconds they were racing down the high street. As Juliet jumped onto the bus, amidst a small crowd of Leete-bound night-owls, Arthur called, 'Tell you what – I'll collect coincidences for you and write them down. You come into the shop every week and pick them up – right?'

She turned – the bus was already moving away – and waved.

'What's yer name?'

'Arthur Robinson.' (A shout.)

'See yer.' (A thin scream.)

*What a girl! Not a word about three-fifty on seats and coffees!*

His thoughts went with relief to Brenda, who was at this moment probably trying a new hair-do in front of the glass or painting her nails – or even (thought Arthur tolerantly) out with someone else. He was not jealous.

# 9

The workmen at the Cowshed having driven off to their lunch in a large car belonging to one of them, Frank was taking the opportunity to sweep the floor of his living-room, on which they had allowed much litter to accumulate. He was also quoting aloud poetry appropriate to autumn: ' "A spirit haunts the year's last hours / Dwelling amid these yellowing bowers: / To himself he talks . . ." ' *As I'm doing,* he thought, vigorously driving before him empty cigarette cartons, fragments of plaster, whitish dust and greasy paper. He was content, though somewhere at the back of his mind lurked faint uneasiness at the fact that no other man within many miles was at that moment quoting Tennyson while sweeping with a twig broom the floor of a disused cowshed in which he proposed to live.

To banish this slight sensation, he began to think of Juliet. *I wish I could do something about that child: she bothers me. The best thing would be to get old Addy to put up the money to keep her at a university. (We won't bother with grants.) I could do it, I suppose, but then there would probably be gossip, certainly in*

*Wanby. Everybody's so used to my being in love with the wrong person.*

Whistling, he put the broom away, and set about brewing some herb tea. As he did so, a thought hit him, solid as a brick and with much the same effect: *I lead an unnatural life and I'm getting old maid-ish.*

Instantly, other thoughts leapt to his defence: *Hell, why shouldn't I? I'm comfortable. I'm not utterly useless – there's the Society to prove that – and the belief that bachelors are 'selfish' is old-fashioned. I do no harm (that's a feeble one, if you like) . . . perhaps I'm getting a bit bored with my own comfort. Perhaps I'll meet a new mermaid . . .*

He was astonished at the force with which he thought: *God forbid.*

His thoughts, as he sipped the dark-green liquid and stared out over his meadows, returned to Juliet.

*She's virgin soil. I've never heard her utter a word showing she has been influenced by anyone or anything, except this mysterious something that demands so much solitude. And mathematics. Oh, and that Bach the other night.*

*But the lack! There's such a lack there: lack of ordinary human responses, human tastes, human desires . . . That would be something to occupy me, teaching Juliet to be human. I'll teach her to look, and to hear, and to feel, until she's a human creature.*

He was smiling as he went through to the little kitchen that had been added to the long, low shed. He felt full of energy and interest. It would be a Good Work.

Perhaps there is something about an unusual female which arouses in males the desire to instruct and to change. It was

well for Frank Pennecuick and Arthur Robinson that neither
of them knew what they had taken on.

Arthur was finding that his search for coincidences was quite
as embarrassing and tiresome as he had expected.

At the end of the first week, however, he had perfected a
system; had bought a notebook; and was growing accustomed
to sitting down at café tables or leaning on bars, and saying
to strangers: 'I say, excuse me, but I'm writing a thriller and
the plot turns on a coincidence. I wonder if you can help me?'

He did not want trouble. He chose the more unalarming-
looking of the young, and the more soppy-looking of the elderly,
avoiding members of HM Forces, and gangs of either sex. An
hour a week was quite enough to give to his odd search. In a
fortnight, his job in the bookshop would be up, and he would
go into Uncle Bill's office. Free time would be scarcer after that.

Then, gradually, he learnt that no one is 'ordinary'.

Every individual he spoke to showed some narrow, delicate,
almost colourless streak, personal as a fingerprint, that set them
imperceptibly apart from everyone else. Even within the most
apparently moulded type there appeared these variations, infant
shoots of oddness and individuality. There had been the elderly
man who accused him of nosy-parkerism, muttered about a
free country, and threatened him with the police. This was the
evening on which Arthur nearly abandoned the project. But the
embryo novelist heard the shy notes and saw the faint gleams
behind the halting sentences and the clichés.

As for stupidity . . . perhaps he did not make enough allowance for the slightly alarming effect of clear dark eyes (not
exactly glaring, but magnified by thick spectacles) fixed with

severe attention upon the victim. Usually his spiel about the thriller and the coincidence was greeted with an open mouth and 'Pardon?'

'Eh? Say it again slower, son.'

'I dunno what you're on about.'

'How very interesting! My nephew writes. He hasn't had any luck so far with *publishing*, poor boy, but he isn't discouraged. So *you* want to be a writer too, how *thrilling*! I wonder if you'd like to meet Andrew?'

'Coincidences? Funny you should ask me that. Only this morning I was saying to Mrs Bender who lives next door to us no it wasn't this morning it must have been Monday because I'd just come from the launderette well I was on my way back as a matter of fact and I ran into her just as I was going along Bowie Road . . .'

From the mass of examples collected during one week, there shone out, large and lucent, one jewel.

It came from a tramp, an old man with a flowing beard who was covered, or rather packed into, layers of rags, glimpsed by Arthur on his way home one cold evening as he hurried past a coffee stall.

The handsome, ravaged profile outlined against the lights in the little place caught Arthur's attention, and he paused; approached; ordered coffee; and addressed the towering ancient with his tale.

There was a pause. Arthur noticed that the old man's nose was purple and threaded with crimson veins. He was prepared for retreat. Anything: a blow, a roar of rage, a shout of laughter.

'I know of one,' said a hoarse voice at last, while bloodshot eyes were fixed dreamingly upon Arthur's own. 'It happened in

Bulgaria to a man I knew. He murdered his cousin. Wrapped his body in a rug and threw it into the river. But the crime haunted him; yes, it haunted him, and he couldn't sleep. He used to walk along the seashore at night, up and down, up and down,' went on the broken, educated voice somnolently, 'and presently he noticed something dark lying at his feet and rolling to and fro in the waves.' Pause. 'I suppose you haven't such a thing as a cigarette about you?'

Arthur, mesmerized, handed him a nearly-full packet.

'Ah thank you – very kind – and it was the rug. The body had gone; the fishes had got that; but it was the rug.'

He lit a cigarette shakily, and stowed the packet into his rags.

'Thanks for telling me,' Arthur said at last, and the old man gave a mocking wave of a long-fingered hand and turned his back.

Arthur hurried away. It was not until he was nearly home that it struck him that the story might be made up.

He shut the gate of his home with a sensation of safety and relief. The rags, the great beard, the voice: all had seemed to open before him a chasm in which wandered souls once sure of themselves and safe but now preferring this twilight to the light of day.

Juliet came into the shop on a busy morning with such an air of meaning to be attended to at once that Arthur's sole customer, a sturdy lady choosing *a nice book about dogs* gave her a haughty glance.

'Oh hullo. Be with you in a minute,' Arthur muttered. When the lady had gone (having deliberately prolonged her choosing, *to teach that girl a lesson*), he turned round to find Juliet at the other end of the shop.

He hurried down to her, and held out his notebook.

'Here – they aren't much good, I'm afraid, except one I got from an old tramp. That's a beauty. Hurry up – there's another person waiting.'

She had snatched the book from him and was already reading the carefully written pages, with an effect of *eating* them, so intense was her concentration.

'Pure,' he thought he heard her mutter, and saw her give a little nod, as he rushed off, thinking, *Well, I'll never know what that meant, so shan't waste time wondering.*

As the second customer left, there wandered in a tall man, shabbily dressed in brown. Arthur did not approach with helpful enquiries; he had been told to encourage browsing, and this one looked like a browser.

Instead, the brown man went straight to Juliet.

'There you are,' he said, and she said, 'Oh – hullo,' impatiently.

'Are those the notes your friend was collecting for you?' the brown man asked, while glancing pleasantly towards Arthur.

'Yes. Not much use except for one,' raising her voice and nodding at 'your friend'. And she was at the door.

'I suppose you can't join us for coffee and tell us how you got this material, which I'm sure will be useful to Juliet,' the browser said warmly, turning to Arthur.

'Oh – thanks. But that's impossible. I'm in charge, see, until the other assistant comes on at one. But thanks all the same.'

'Some other time, then.' He hesitated. 'Juliet doesn't mean . . . It's just that she's – well, a very unusual child, and one mustn't expect ordinary behaviour from her.'

'I don't.' And Arthur grinned.

The brown browser smiled too. 'Yes, I know. But I think it possible that some day you'll be proud of having helped her.'

Arthur looked steadily at him through spectacles which performed, for him, one of those warning or menacing effects produced by the markings on certain butterflies.

'You her boyfriend?' he demanded sternly, feeling protective towards Juliet Slater, and was reassured by a wholesome laugh.

'Good God, no, I'm just a kind of elder brother or something. That respectable enough for you? Come to that – are you her boyfriend?' on an unmistakable note of hope.

Arthur shook his head. 'No fear.'

Frank smiled and turned away.


Juliet's parents had no religious or, for that matter, tender notions about Christmas.

'We–always–go–to–my–sister's, see? A–bit–of–company,' Mrs Slater had been saying, ever since Juliet could recall. Mr Slater refrained from complaint as long as he was allowed, for once, to drink too much, in the company of a brother-in-law as large, morose and habit-clenched as himself.

'Don't s'pose you'll be comin' home for it, then,' stated, rather than questioned, Mrs Slater a week or so before the festival. It had been arranged between them that Juliet's telephone call to the neighbour's house should be made on the same day and at the same time every week, as this avoided Mrs B having to go next door to summon Mrs Slater.

'No, Mum.'

'People'll think it's a bit funny.'

'Will they?' Indifferently.

'You're welcome, Julie, 'spite of running off like that, you know that.'

'Aunt Addy'd have a fit. She's got this here nephew. And some other people coming to stay.'

'Don't she think it a bit funny, you not wanting to be with us Christmas-time and you our only one?'

'She don't think I'm your only one.' Juliet was suddenly irritated by her mother's soft whine.

'Wot? Wot you say?'

'I said she don't think I *am* your only one.' There was a grin in Juliet's tone.

'Oh Julie! You been telling her lies?'

'Had to. Now don't go on about it, Mum, it's done now.'

'Oh Julie! Wot you been and told her?'

'Nothing you need worry about. You have a nice Christmas with your other four kids.'

'*Julie*! You never!'

'Yes I did – and so'd you if you was half off your trolley wanting a bit of peace and couldn't never get it . . . Now don't cry, Mum. I'll ring you Christmas Eve. And there'll be something nice for you and Dad in the post. Cheerio.'

'Julie—'

But Juliet had replaced the receiver.

Miss Pennecuick had invited the Masseys, Frank, and a married pair, old friends of hers, to stay until New Year's Day. The Harding-Grays were amiable and pleasant enough, but hardly 'added to the gaiety of nations', though nations were their chief topic of conversation. Priding themselves upon keeping their minds alert, they remorselessly read their newspaper from front to back every morning over their breakfast trays (omitting only the sports pages), and arrived at luncheon primed with the difficult names, correctly pronounced, of the Arabs or Vietnamese present at the latest hopeless conference table.

From the 'newest industrial deadlock' to black holes and the bouncing universe was, for the Harding-Grays, only a step, and they did not seem to realize that other people might have weaker nerves and digestions than themselves.

'Well, at least they didn't grumble about permissiveness,' said Clemence. She and Frank were indulging in a little good-natured mockery of the departed guests on New Year's morning.

'Yes, we were spared that. They rather approved, trendy old donkeys.'

'I thought "Three cheers for Aunt Addy" when she came out with: "Well, my dears, I can't do anything about all these things so I shall just ignore them."'

Frank was staring out at the silvery trees. Hoar frost, one of the rarest and most beautiful of natural spectacles, had descended, as silently as a New Year angel, in the night. A sudden sense of enjoyment in Clem's company came to him, and with it the realization that his own mood was usually so lofty as to lower the spirits of others.

*Man's Fate . . . The Origin of the Universe . . . I almost never feel actively cheerful*, he admitted to himself, and laughed aloud suddenly, and got up from the window seat.

'What is it?' Smiling, as she looked up from her knitting.

'I was just thinking I'm a bit of a Harding-Gray myself.'

'Oh you aren't . . . but you do hardly ever laugh out loud.'

'I'm going to take young Juliet out for a walk. She looks liverish to me. Coming?'

'No thanks. I must write some letters.'

*Not though the hoar frost was so pretty, not though an hour of his company was precious. Not with Juliet Slater.*

'We'll be back for lunch.'

He smiled at her as he went out, leaving her glad to have heard the unromantic word. One did not fall in love with a liverish teenager.


Frank ran upstairs and tapped on Juliet's door.

'Juliet? Coming for a walk?'

'All right,' after a pause. She opened the door. She was putting on her cape. Her books were open on the table, and Frank felt such a strong curiosity about what she might be reading that in two strides he was across the room and bending over them.

Juliet said impatiently: 'Get your skates on.'

'Sorry. What's this? *The Challenge of Chance* – any good?'

She shook her head.

Frank forgot to watch his speech, and said, like anyone else, 'What an odd book for a girl to be reading.'

'He – that boy – you know, Arthur in the shop – told me about it, so I tried in the library. But they hadn't got it, so I bought it.'

'Bit of a waste of money, was it?'

They were hurrying down the stairs.

'S'pose so.' Clang! went the armour, the grin vanished. They were crossing the hall in the sunny winter silence of the house.

'Have a good promenade!' cried Antonio, as two faces peered round the green baize door.

'Thank you,' Frank called, turning to smile at this unbutler-like valediction, and shut the front door on himself and Juliet.

'Surely,' said Rosario to his brother, 'he will not sleep with her in the icy fields?' (He did not say 'sleep'.)

'No, they will go to his hovel. He is crazy. Though, should they sleep in a hedge, it would be suitable. Icy fields, icy girl.'

Guffawing, they returned to their region.

Here were trees masked in stiff silver up to their highest twig, a lane gleaming with ice splinters, and an air so cold that it bit. Cold gaiety danced over field and sky from a white-yellow sun. There were the usual distant cries of distress and protest from cars skidding, cars stuck, cars run out of petrol, cars. Otherwise Juliet and Frank had the world to themselves.

*Here*, he thought, *is the morning to start nourishing those starved buds of feeling.*

Yet he did not know how to begin, and actually felt a little nervous. *Would this inarticulate adolescent find him 'soppy', or the contemporary equivalent, if he pointed out the beauties surrounding them? Best begin on something solid . . .*

'Juliet, have you thought any more about going to university?'

Their footsteps were making a light crunching noise in the frost as they marched along.

She glanced up at him.

'They said I ought, at the comp. I told you. But Dad . . .'

'Hey – I thought you said you didn't have a dad.'

This, the second slip, was not going to be ignored.

'Oh,' and she grinned, 'don't you go grassing on me, will you?'

'I won't. As long as you tell me all about it.'

'You blab to *her*, and I won't never tell you another word about anything ever again.' She had stood still suddenly, and her eyes flashed with anger.

'I won't, Juliet, I promise. It would only hurt her and . . . upset everything for your future, perhaps. But won't you tell me? As your friend?'

She considered him steadily, and then began to march on in silence.

'See, I had to get away,' she began suddenly. 'Get a lot o' time to meself. Think things out. About what interests *me*. Dad've pushed me into a factory. Not for the money, he's an engine driver, we got enough. No. He just thinks I ought to be workin' and everythink else is a waste o' time, university included.'

'I see,' Frank said, really moved. The passion of the artist or scientist for solitude! The young Mozart, the young Poe, every gifted creature who had ever been frustrated, Frank knew how they felt; and throughout time, and all over the world in which they were strangers, he sorrowed for them.

'Stoppin' me tryin' to work something out,' she said suddenly.

'About coincidence?' he dared, following an intuition.

But all he got in reply was: 'Not sure . . . s'pose so,' and a long pause.

He almost held his breath. All suspicion that his imagination was at work, magnifying a small situation into something important, had gone. He saw an ignorant child, burdened with a gift that was too great for her. And what was the gift?

A richer light poured suddenly over them, making the fields sparkle as if scattered with powdered diamonds.

'There's the sun!' he exclaimed, and Juliet said crossly, 'Go on!' and then laughed; they both laughed.

'Well, he hardly looked like himself before, did he?' said Frank, yielding to that streak of whimsy in which he usually indulged only with Clemence. Juliet was staring straight into the white radiance, *Like an eaglet*, he thought, *like an eaglet. Leave things, now. Don't push too hard.*

'At a university, you know,' he began '(we'd better turn back or we'll be late for lunch), there would be people who could help you to – think out whatever it is you want to. People trained to do it. Would you like me to suggest to Aunt Addy that she send you to one?'

She turned on him; a small hooded figure suggesting some dwarfish norn, and snapped: 'I don't know what it is I *want* to work out – so how could they help me? Not if *I* don't know? 'Sides, I sooner work it out for meself.'

'But they could help you to think, Juliet. That's their job.'

'I can think, all right.' She was climbing swiftly over a stile, declining his offered help. 'Trouble is—' She landed carelessly on the ice below and slipped, and he caught her before she fell. *Frail as the robin's bones*, he thought, *nothing of her.*

'There.' He set her on her feet as if she were a child.

'Wasn't lookin'.'

'Go on with what were you saying—'

'Trouble is,' and she turned and looked up at him, 'I got to find out what I'm thinkin' *about*.'

'They could help you to find out.'

But she seemed to have lost interest. 'Oh, it'd be all yaketty-yak – it always is,' she said roughly. 'I can't spare the time.'

'No . . . Well, I'm – I'm your friend, anyway. You do believe that?' He knew what he would hear.

'S'pose so.'

But with it went a smile, the one differing from the defensive grin, and they finished the homeward walk in amiable silence, broken only by one or two cautious remarks in which he pointed out the beauties of Nature.

Clemence spent most of that afternoon writing to the only man who had ever proposed to her.

The house was silent.

A freshly arisen east wind whipped the frost about; and the sun had gone in. It needed a strong effort of Clemence's will to sit down at the handsome, elderly desk (born 1903) in the library, and start '*Toddy dear*'.

'Toddy' was Edward Rossiter, his baby attempt at Teddy. He was thoroughly likeable, solid and desirable in every way except one: she did not want to marry him.

He was in South America, managing a branch of one of the great English banks. She wrote to him every month. She suspected, from casual observations in his recent letters, that he was becoming interested in another young woman, a member of the English colony in Lima, and she was jealous: she had been keeping Toddy in cold storage in case Frank suddenly married one of the Fionas.

# 10

'A thoroughly dull visit,' pronounced Mrs Massey as the car sped away from Hightower. 'But the food was good . . .'

'Yes, Maria can cook.'

'. . . and that's another thing, they're colourful, a picturesque family, I should have enjoyed seeing more of them. If only Addy weren't so *conventional*! Anyone else would have had them in for drinks one evening, and heard something *amusing*, for a change. But not Addy. I can just hear her "Being familiar with the servants" – oh no.'

'Grandmamma, what do you think of Juliet?'

Clemence did not try to hide her strong wish to hear the verdict.

Mrs Massey's private opinion, Clemence knew, was that Frank was a cranky fool and that her grandchild was 'going the wrong way to work'. But she never let slip a word of unkindness about Frank, or gave Clemence advice that went against the grain of the latter's nature. In this case, and in this alone, she let the wisdom of love prevail.

'A most peculiar little creature,' she now snapped. 'That appalling accent and no looks . . . And yet there's something striking about her, something really unusual.'

'Do you . . . think Frank is . . . off again?'

'I think not. She's *too* odd and bony and mysterious – like Ottolie – only she *wasn't* bony. (Such a *name*, too. So *irritating*.)'

'You don't think he's likely to marry her?'

'Most unlikely,' was the decisive answer.

Mrs Massey thought that Frank would not endanger the inheritance of his great-aunt's fortune by such a piece of rash-ness, but she said instead: 'She's very young, and extremely dependent on Addy's kindness, and that would appeal to his chivalry.'

Clemence did not answer, but a long sigh seemed to breathe out into the dimness.

'Yes,' she said thoughtfully at last, 'entirely dependent. Do you think she's on the make?'

'Impossible to say; she's "cagey" as the young say nowadays, never gives anything away. She's certainly got herself comfort-ably placed. I should think Addy will leave her a great deal, if not everything.'

'And cut out Frank? Oh no! She couldn't be so – so unjust.'

'She's besotted. I'm sure I can't think why. The chit gives *me* the creeps – she has such peculiar eyes. I never saw any like them. It isn't only that very pale greenish-blue, though that's unusual enough, I don't know what it is . . . when she looks at one . . .'

'But she hardly ever does – not really look.'

'I know. It's when she *does* look, it's as if she were directing rays onto you or something, that go right through you, not inquisitively, nothing so ordinary as inquisitiveness. I felt on one occasion as if I were being taken to pieces.' (This remark was accompanied by swelling bosom and deepened voice.)

'There *is* something very – cold – about her. Perhaps it's just being very clever,' Clemence said.

'Oh nonsense. When she *does* condescend to utter, she sounds mentally defective to me.'

Clemence gave her an affectionate glance. 'Are you warm enough, dear?'

'Of course I'm warm enough,' defiantly wagging the stableboy cap, which was allowing her ears to feel frozen. 'Oh dear – another week to get through,' as the car drew up in front of their cottage. 'If only someone amusing would drop in. Not that there *is* anyone amusing in Wanby.'

Clemence competently housed the car for the night and joined her grandmother, who was sitting close to a pleasantly glowing fire, in the small, white-walled living-room with its dark beams and chintzes and ancient Chinese and Japanese wall plates.

'At least this place isn't damp,' Mrs Massey observed. 'But the *quiet*! Really – so depressing.'

'I'm going to have some orange juice. Do you want anything?'

'A small whisky, please. Thank you, darling. Aren't you having a biscuit?' she added, as Clemence came back in carrying a tray.

'Not me – I've got my figure to think about.' Clemence set down the tray.

'Oh, there's more to *it* than figures,' darkly.

Clemence mentally responded: *Yes, Grandmamma, I'm quite aware of that. And I haven't got* it.

Mrs Massey was thinking: *And what a pity you haven't, my poor pet!* It, *as that woman Elinor Glyn used to call it.* She thought it wiser to change the subject.

'If I were younger and had the energy, it would amuse me to investigate that girl's background. It sounds fishy, to me.'

'Juliet? Oh Grandmamma. Why?'

Clemence was anxious to be fair to Juliet; she held the code of 'fair play', instilled, if only by fading tradition, by the excellent girls' private school at which she had been educated.

'I'm sure she's lying,' Mrs Massey went on.

'I don't see how you can possibly tell.'

'I *feel* it.' Mrs Massey gestured dramatically. 'Addy ought to be protected. Goodness knows, she isn't capable of protecting herself.'

'I think she's very well protected – first-class accountant and so on.'

'Oh that sort of thing – of course. It's her poor silly old feelings I'm worried about.'

Clemence let these observations drift into silence. If Juliet were a liar, and out for herself, and the facts were discovered, what difference would that make to Frank's obsession? Judging by Clemence's experience of his previous infatuations – none. He had never loved his nymphs for their moral qualities.

In spite of her anxiousness to be fair to Frank's collection of dryads and moon-spirits, Clemence referred to them, in her own mind, as 'those useless wets'.

# BOOK TWO

# 11

The days began to lengthen and whiten, with snowdrops and blackthorn and lingering evening light.

Frank was always aware of the wish, growing stronger rather than declining, to proceed with the humanization of Juliet: this was partly caused by the awakening of the year in its immemorial beauty, and partly by the fact that his great-aunt's health was declining rapidly.

'Excitement is the thing to avoid,' Dr Masters said to him, one morning late in March. 'Any kind of agitation. It's a vicious circle; the heart condition tends to induce excitement, and the excitement weakens the heart. And I'm afraid she *is* deteriorating, every week.'

He paused. He had the admirable bedside manner inculcated by precept and example in medical students fifty years ago.

Frank looked steadily into the kind, clever old face.

'I'm afraid there's very little to be done, Frank.' Dr Masters went on, 'Of course, I can't speak definitely, but I can tell you what you already know. We' – Dr Masters meant the medical profession – 'can postpone decay and death but we can't stop them, and in Addy's case I'm afraid the limit has nearly been reached.'

'I'm very sorry. She's been good to me; I've always been fond of her: my own mother died when I was six.'

'Pity Addy never married. Made for it. Extraordinary, the way things go. Do you think she's been happier since that odd-looking girl came here?'

'Oh yes, in a way (I'll see you out), though she worries about her; Juliet sits up late, chain-smoking, that sort of thing.'

'Well, I hope the girl's provided for, that's all, otherwise she'll be in a hole.'

Frank ran upstairs to Juliet's room.

'Yes,' called an absent voice after the inevitable pause.

'It's me – Frank. I want your mother's address.'

Another pause, and the door opened six inches showing a yellowish face and bloodshot eyes; Clemence would have been comforted.

'What for?' Sullenly.

'I want to talk to her. Come on, Juliet, this is very important, it may affect your whole life.'

'I got something I got to work out – been up most of the night.'

'Yes, you look it . . . Come for a walk for ten minutes – it'll do you good.'

She glanced back at the open pages of the books on her table, their whiteness reflecting the white glow of the spring sun, and some emanation from the young light seemed to call to her own youth.

'All right – but I don't say I'll tell you nothing. 'T'isn't any of your business, and,' the expression became sulkier, 'I'll have to ask *her* first.'

She was taking down her cape from its place behind the door.

'All right – only hurry up, and don't upset her. Dr Masters has just been telling me she must avoid excitement of any kind.'

Juliet made a face, and skimmed away.

'Oh, it's you. What do you want?' Sarah opened Miss Pennecuick's door grudgingly.

'Is that my girlie?' A faint voice from the bed.

'Now don't you go tiring her,' Sarah muttered.

The spring light was merciless to Juliet's benefactress, in a housecoat adorned with delicate lace which deepened the greenish-yellow tint of her face, over which she would permit only the lightest veil of powder – ladies did not 'paint'.

She held out trembling arms.

'Come and give old Auntie a hug, my baby.'

There was no strength in the clasp; the arms folded themselves about the shrinking Juliet with an effort.

'What is it, love? Come to sit with me for a little while?' she gasped.

'Frank wants me to go for a walk.'

'Oh . . . I was so hoping . . . Well, you go, darling. I wish I could have got the car out for you.'

'I *like* walkin', Auntie,' Juliet was already at the door. 'Bye-bye.'

'Tell him to take good care of you, my precious,' came the feeble voice.

Sarah muttered: 'And you be back in good time for luncheon. Keeping everything hanging about. Shouldn't wonder if she isn't setting her cap at him,' picking up a half-finished baby's jacket which she was expertly knitting.

'Oh *no*. Frank is thirty.'

'Ought to marry Miss Clemence, if you ask me,' Sarah said suddenly.

'Clemence, yes. Clemence is what I hope for, Sarah . . . But I also want my baby to be safe before I go.'

'Who's talking about going? Here, let's have a bit of music to cheer us up.'

A blare of sound, threaded by the voices of apparently imbecile adolescent females, sprang from Radio 2.

Frank and Juliet turned down a narrow way signposted FOOTPATH TO MOPP'S END.

But before this alluringly named region was attained, they crossed a big meadow glistening with dew; went along another path, and then into a lane under blackthorn covered in frail, milky blossom.

'Too early for scents yet,' he observed. 'The may won't be out for another fortnight . . . look at the buds . . . and then we'll need a week of hot sun to bring out the scents.'

This brief walk was being undertaken to discuss practical affairs. But he never lost an opportunity of sowing seeds on that stony ground. He glanced at her. Her face had settled into its usual remote expression.

'How beautiful that thorn is against the blue!' he exclaimed, pausing and staring upwards. The damp, ordinary little lane was full of the frenzied chinking and whistling of nesting birds. 'Do see, Juliet.'

She paused and turned back reluctantly; looked first at him with impatience, then slowly tilted her head to look at blackthorn and sky. He waited, feeling an excitement that reason told him was foolish.

'It's . . . I . . .' she said flatly at last, and glanced at him. 'It's beautiful, I s'pose, like you said. But I . . . I . . .'

'"I see, not feel, how beautiful they are!"' he quoted as they walked on. 'Is that it?'

Then inevitably: 'S'pose so.'

'You were going to give me your parents' address?' he said pleasantly in a moment.

'Why j'oo want it?'

'I'll tell you. I'm afraid Miss Pennecuick is fading . . . Juliet, she may die quite soon . . . in fact, Dr Masters only an hour ago warned me that she may . . .'

'She won't!' exclaimed Juliet angrily, stopping in her swift stride. Was all her new-won peace to be swept away? 'What's that got to do with Mum, anyway?'

'I assure you that my aunt may die sooner than any of us thought likely. That's why I want to see your parents.'

He made no attempt, now, to avoid using the plural.

'What *for*, Frank?' She turned, goaded, and stared at him.

'Because I want to have your parents' approval and consent – have them backing me up – in case there's any trouble about her will.'

'Trouble? What d'you mean – trouble?'

It was plain to him, as he stared helplessly at her, that for all the plotting, she had never given a thought to the future. She had assumed, as a child of eight might have done, that her refuge, secured by clumsy lies and based on her benefactress's gullibility, would continue undisturbed.

'I mean this.' They walked on, skirting a wide pool of rain reflecting the changing sky. 'If she does go soon, and she leaves you a lot of money in her will, which she may well do, there

may be protests, and even – er – going to law about it, by other
members of the family.'

Juliet appeared to reflect.

'Nothing to do with them, is it?' she said sulkily at last.

'Isn't it? You'll very soon find out that people find it *is*
something to do with them where money's concerned.'

'Who'd make this here trouble, then?' the tone was contemptuous, half disbelieving.

'Oh . . . old Cousin Harry and his family. He isn't a bad old
boy, but his daughters, Phyllis and Althea, might plead undue
influence.'

'What's that?'

'They'd say you worked on Great-Aunt's affection for you,
and persuaded her to leave you the money.'

'Never said a word! Never thought about it.'

'No. *I* don't think you did, Juliet. And a matter of fact, I come in
for most of the dear old thing's money, as her nearest relative—'

'Then I'll be all right, won't I,' she said indifferently.

This silenced Frank.

It implied so much. She accepted the fact that he was her
friend and that he would look after her. It was as flattering
as a caressing head-butt from a normally ill-natured dog, and
he swore to himself that her casual acceptance should never
be abused. *I'll stick to her for her lifetime*, he vowed. *I'm most
certainly not in love with her, I'm not certain I even like her. But
I do feel I've been – entrusted with something unique, which trusts
me, and I'll keep the trust.*

'I want that address, please Juliet, just in case.'

'All right,' after a pause, and sulkily, 'but you remember what
I said about grassing to Auntie.'

'Are they on the telephone?'

'Course not. Why should they be?'

'Well – people are.'

'My dad likes a bit of peace and quiet – s'pose Mum might like one, but he won't have it . . . Ooh, look! There's a squirrel.'

She stopped, her gaze fixed on the creature, tail curled over its back with sunlight shining through the silvery hairs. It was squatting on a fallen beech and studying the pair of them.

He made an involuntary movement, and she hissed: 'Don't! Very nervous, they are.'

The squirrel, with the apparent aimlessness of wild creatures, darted away.

'Pretty little things. But I like the native red ones best,' he said as they walked on. 'We'd better be turning back – we'll be late for lunch.'

*Animals*, he was thinking, as they went swiftly homewards. *They seem to be the only things outside her mysterious 'work' that she takes any interest in. There were the questions about Bach, but she seems to have forgotten those. She was feeding the squirrels in that park when Aunt found her . . .*

Meanwhile, the twenty minutes between here and Hightower could be put to use. 'Look at the grass,' he remarked, as they crossed one of the verges bordering a secondary road. 'It was cut probably yesterday afternoon. The tips of the blades are square; uncut ones are pointed.'

She looked downwards.

'Square,' she said in a minute, 'like you,' and gave him a mischievous glance.

He laughed with pleasure. 'That's the last thing I am. Now see this—' They had entered the great meadow. 'Someone's been here after us. This path was hardly noticeable when we first came through. It's been pressed in more deeply. See.'

He felt that the more impersonal word was less likely to irritate her than the imperious 'look'.

'Yes – kind of faint-like. Don't let's walk on it,' and she moved aside into the long grass thick with buttercups.

'Why not? It's meant to be a path.'

She did not answer, and he suddenly felt in need of lunch.

## 12

George Slater, having woken at eleven, was sitting up in bed sucking down tea and reading the *Daily Mirror*, when the front door chimes sounded.

He ignored them: Rose was in. He concentrated on the photograph of one Brenda Beezeley, who had Disappeared, and was the object of police suspicions of Foul Play.

Rose said: 'Drat – who can that be, this time o' day?' and got up from her chair in the kitchen, where she had been about to open a tin, and rolled along the passage to the front door.

Mr Slater continued to read down a column headed WHERE IS BRENDA'S BODY? but, unwillingly, part of his attention was given to a prolonged mumbling which was just audible from the front door.

'Yes?' Rose Slater looked up at Frank with large, softly gazing eyes. Her face was also large and soft. She was shapeless, and covered in drooping, clean, bright clothes, the whole protected by a plastic apron. Her bedroom slippers were new and coloured, and her hair rolled up in pink curlers; she suggested a woman not quite in bed and not quite out of it, and Frank supposed that some men would like that. And when she had been nineteen, he thought, she must have been unusually pretty. But – Juliet's mother!

'Good morning,' he began, as she stood silently gazing and irresistibly suggesting to him one of the cows in a meadow at Wanby. 'I'm a friend of Juliet's – your daughter – you *are* Mrs Slater?'

'That's right.' Amiable tone, but no movement or smile.

'Well – may I come in for a moment, and have a word with you and her father? My name's Frank Pennecuick – I'm great-nephew to Miss Pennecuick, the lady your daughter is living with.'

He was prepared for an exclamation – *Oh, Juliet isn't in any trouble, is she?* None came. Nor was there a sulky *We don't want to hear nothing about her, thank you.* Instead, Mrs Slater rotated – that was the word her movement suggested – in the direction of a closed door on her right, and mumbled: 'I'll jus' ask him,' and opened it, and went in.

He waited at the open front door, studying the neatness and brightness of the tiny hall. The stuffy air was pierced by the song of a bird, accompanying a cacophony on the radio. The chill spring wind blew against his shoulders. Listening intently now, he caught the sustained mutter of a conversation behind a shut door: a kind of whining rush broken by occasional mono-syllables, like rocks impeding the flow of a stream.

After a pause of quite eight minutes, the door opened, and Mrs Slater came out. She had been crying.

'Come in, will you, please,' keeping her head turned away. 'In 'ere,' she added almost inaudibly, standing aside.

When he was in the room, he heard the door shut softly behind him, and was so full of indignation over that tear-marked face that for a moment he could not get a word out; he stood staring at the big man sitting up in the big double bed. And when he did speak, he said, not 'Good morning', but: 'I should prefer Mrs Slater to be here, please; I want to talk to you both.'

'Morning.' Mr Slater never took his stare from Frank's face. 'Oh – all right.' He opened his mouth wider, and sent out a mighty shout: 'Rose! Chap wants a word.'

Frank received an impression that 'chap' had been substituted for 'gentleman' out of principle, rather than from insolence. The room was tidy, except for Mr Slater's large underclothing flung on the floor. It was furnished in bright colours, and was very clean, and stiff.

'May I sit down?' he asked, as Mrs Slater, with hastily repaired face, hurried into the room and she muttered, 'Course', and pushed a pink mini-armchair at him. He waited, standing, until she had rolled herself into its twin, muttering, 'May as well be comf'able.'

Mr Slater folded the *Daily Mirror* and said: 'Only to be expected, is what I say.'

'Oh – er . . .' Frank sought for a suitable reply. Could this apply to Juliet?

'This Beezeley girl. Ask for it, girls do. Out all hours, dressed any'ow, talk to anyone what chats 'em up instead of acting quiet and walking off 'ome, and then don't like it when they get murdered . . . you read about it?'

'Er – no. Murder doesn't interest me, as a matter of fact.'

Frank perceived that the subject had been introduced as a kind of social ice-breaker, the Slater equivalent of 'Do-you-know-the-Rowden-Smiths?'

'Ah. I like a good murder. Interestin'. The police work and
that. But this one isn't much good. Straightforward. Soon's
they find the body they'll be home and dry.' A slight movement, altering the shape of Mr Slater's mouth, appeared at
its corners. 'Though dry isn't the word, reely. Drowned, they
think she was. The frogmen are out.'

*The frogmen are out.* The sentence might have come from
some thriller. Frank roused himself from an instant's fantasy.

'Mr Slater, I want to talk to you both about Juliet,' he began,
'and I'm going to be frank with you. I don't want you to – er –
misunderstand my interest in her—'

'That's all right,' Mr Slater interrupted. 'She isn't that sort.
Clever, but never looks at boys nor had boys look at her, so far
as me and her mother knows.'

Here Mrs Slater gave a watery smile and said: 'Julie and
me says she's no more interested in boys than if they was
elephants – not so much, tell you the truth, she always says,
it's a kind of—'

'Belt up, Rose,' Mr Slater commanded. 'Besides,' to Frank,
'you're old enough to be her father.'

This was not heard by Frank with pleasure. 'Well. Perhaps
more like an uncle. That's the way I've come to feel towards
her. Not as – er – close – as a father. Now this is the
point' – he leant forwards – 'and we must be realistic about
it. The old lady, Miss Pennecuick, my great-aunt, is failing;
her doctor told me only a few days ago that the end may
come at any moment. And she may have left Juliet money
in her will.'

He paused, studying the faces turned towards him, and
expecting exclamations of excited greed. What he had not

expected was a manifestation of that now almost extinct and forgotten quality: pride.

Mr Slater's expression changed not at all, but he said in his hardest tone: 'Oh she may, may she? Well, for all me and Rose cares, she can keep it, we can do without it, thank you all the same. Rose! Hot us up another, will you?' and he thrust the teacup at her. 'I can keep me family all right, and Julie can go out to work, like any other bit of a girl.'

Mrs Slater rolled hastily out of the room with the teacup.

'Any money will be left to Juliet,' Frank said, gently emphasizing the name. 'Of course, if she wanted to share—'

'We don't want nothing!' Mr Slater dashed his hand down on the *Daily Mirror*. He had become plum-coloured in face and neck. 'Let her take the old girl's money and do what she likes with it. She won't go to the bad, that's certain sure, not with her looks.'

'No . . . but she might go to university, Mr Slater.'

'She could o' gone to one of them places without any old lady's money. She got five of them A levels, most unusual they said, up at her school. Wanted her to go on there, on some grant, but I wasn't 'aving it, wasting her time when she could o' been earnin' good money. Why, I seen adverts for bits o' sekerteries for three thousand a year and more. And *more*. I ask yer.'

He almost snatched the refilled cup from his wife, sipped, then set it down on the bedside table, growling: 'Burn yer blasted mouth, now.'

'Oh George, you've spilt it! I just polished that.'

'Then you can polish it again. Give yer summink ter do.'

'I *got* things to do.'

'Go and do 'em, then,' Mr Slater instructed without a trace of ill-temper, but Rose was leaning back in the pink mini-armchair.

Frank persevered. 'Yes, she's an unusually clever girl – outstandingly so. But about this money. What I want to make certain of is – if she does inherit something handsome, and if Miss Pennecuick's relations contest the will – er – make a fuss . . .'

'Oo'll make a fuss? What right 'ave they got? Old girl leaves it to Julie, it's hers by right. That's the law, isn't it? I'd like to see anyone sticking their pissing nose into her affairs!'

'Now, George. That's ugly,' Mrs Slater said placidly. 'Language . . .' And to Frank's surprise Mr Slater muttered, 'Oh all right . . . sorry. But just let anyone try doing my girl out of her rights, that's all. Not that we *need* it, mind—'

'Well then, if we're doing all that well, p'raps you'll see your way to me havin' that cork lino for the kitchen,' his wife said, with an effect of tartness.

He waved a hand impatiently: '*I* don't want nothing to do with any money, mind yer. But if you come 'ere to find out if we'll stand by our own, course we will. Stands to reason. I don't like 'er much—'

'George! What a thing to say!'

'—but she's me own flesh and blood, and 'sides' – here was thrust out, gaunt, and harder than tempered steel, the expression of one of those bedrocks of the British character that has *not* been destroyed – 'it wouldn't be fair.'

He brought his fist down slowly, with impressive effect, upon the already crumpled *Daily Mirror*. Rose twitched the paper off the bed, murmuring, 'I want a read of that, looks like it's been in the dustbin already,' while Frank stood up, divided between a desire to laugh, and incredulity at such a pair having produced Juliet.

'Are you in touch with Juliet?' to Rose.

'Phones regular once a week.'

Then she hesitated and Frank wondered if she was about to refer to Juliet's lies. But, after a stealthy glance at her husband, who was glaring at the *Daily Mirror* as though compelling it back onto the bed, she only ended in a murmur: 'Keeps in touch, I will say that.'

Frank made a little bow to Rose and turned to leave.

She accompanied him.

'You mustn't take too much notice of him,' she said, as they stood by the front door. 'His bark's worse than what his bite is . . . I wish Julie'd get married or even engaged, that's what I'd really like . . . All the other girls . . . She's a funny one, and no mistake. I don't s'pose she's got anyone down there?'

'Not so far as I know, Mrs Slater,' gently.

'No . . . I didn't s'pose so. Oh well, all come out in the wash. Good morning. Thanks for coming . . . I s'pose you couldn't fancy a cup of tea?'

He shook his head smilingly, thanked her with more words than he would have used to most people, and, catching sight by good luck of a cruising taxi, hailed it, and directed the driver to King's Cross.

His mind was full of the awfulness of marriage. These thoughts were more insistent than the reflection that his interview with Juliet's parents had gone better than he had anticipated. But he suddenly felt a wish to talk it over with someone. He decided to take Clemence out to lunch: she was such a good listener.

St Alberics, like every other place in England large enough to call itself a town, had recently opened a restaurant for 'natural' foods, and this, of course, was the one to which he took her.

She, soberly pleased at being pounced upon as she was leaving Dr Masters's surgery at ten minutes to one, did not like the Cool Cucumber, but did not, of course, say so.

She surveyed the trays of glowing grated carrot and pearly rings of raw onion, and the bowls of chopped cheese set beside cartons of natural yoghurt, without any vulgar rising of the salival juices. There were also those little wooden barrels full of nettle wine and dandelion wine. She would have relished a glass of rosé.

But he was handing her a wooden spoon and fork and a beech-wood bowl, which she had to fill with a meal; cold, moist, and good for you.

In comic despair, she studied the back of her host's head, shapely below its curtain of thick, curling, shoulder-length hair. What would happen, she wondered, if she slammed bowl, spoon and fork back in their racks, and demanded to be taken somewhere where one could eat the kind of food *she* liked?

But of course she would do nothing of the kind.

'I saw Juliet's parents this morning,' he announced when they were seated and he had poured out two generous glasses of dandelion wine. 'The most extraordinary pair – I don't mean eccentric, I mean extraordinary in having produced Juliet.'

He attacked a mound of shredded vegetables, while giving her an account of his visit and of Juliet's lies. (She suppressed an impulse to burst out: *How do you really feel about her, Frank?*)

Instead, 'What was the point of going to see them?' Dutifully chewing raw carrot. 'I mean, how does that help her?'

'I want them on my side – *her* side, that is.'

There was a trace of defiance in his voice. He was now more anxious than ever that his interest in Juliet should not be misinterpreted.

Clemence's clear blue eyes met his own with their usual calm, and the defiance subsided. Good friend that she was, she always understood: she was 'the thousandth man that sticketh closer than a brother' – but never so close as to be a nuisance, he thought.

She, meanwhile, wanted to exclaim: *But she told Aunt Addy!* and *She must be thoroughly untrustworthy*, and, fatally, *Frank, how can you care about what happens to such a little liar?* And of course she exclaimed not at all, but assumed a gentle, questioning expression which encouraged him to continue.

Which he did.

'You see' – he spoke slowly and with concentration – 'there's this something, some problem she has; I gather from hints she's dropped that it's something to do with coincidence – scientific. Anyway one or two books have been written in the last few years about coincidence but she's only lately got hold of those, she told me. She's been thinking about it, this question, ever since she could think at all, in a vague kind of way, not really knowing what she was puzzled about—'

*Yes, I must face it. He's Off Again*, the Thousandth Man was thinking dismally. *But it's in a different way, this time.*

'—and now the question, whatever it is, absorbs her to the exclusion of all other interests.' He drew a carton of yoghurt energetically towards him and reached for some very brown sugar.

'But what *is* it, Frank?'

'She doesn't *know*. Haven't you been listening?'

'Of course I have.'

'Have some more—' He pushed the carafe at her.

'No thank you. I – I haven't quite—' She held up her glass. 'But if she doesn't know, and can't tell you because she doesn't, how can you help her by seeing her parents?' She glanced at her watch.

'I can get their support if the Barrows make a plea of undue influence over Great-Aunt's will and—'

'And what? (Frank, I'm sorry but I must go. We've got someone really ill, one of what Edward calls his "heavies", coming at two-fifteen sharp . . .')

'And I can guarantee quiet and solitude for her to work at her problem.'

'But that means – adopting her. Or . . . something.'

Clemence, standing up to slip unaided into her coat, turned to stare at him. *Or something*? Not . . . her stomach seemed to turn over.

'Exactly,' he said, in the tone she had heard from him only two or three times in the twenty years of their friendship. 'I believe she's a genius, and I'm going to see that she gets her chance.'

'Well, dear. What kind of a day?' her grandmother asked, when she got home that evening.

'Oh, so-so. Frank took me out to lunch.'

'Raw salad and that unnatural cutlery?' Mrs Massey said tartly. 'Why couldn't he have taken you to the Santo Alberic and given you something eatable? He can afford it. He really is one of the most trying . . . no, *the* most trying man I've ever known. And so *silly*.'

'But sweet, Grandmamma. And kind. And – and good, too.'

Mrs Massey made the sound written as h'mph. The qualities her granddaughter had named did not attract her in the male.

'Of course, if that's what you *like*, dear.'

'It's the best basis for . . . the kind of marriage I want.'

Clemence was leaning forward, holding her large capable hands out to the fire, and looking into its flames, and she now repeated the conversation at lunch.

'Do you – er – think any progress has been made?' Mrs Massey ventured to ask at last.

'Absolutely none, I should think,' was the quiet answer, and then she burst out: 'It's absolutely the *end* having some dotty *idea* for a rival!'

'Really the best advice I can give you, dear – and I've seen a good deal of the world, you know – is to find someone else, and quickly. I've always said, and I say it now: the best cure for A is B.'

'But I want Frank,' Clemence said.

## 13

'I've found another coincidence for you, a really good one,' Frank said to Juliet, on a walk they were taking some days later. It was suddenly high spring; emerald leaves and pink and white blossom tossing in a tearing, cool wind, and the sun silver-white in the changing sky.

Round came her head, with the eyes full of light. She said nothing.

'Yes, in some book of memoirs – can't remember whose. A man had bought his wife a superb painting of a grasshopper by some very famous painter, Picasso, I think; and that night when she went to bed she found a grasshopper struggling and buzzing under the bedclothes. I thought it very odd indeed, and just up your street.'

'Pure.'

'What?' He was not quite sure that he had heard the muttered word correctly; it was so unexpected.

'Nothing. That's interestin'. I – I liked what you told me about the robin, too. Superstitious, course – Christ, and all that – but I liked it. Dunno why.'

*No*, thought her would-be mentor, *you don't know why, and for a very long time you won't.*

Juliet's road was going to be immensely stony and immensely long, and perhaps at the end of it all his cautious feeding into her of the nourishment he believed a human creature must ingest in order to be human (if these treasures were not in the spirit from birth) might have been wasted.

'There's *two* robins!' exclaimed a voice at his side almost unrecognizable from excitement. 'And we was just talking . . .'

'Yes. It is the mating season, dear,' he said gently. It then occurred to him, with one of those flights of fancy more usual in women than in men, that perhaps for Juliet there never would be a mating season. It was the kind of thought for which, among other qualities, Clemence wanted him for her husband; such perceptions complemented her own sober and unimaginative temperament.

'You goin' off to the Cowshed now?' Juliet asked, as he paused at the crossroads, one road leading to St Alberics, and the other back to Leete.

'Yes. As usual, I've got to see a man . . . I only came up to drag you out for a walk. You'd sit stewing over those books all day if someone didn't, and there's no one else to.'

'It's better stewin' than what it is sittin' with poor old Auntie. That does get me down, if you like.'

Miss Pennecuick had taken to her bed, and did not seem likely to rise from it again.

He looked at her curiously. Did she have no feeling of affection towards the woman who had rescued her, and given her solitude and silence so that her strange powers could develop?

'Yes. It must be very tedious,' he said drily, moving in the direction of the small shop selling ice cream and cigarettes that adorned the otherwise charming break in the lonely little roads. 'I left my bicycle here. See you later this week.'

'All right' – and she turned back slowly down the Leete road.

'Juliet?' he called, as he rode past her a moment later. 'Don't be too long, will you? You know how it upsets Great-Aunt if you aren't there when she wants you, especially lately.'

'Oh all right. But it's a dead bore.'

The thin voice floated after him, its discontented note contrasting with the bloom over tree and hedge.

When he was out of sight, she dawdled. The wind lifted her hair and sent it flying out behind her, and the chill air had brought colour into her face.

The white grasses of winter had mysteriously vanished, the last bronze and copper leaves had blown away, and emerald, emerald had everywhere replaced the dun and pallor. The air bit, but it smelled sweeter than any scent that man could concoct; the wild rosebuds, long and pointed with deep pink, were lifting themselves in the hedges.

Juliet wandered on, slowly on. For once her brain was quiescent, and that mathematician's inner picture of the world which is 'presented in the form of inter-related quantities', was replaced by one presented by her senses. Not fully, not with the mysterious splendour that brings tears (as Frank's friend the poet would have seen it with his inward eye) – only faintly and, compared with his vision, a ghost-like entity. But she felt the difference: it came upon her like a revelation; she experienced an emotion almost completely unfamiliar, and only dimly present in the past while she was talking to the pet bird in her former home, or watching wild creatures at play. The world of Nature, Mother of all the Goddesses and of Man, broke through the framework imposed by science, and with it there came a new happiness.

She wandered slowly homewards, seeing everything, breathing each waft of cold sweet air, treading with pausing feet the dry road already lightly filmed with summer's dust.

So when Sarah, shaking with indignation and almost purple with rage, saw from her place by the gate in Hightower's wall her mistress's detested protegée 'dawdling along as if tomorrow would do', she broke into a shrill tirade:

'Where you been, you wicked little beast, you? Bone-selfish, that's what you are, crawling home like some snail, and that poor dear nearly out of her mind wondering where you was. You know's well as I do the doctor says she got to avoid all excitement. All excitement, he said.' Sarah was now tottering beside Juliet, as the latter began to hurry along the path leading to the house. '*That's* what he said, and Mr Frank ought to know better, taking you out when she's about as bad as she can be—'

Juliet broke into a run, flinging an expletive over her shoulder, and Sarah uttered a gasp of outrage, while beginning a shaky attempt to run herself.

The front door was open. Juliet rushed through, across the hall where Pilar, polishing, gaped at her, and up the stairs, two at a time. The unfamiliar happiness she had just experienced was fading; in seconds, it would be forgotten. All she wanted was to get the interview with Auntie over, and get back to her table and books.

She rapped loudly on the door, hearing as she did so a peculiar sound, a kind of loud gasping. She opened the door violently, her anger rising, and darted across the room to the bed and stood there, silent and sullen and trembling with rage.

'Wh – wa – wh – late – wh—' choked a voice out of the face almost unrecognizable from age and agitation. 'I – wh—' The eyes behind the spectacles were fixed in a piteous glare upon her face. 'Oh have you – I – got so—'

'So what? I'm late!' she burst out. 'I only been for a *walk*, haven't I? Anybody'd think I been taking drugs or something – off with some boy – only for a bloody *walk*, and you knew it, and it was your Frank called for me. There's never a minute's peace in this place, it's worse than what it was at home—'

'Juliet' – in a cracked, sobbing voice – 'baby—'

'Yes, that's about it – "Juliet baby" – and treated like one, too. Makes me sick – I'm going on seventeen, not a kid of nine. I can't get a minute to meself, not to *think*, that's what I want to do, *think*. How can I think, with you after me all the time, worrying and moaning?'

Miss Pennecuick uttered a loud cry, and lifted a violently shaking hand as if in fear of a blow, while tears rolled down her face; her heartbeats were shaking her nightdress.

'That's right – now blub. Oh, I'm off, I can't stand no more of this—' and Juliet turned and ran out of the room, swerving to avoid Sarah who, breathless, had just reached the door.

'You wicked girl!' as Juliet swept past. 'After all she's done for you!' Her voice was lost in the slam of the door.

Juliet tossed back her hair angrily when she stood in the welcome silence of her room, and muttered an ugly word;

but the sight of her work table, with books and instruments arranged upon it in the order that was never changed, immediately soothed her.

With strong satisfaction, she saw the figures, spread on a sheet of paper, on which she had been working when Frank's knock interrupted her; and, pulling the chair towards her with one foot, she sat down before them. The May airs floated, sweet with the scent of blossom, through the window: she did not notice them, nor lift her head to listen to a distant cuckoo's cry.

With both hands held against her skull, so large beneath the masses of hair, she sat, staring unseeingly at the paper, motionless as stone.

'What is it?' she called faintly, in answer to a dramatically loud knock on her door. She did not start nor look up.

The door was flung open. Sarah stood there with, behind her, the flushed faces of Rosa and Maria.

'She's been taken very bad indeed,' Sarah shouted. 'Very bad, she is. I phoned for Dr Masters and told him to stop on the way at that place' – Sarah meant the Cowshed – 'and pick up Mr Frank. And *you* come along, too, and stay with her, seeing it's all your fault, God forgive you.'

Juliet got up and came over to her, meeting the shocked gaze of the two girls with a defiant stare.

Along the passage the four went; she could smell lunch cooking and, suddenly, felt hungry.

At Miss Pennecuick's door, Sarah turned on the two maids.

'You be off downstairs and don't you leave that hall for *one second*. I want the doctor in the house the very instant he comes. And none of your chattering and giggling, neither.'

'Oh no, Senora Sarah!' Two shocked voices, and tears welling into four dark eyes. 'Of course we don't make laughing. She been so kind like a mother—'

'Yes, all right, never mind all that . . . You just be off and mind what I say. *You*,' to Juliet, 'I hope God'll punish you, that's all,' and she noiselessly opened the door.

The scene was quiet enough. Antonio and Rosario were at either side of the bed, the younger man clasping Miss Pennecuick's hand as he knelt beside her, and Antonio reading slowly aloud, his deep voice reverently softened to the occasion: '"He leadeth me beside the still waters. He restoreth my soul: He leadeth me in the paths of righteousness for His Name's sake. Yea, though I walk through the valley of the shadow of death"' – the voice sank, became full of awe – '"I will fear no evil: for Thou art with me; Thy rod and Thy staff they comfort me."'

His eyes were fixed upon Miss Pennecuick's worn prayer book, the gift to her, when she was twelve, of her mother; his expression, with lowered lids, was all solemnity and sorrow.

Miss Pennecuick's eyes were shut, but as the quiet sounds of entry came, she stirred. 'Jul . . .' she mumbled, and a speck of saliva came from the corner of her twisted mouth. 'Where's my baby?'

'Go on – speak to her,' hissed Sarah, giving Juliet a savage push towards the bed.

Juliet stumbled, turned, and pierced Sarah with a look that made her draw back, then went slowly forward.

Antonio let his voice fade off: '"Surely goodness and mercy shall follow me all the days of my life,"' and stood in silence, his eyes fixed upon the book, which he gently shut.

Rosario, with a delicacy and tenderness unexpected in so carnal a creature, was gently stroking the hand he held, his eyes fixed mournfully upon the unrecognizable face.

Juliet stood, staring. *Christ, she looks ugly*, she thought. *Like some old guy what's going to be burnt.* She forced herself to speak softly:

'Auntie? It's me – Juliet.'

'Jul . . .' The mauve lips tried to form words but failed; the head moved from side to side.

'Take her hand – go on – take it,' Sarah whispered fiercely.

Juliet reluctantly put her fingers about the skeletal wrist; then, in imitation of Rosario, began to stroke it. She had to bend over the bed; the position irked her, so she knelt – and that was more uncomfortable still, from its unfamiliarity. She half turned: 'Get me a stool.'

Antonio noiselessly carried up one of the tuffets kept in every room where Juliet would expect to sit down.

Juliet settled herself, and the familiar position was welcome. Miss Pennecuick's eyelids came down, shutting her faded eyes into their dark little caverns, and she seemed asleep.

'How long'll the doctor be?' Juliet did not bother to lower her voice, and Rosario's eyes fixed her in a shocked stare.

'Never mind. You stay where you are,' Sarah whispered.

'I'm hungry.'

'Yes, and she's dying. Now you shut up. Your place is there.'

Sarah sat down in the chair which was her own, and there was silence but for the tick of the clock. Some twenty minutes passed, during which Sarah once made an imperious gesture, and the young men tiptoed out, with last, awed looks at the still figure in the bed.

As Catholics, living a full family life, they were used to such scenes at the bedsides of elderly aunts, grandfathers, cousins and in-laws, and, while perhaps there was some acting of a part, there was also true grief, true religious awe, and none of the fear mingled with embarrassment which might have been felt by English servants.

Sarah suddenly sat upright. She had heard the front-door bell.

Even as she was struggling up from her chair, there were sounds approaching, and then the door opened quietly and there was Dr Masters, with Frank's grave face behind him.

'Oh, Mr Frank—' Sarah began. 'Oh, Mr Frank . . .'

'Now you go out with Mr Frank while I have a look at her,' Dr Masters said kindly, putting his hand for an instant on Sarah's shoulder, 'and send one of the girls up – Pilar would be best. You go too,' he added to Juliet, 'but stay outside in case she wants you.'

Juliet sprang up, dropping the hand she was holding, and darted to the door. Dr Masters's glance went after her, then he turned to his patient.

When Pilar had hurried in, and shut the door, the three stood on the landing in silence, Frank softly patting the sobbing Sarah's back while Juliet stared over the balusters down at the dining-room door.

In a moment, restless with hunger, she said to Frank: 'You got home before he came for you?' jerking her head towards the shut door.

'Just. I was starting to make lunch.'

Her grin flashed. 'Don't talk about lunch! I'm starving.'

Frank let quite half a minute pass before he said deliberately, 'Juliet, I sometimes wonder if you're human. A human being, as most people understand the words. Even if you are "starving", can't you keep the fact to yourself? No, it's no use. You can't understand.'

'Can't help being hungry, neither. Still,' defiantly, 'I done a bit of work since I got in.'

# 14

The bedroom door opened noiselessly. 'Frank?' said Dr Masters. 'Asleep. Here a minute, will you.'

Frank went in, and the door shut again. Sarah continued to sob, and Juliet ran downstairs and pushed open the door of the servants' quarters.

'She's better, she's asleep,' she announced to the doleful group seated around the big room, 'and Mr Frank says will you bring in the lunch.'

'Good – good.' Rosario produced a surprisingly robust smile. 'We must eat to keep ourselves strong for the grief to come,' which, judging by various signs, they had already been doing.

Antonio now made imperious gestures, and bustling began.

Pilar timidly approached Juliet, who was already at the door.

'Oh, Mees – what you think will happen to us, to me and all of us, if she die? We don't weesh to go home. No work, not much food, no fun and our muzzer is very, very old—'

'God knows. But you make up to Mr Frank, he's a softie, he'll look after you. Oh, there's the bell.' Juliet always thus referred to the gong, which Rosario was striking softly in the hall. 'Mr Frank's the one.'

She was gone, leaving Pilar, as a good Catholic girl, shocked by advice which she had misinterpreted.

When they were seated at lunch, to which Dr Masters had been asked to stay, he said: 'You must have a nurse, and at once.'

'Sarah won't like that,' observed Frank.

'I'm afraid we can't consider the Sarahs of this world when someone's dying.'

Frank glanced at him, but said nothing.

Juliet continued to eat roast beef.

'I was thinking that there'll be no one really in charge,' Frank said presently.

'I know. I *might* spare Clemence, but—'

'Oh, you can't do that. No, I've a much better idea – what about Clem's mother? There's no one in this house who could stand up to old Dolly. She's fond of Addy, and she'd enjoy it.'

Dr Masters smiled drily. 'Yes, wouldn't she. I'll look in on my way home.'

Juliet having bolted a portion of some exotic Spanish sweet muttered something about 'work', and sped up to her room.


For a moment she sat motionless, staring unseeingly through the open window. Then her mind turned away from the 'real' world, into that world of immovable laws which, to her, *was* the real one. Her last thought, as she forgot everyone, was: *Why do there have to be other people?*

At about four o'clock her train of thought was interrupted by irritating sounds. A taxi driving up, distant voices – an imperious old one, debating the fixed amount of the fare from Wanby to Leete. Later, footsteps along the passage and the penetrating old voice:

'Where's that child? Tell her I shall expect her for tea in the drawing-room in twenty minutes. And Pilar – you are Pilar, aren't you? I thought so, I remember that attractive way of doing your hair – *toast* please, and see that it's *really hot*, and the tea made with *boiling* water.'

Enjoyment in giving orders, like Lady Somebody in the second act of a Pinero play, coloured the well-produced tones. But Juliet had not heard of Pinero, and her impulse was to slip into her coat, and run.

Too late.

One of those taps on her door, which were such an irritating feature of life at Hightower: 'Senora Massey, she want you having tea wiz her in the drawing-room.'

'Oh all right. Tell her I'll be right down.'

But first she washed her face and hands with some expensive soap that was a present from her patroness.

She went downstairs smelling strongly of 'Blue Grass'. Her satisfaction in being clean was linked with the austere perfection of the shapes that were her constant inward companions. As well imagine grease or dust coating a droplet of mercury as staining those abstractions; and, vaguely, she liked the same feeling to be about her own body.

Mrs Massey, wearing a becoming dress printed with mauve poppies, was sitting before the electric fire. Her eye fixed itself at once upon Juliet's slacks and T-shirt.

'May I enquire if you think that is the proper way to dress in a house where someone is gravely ill?'

'I been out and didn't think to change.'

Juliet sat down on her tuffet and looked Mrs Massey full in the eye. *What a goblin*, thought the old lady, who was relishing every minute of her position as friend of the family left in charge. She began to pour out tea.

'No milk,' Juliet instructed, and took the lid off the toast dish.

'I hope you are not "slimming", my dear, you are much too thin as it is and it is customary to wait for your hostess to help herself first. Have you never heard of anorexia nervosa?'

Juliet, mouth full of toast, shook her head.

'Then I will not enlighten you,' said Mrs Massey, suddenly bored and eager to get at the toast. Then, after a few moments, when boredom was verging on irritation, the door opened and Dr Masters came in, followed by Frank, and someone in nurse's uniform.

'Everything all right?' asked Frank. 'Oh, I beg your pardon – this is Nurse Judson. Mrs Massey, Miss Slater.'

'How do you do, Nurse, such a comfort to have you here,' Mrs Massey said graciously; Juliet made a vague sound and an awkward movement, and Nurse Judson said 'Good afternoon' in a voice suggesting that it was a bad one.

'Tea – Edward? – Frank? It isn't very hot, but I'm sure you could drink a cup, Nurse. I'll ring for some more.'

'No. No, thank you. We must go to our patient. But if you would get one of the girls to bring some up—'

'Of course.' Mrs Massey rang; and when she looked away from the bell-push, Juliet was not there.

When Dr Masters had made his examination, having expressed the opinion that there would be no serious deterioration that night and promising to telephone early the next morning, he left, taking Frank with him; and there settled upon Hightower that atmosphere of awed expectation which invades a house where a death is awaited.

Towards evening the wind subsided, as if with lingering sighs, in the boughs of hawthorn and apple tree; and pearly clouds clustered about a pearly moon. The servants stayed in their sitting-room with television silenced as a mark of respect, awaiting a summons from the two upstairs whom they already called the Old Ones. They abandoned English, and muttered in Spanish.

About half-past eleven, Juliet was seated at her table with fists thrust into her hair and her mind moving in another world, when her door was flung open.

'You come along and stay in her room,' Sarah burst out hoarsely. 'All night if need be. She don't' – she began to cry – 'don't want . . . me. Just woke up and said so. Took one look at me and that's what she said: "I don't want you, where's my baby? I want my baby." That's what she said . . .'

'But isn't the nurse there?' Juliet did not move; her eyes slid round beneath the disordered pale mass of hair.

'Course she's there, but you get off that chair and show a bit o' feelin' – after what Miss Addy done for you—' Sarah began to cry again as she turned away and went along the passage to her own room.

Juliet went sullenly to the sickroom door, and tapped; it was opened noiselessly by Nurse Judson.

'Yes? What do you want?' Her eyes were full of disapproval.

'Sarah said I'd better come and sit with *her*,' jerking her head towards the bed.

'*I* am in charge here. Still, you had better come in, in case Miss Pennecuick should become conscious and ask for you again.' She rustled aside to let Juliet enter, then resumed her seat near the bedside lamp and took up some knitting. 'You must keep absolutely quiet.'

Juliet established herself on her low tuffet, avoiding glancing at the thing breathing noisily in the bed, and brought a pencil and sheet of paper from behind her back where she had been concealing them. She began to work again at her problem, picking up Miss Pennecuick's prayer book from the bedside table to serve as a rest for the paper.

The single lamp illuminated with its veiled glow the dim, hushed room. Nurse Judson took in Juliet's every action: she had been given a twopence-coloured version of the situation at Hightower by Mrs Massey, and was prepared to see Juliet as a conniving snake.

*What a little oddity! And what was she doing? Sums? At near midnight, in a room with someone dying?* Nurse Judson knitted faster and more accurately in a fit of moral relish. Presently she rose noiselessly and went over to her patient in silent inspection. Juliet did not look up.

'I am going down to the kitchen,' Nurse Judson announced, 'to make a cup of tea. I shall be about ten minutes, and don't you stir out of this room until I get back. And keep your eyes on *her* – not on that whatever-it-is you're doing.'

She went to the door and opened it, then hesitated. The upstart could not be a day older than the probationers at the hospital where she had trained.

'Do you want one – some tea, I mean? If you do, I'll bring another cup.'

She had meant to keep her sentences curt and reserved. But some quality in the eyes now lifted to her own from what she inwardly termed 'those blessed hieroglyphics' caused her to expand a little in speech and manner.

Juliet slowly shook her head, and Nurse Judson went noise-lessly out.

How still the room was now! An unfamiliar sensation began to creep upon Juliet. She kept her eyes fixed upon the sheet of paper.

She could see, without looking, the white gleam of the bedcover, and the breathing thing that lay under it, the subdued tint of wallpaper and carpet. There was nothing to be afraid of.

But she was afraid.

Every vague remark that she had ever heard about death, the Vast Unmentionable of her century, floated in her mind, and in the warmth of the silent room she suddenly shivered.

Her hand hovered over the paper. But it was useless; the dance in her head, so beautiful in its intricacy, would not return. Somewhere outside time and space the dance went on, eternal and still beautiful; but human fear had broken in, and she could no longer enter that world where the dance continued.

She started violently. A deep, snorting noise had burst from the lump beneath the bedclothes, and Miss Pennecuick moved, and threw out an arm. Juliet sprang up and crept to the bed, and stood fascinated into objective curiosity that drove out fear.

Was she going to see death?

Miss Pennecuick's lips writhed uncertainly. Then her eyes slowly opened, and they were those of a sane and sorrowful old woman. She looked full at Juliet, standing in the glow of the lamp, with its light on her expressionless face.

Miss Pennecuick's lips writhed again, and she made a distorted attempt at speech. Then her voice came out on the silent air, soft and hoarse:

'You never cared for me at all, did you?' she said.

A choking sound followed. And then all expression left her face. Her head rolled slowly sideways on the pillow, and was still.

# 15

Juliet did not move. *Auntie must be dead. Was that all? – And her voice quite ordinary. How funny her eyes looked. And her face . . .*

She heard the door open.

'I think she's dead,' she said, not lowering her voice and without turning round. She continued to stare at the unrecognizable face.

Behind her there was a soft exclamation, and the sound of a tray being set down. Then Nurse Judson was at her side and bending over the bed, and taking certain actions with the body.

The nurse stood up with the faintest of sighs.

'Yes, she's gone . . . what happened?' she asked in a subdued voice.

'Nothing much.'

Juliet softened her own voice in imitation; apparently one did this when someone died.

'I was sitting thinking, like, and she made a funny noise and opened her eyes and looked straight at me . . . quite ordinary – well, you know, sane, I mean – she looked . . . and then—'

She broke off. *Did the old woman's sentence, spoken plainly and sadly, mean that she had not been left any money? But Frank would look after her.* 'Did she say anything?' Juliet shook her head.

'Well.' Nurse Judson swallowed her indignation. Was the girl made of ice? 'You had better be off. It's' – she glanced at her wrist – 'after twelve.'

She turned again to the bed and slowly, with the gentlest of movements, drew the coverings over the face. She did not look again at Juliet, and the latter, subdued by the events of the last minutes, went slowly to the door.

Out of the corner of her eye, as she turned to go, she saw Nurse Judson kneel briskly down, and sink her neat head into hands clasped upon the counterpane.

*Praying,* thought Juliet, skimming along the dim, hushed passage. *So that was another thing you did when someone died.*

'Yes, just before twelve last night,' said Nurse Judson, following Rosa with the morning tea into Mrs Massey's bedroom. 'I had gone out of the room for a few minutes to make myself a cup of tea. Miss Slater was there. She says it was very quick – these cases so often go off quicker than we expect, or else they linger . . . I'm going to phone Doctor now. I have . . . made her all tidy.'

'Very sad, poor dear Addy.'

Mrs Massey allowed the words 'a merciful release' to remain unuttered. It wasn't a merciful release. Except for the weakness of the last years, Addy's life had been very comfortable. *Plenty of money – though, poor dear, she had never known how to spend it and always three or four servants.* If a vague idea went through Mrs Massey's mind that a body untouched by the body of a man – and a heart that had suffered a pain other than physical pain, from its stored-up treasures of love unreturned – could be a burden that it was a mercy to be freed from, she dismissed the thought with the familiar: *Poor Addy, no one ever looked at her.*

She went on at once: 'Well, thank you very much, Nurse. I'll just drink this, and I'll be down.'

'Yes . . . I expect Doctor will want me to be off – I've another case this afternoon.' Nurse Judson saw no reason why healthy old ladies of eighty-odd should linger in bed, and she knew she must force herself to have a word with Dr Masters about her ten-minute absence from the sickroom. 'Don't cry, it upsets people,' she added sharply to Rosa, who was sniffing. 'Nothing to cry about . . . good long life . . . every comfort . . . and she was a believer.' (Mrs Massey looked remote.) 'Well, good morning to you, Mrs Massey.'

Mrs Massey saw with relief the door shut upon Nurse. Now she had the management of Hightower and its inmates to herself – at least until Edward Masters and that sloppy Frank arrived. And for the moment, there was Rosa to be comforted, and that little chit to be kept a watchful eye on and instructed in the proper way to behave.

'Don't cry, please, Rosa, there's a lot to be done. Just hand me my dressing-gown – thank you, my dear.'

And Mrs Massey climbed zestfully out of bed.

She was too well mannered and sensible to make a show of grief. If any such temptation assailed that part of her nature which relished drama, she rebuffed it with the realization that no one was going to believe in hysterics about poor old Addy.

When she had finished telephoning Dr Masters, and received his soothing reassurances about that ten minutes' absence, Nurse Judson drove briskly away in her little car.

*

Juliet awoke late, which was unusual. She was instantly irritably aware of what had happened, and conscious that she must let her parents know – *in case I have to—*

But the thought *go home* refused entry to her mind. *Frank'll see I'm all right* replaced it.

Nevertheless, while she dressed she could not cease from wondering if Auntie had known all along about everything. The advantage taken. The scheming. The long-nurtured plan to use Hightower as an escape. The lies about her family.

Most disturbing of all, had she known the truth expressed in her last sentence?

*She'd never get over that, not her,* Juliet thought, sweeping the brush through her hair.

As she ran downstairs she felt an air of activity in the house. There was a sense of someone about to arrive or depart: the bells door, telephone and servant had it their own way; they were in command except along the passage leading to Miss Pennecuick's room. There the silence began.

'Gently, please,' Mrs Massey, seated in majesty before the coffee pot, instructed as Juliet darted into the breakfast-room. Her voice was deep, a finger raised. 'This morning is not like other mornings.'

'Sorry and all that.' Juliet helped herself to porridge and cream.

A meaningful pause. 'Good morning, Juliet.'

'Oh . . . mornin',' spoken with her mouth full.

'Really, my dear, if only you could realize what a help in life good manners are to a girl. *I* have always found it so.' Mrs Massey crunched into a piece of toast, and picked up the *Custodian*. 'Now, the one thing you have to remember this morning is not to go running off somewhere; we may need you. There is nothing to be done until Mr Pennecuick arrives and . . . the officials. I shall be in the drawing-room if I am wanted. I suggest that you go into the garden and find some flowers for our dear old friend. She would have liked that.'

Juliet, skimming towards the garden, had become pale. She did not want to look again at Auntie's dead body, and as she pulled up narcissi, dandelions, anything she could find, she looked forward to Frank's arrival. *Soft as he was, he was better than the old bitch* (meaning Mrs Massey).

Re-entering the house and wondering how to avoid going into *that room*, she met Pilar.

'Oh, Mees . . . you have flowers too. This afternoon I go by the bus into St Alberic with Antonio to buy a good bunch from us all, me and my brothaires and sistaires.'

'Good idea,' Juliet mumbled, and thrust the ragged cluster at her. 'Put these with yours, will you?'

'You cannot to see her,' Pilar said at once, sympathetically. 'Me too. I fear to look on the dead. And' – her voice sank – 'that man is there now. He just come.' Her face darkened over, like a small sun eclipsed by a cloud.

'What man?'

'The man . . . who do all the arrangements.'

'Oh. Well, course we can't go up while he's there,' said Juliet hastily. 'Put 'em in water, will you? Cheerio,' and she made headlong for her room and her table, thinking, *I'm not going in there unless someone shoves me.*

Death, and the uncertainty of her own future, and even a slight sensation of regret for silly old Auntie, broke, that morning, through the delicate web of ideas in her head.

At last she put books aside, snatched her cape off the door, and hurried downstairs. But, hurry as she might, she saw Frank in discussion with a man in a black suit standing outside *that door*. She rushed on towards the drawing-room and Mrs Massey.

Mrs Massey looked up over her spectacles from an article on abortion. Her expression was disapproving – as well it might be, but not for the obvious reasons.

'Going *out*?'

'Yes. I got the flowers. Thought I'd go and phone me mum.'

'Surely you can perfectly well do that from here?'

'I want a breath of air.'

'Oh very well.'

Mrs Massey, who was awaiting Frank's descent to hear what had been arranged, was giving only half her attention to Juliet with her mind on a most interesting article, to be read next, on transvestitism, and Juliet hurried on to the much vandalized telephone box at the crossroads in Leete, and was relieved to find it unoccupied.

'Mum? It's me, Julie.'

'Oh hullo, love. You all right?'

'I'm all right. It's her – Miss P. She's passed on.'

'No! Fancy! Poor old lady. I hope she didn't suffer much. When was it?'

'Didn't suffer at all, not what I could see. Went out like a light.'

Juliet's voice did not change, but vividly through her mind's eye there passed a picture of that last mournful stare, and she heard again the final sentence. Impatiently, she dismissed both vision and words. But then there followed a disturbing conviction that she would remember both for the rest of her life.

'You comin' home, then? You know you'll always—'

'Shouldn't think so. Frank, you know, Frank says—'

'—you'll always be welcome in your own home, but your dad says I got to make you understand that if you come, you got to get a job. Though if you been left a bit of money, I s'pose—'

'How's Bertie-bird?'

'Oh, he's cheeky. "You're cheeky," I tell him. "Aren't you cheeky?"'

Juliet forgot her mother at once, marching home with her woollen cap (knitted by that same mother) pulled off and her great brow, already marked with the faintest of thought-lines, bare to the scented air. The sweet wind entered her nostrils and, for once, she thought of nothing.

Irritation returned when she had to press the bell at the gate. She prepared to dart past whoever opened it (at least it would not be Sarah who was prostrate in her room).

It was Antonio who stood there, wearing the air of solemn importance which he had assumed since the death of his mistress.

He fell into step beside her. 'All is arranged,' he announced. 'The burial is on the day after tomorrow. Wednesday the day is. And tomorrow the family come.'

'What family? Oh yes – Frank did say something.' *The ones what might make trouble.*

'Is a cousin of the Senora. Mister Barrow. And his two daughters come, Miss Barrow and another Miss Barrow. All very old, I think. We all go to the burying, and I come home first to arrange much lunch because all will be very hungry. Then in the afternoon the man of business read the will.'

'Oh yes – the will.' They were nearly at the front door.

'We wish to hear that, because we think perhaps she leaves us some money. A very kind old lady. But still' – up went his eyes – 'we have no home in England. Bad, bad. In Spain, much secret police, no work, not much food. We like to stay in England.'

Juliet nodded absently, and was making for the stairs when he added, 'La Senora Massey wish you go to her in the drawing-room.' Juliet turned irritably.

Mrs Massey, to an observant eye, appeared to have swelled. This was because Frank, in telling her the arrangements for the funeral, had thanked her cordially for her calmness, authority, reliability and unselfishness in taking charge of Hightower. (It had occurred to him that bossiness and enjoyment of drama had also been exercised, but naturally he did not refer to these qualities.) And Mrs Massey had swelled.

'There you are, Juliet, you really must not run off like this, you know—'

'I told you – I went to phone Mum.'

'At these times one never knows – now please don't *hover* like that, sit down, and I will tell you about the arrangements.'

'Antonio told me. It's on Wednesday and some old cousins of hers are comin'.'

'Then he had no business to,' retorted Mrs Massey. 'Those young people are too fond of gossiping.'

(She ignored an inner voice reminding her of sundry cosy exchanges with Pilar.)

'Must I go?' Juliet blurted, taking out her cigarettes.

Mrs Massey stared for perhaps half a minute.

'Most *certainly* you must go,' she pronounced at length. 'Not only would it be considered very, very strange and *ungrateful* if you did not, but I should think that you would *wish* to.'

Juliet was silent, lighting a cigarette.

Mrs Massey was not usually observant, but she noticed that the girl's hands were trembling slightly.

'I never bin to one,' Juliet said. 'A funeral.'

The old friend of the family was ready to be the consoling angel; what she would not endure was opposition.

'Yes, well, but there are such things as duty and affection, you know. You may give me one of those,' indicating the cigarettes.

Juliet, who had anticipated a tirade against the risk of cancer, was surprised, but held out the packet and even supplied a light, and for some moments they smoked in silence.

Then Mrs Massey said: 'Have you any black clothes?'

'Course not.'

'But I suppose you have a black wrap or jacket or something. Even nowadays, when full mourning has gone quite out, it is customary to wear *some* sign of grief and respect. Go up to your room at once, please, and see what you have that is suitable. And don't get buried in those books . . . I know what you are.'

This was the last thing Mrs Massey knew.

But Juliet fled, glad of the excuse. In a few minutes she was back, announcing: 'Not a sausage.'

'I sent you to look for something black, not a sausage.'

'I mean, I haven't got nothing black.'

'"Anything black". Then you must go into St Alberics with one of the girls this afternoon. Ring the bell, please.'

After a prolonged discussion, in which Juliet did not join, it was arranged – with many warnings about not dawdling, not staring in shop windows, not spending more than two pounds fifty, not wasting time gossiping with acquaintances. Pilar was the chosen escort.

Juliet sat on her tuffet, smoking and musing, in a mingling of dreaminess and furious impatience.

'Juliet! Are you asleep? I have spoken to you twice.'

Juliet looked up, with the old, familiar sensation of sullen near-despair she had known since childhood. No one understood.

'Sorry.'

'You will catch the two-thirty bus, and have a black scarf here in time for tea. You will wear it with the plainest dress you have – *not* those trousers, please. Now there is only half an hour until luncheon – why don't you sit down and read the paper? There has been a terrible disaster in—'

But Juliet was at the door. Even half an hour could be used in following that train of thought, and she was not interested in the disaster in the paper.

Another girl, coming down to meet the Barrows at teatime, might have anticipated a trio 'on the make', their rapacity showing in their faces. Juliet, the black scarf knotted clumsily about the neck of her T-shirt, had no such thoughts.

A grey skirt, too long and not in perfect freshness, swung its cheap folds about her calves; her hands smelled strongly of 'Blue Grass'. She was still in thrall to that drifting, dreaming speculation which promised to be fruitful; her brain seemed to be divided into two parts: the one unwillingly busy with people, situations, annoying details and voices; the other floating easily, luringly, in 'strange seas of Thought'.

'Ah, there you are. Phyllis, Althea, George, this is Juliet Slater, poor Addy's young friend.'

Juliet looked at the old man and the *two scraggy old trouts*, which is how she saw the Misses Barrow. She nodded and muttered 'Hullo', at which Mrs Massey glanced briefly at the ceiling.

'Now you can make yourself useful. Pass Miss Barrow the cake, please,' indicating Althea with a nod.

The elder sister glanced up wistfully at the odd, plain girl. *Poor child, she looked lost and lonely. Perhaps this time . . .* Anthea Barrow had never managed, somehow, to get on with young people, but perhaps this girl was missing poor Addy, and there might be a chance.

Phyllis Barrow looked at Juliet's hair. Here was youth. Youth to be disliked, disapproved of and envied. *It was a scandal if a common little thing like this was going to get a lot of Addy's money.* The empty heart seethed in jealousy and pain.

*Queer girl. Looks clean,* thought old George Barrow, chewing egg sandwiches. *Hasn't got that forehead for nothing . . . Like to talk to her, if I get the chance . . . But Phyllis wouldn't like that . . . If only my girls had had brains . . .*

Voices were subdued, there were smiles, but no social laughs. Everyone was aware of the thing lying upstairs in that shockingly shaped box smothered in flowers.

Mrs Massey was not giving in to corpses, though of course one must behave properly towards them, and she kept up a flow of pleasant commonplaces, seasoned as usual with enough tartness to make them entertaining.

She was aware of an occasional admiring glance from the old man, who realized the triumph of her social sense over the primitive fear stalking the house. She was conscious, too, of her own pale skin and elegant dress. *Vanity,* thought Mrs Massey, *is one of the great supports in life,* and she rippled, rather hoarsely, on.

\*

In the evening, the return of Frank slightly lifted from Mrs Massey the burden of maintaining civilization; his easy, natural behaviour was soothing to everyone.

But how tiresome he was with the chit, sending her off to her room soon after dinner, 'because tomorrow will be a tiring day'.

When Juliet had disappeared, after a curt 'Night all,' Mrs Massey gave a small and chilly laugh.

'One feels one should apologize – but you can see what class she comes from. Poor Addy, she was sadly taken in.'

'She has pretty hair,' Althea said timidly.

'That is a gift from Providence, and no credit to her,' said Mrs Massey, who never hesitated to introduce this vague entity when she needed backing up.

'Yes, her manners *are* bad,' said Phyllis, smoke wreathing out from her large, sour face. 'No father, I think you said?'

Frank remembered the monumental figure seated in the bed, and thought that, in the physical sense, Juliet had too much father.

'No father, and four brothers and sisters,' he lied smoothly.

'Addy picked her up in some park or other, feeding squirrels. Just the sort of thing . . . well, she's gone, poor dear soul, and one mustn't. But anyone could have seen with half an eye that the girl was on the make,' Mrs Massey said.

'At fourteen?' Frank snapped, and Mr Barrow, who was secretly on Juliet's side because of her hair, said hastily that she looked clever.

'You're quite right, she is, she got five A levels,' said Frank. *Heavens! How plain the two poor women were!* He thought, suddenly, and with pleasure, of Clemence's slenderness and brown curls.

Mrs Massey observed that good manners and attention to dress were of more use than A levels, and this led to a discussion between the men on contemporary education.

So the evening passed. A slight rain was drifting through the foliage of the elms, and the darkness smelled sweet of new grass, and budding wild flowers and wallflowers and iris in the great garden.

Juliet sat beside her open window, gazing into the dimness, breathing the sweetness of the air, vaguely hearing the rustle of the rain. Vaguely, too, she felt a power for which she had no name, rising about her: it was the aura surrounding a tall young maple which looked with myriad leaf-eyes into her room, and soothed her tumult of dreamy thoughts. It was benevolence.

# 16

Before the procession of black cars, the foremost laden with its tribute of glowing bunches and wreaths, rolled through the gates of Hightower, Frank drew Juliet aside.

'Don't think about what's being done when we're standing by the grave,' he instructed calmly. 'Think about the wild flowers, and the weather.'

'Why?' she demanded at last; she was very pale and looked plainer than usual.

'Because you're frightened. And I don't want you to be.' (*In one way, I don't, that is*, he inwardly finished the sentence.)

She was silent, looking away at a tall chestnut in blossom.

'Aren't you?' he insisted.

'It's creepy,' she said sullenly.

'That's a natural response. But it'll soon be over. Do as I say – think about the weather. It's very old, and it's always there. I think you'll find that – comforting.'

'All right. But I better remember to keep me face sad,' and Frank stifled a laugh as there slowly emerged from the drawing-room the Barrows, Dr Masters, Clemence, her grandmother (elegant in grey and black) and Sarah (with hand-kerchief conspicuous). The Spaniards joined the procession in the hall; they were to be accommodated in the final car.

Juliet tried to follow Frank's advice. But although the rain of the previous night had drawn out subtle scents from grass and wild roses, and the sky showed every change of a fitful spring, from violet-grey to purest azure, she could not let these comforters take charge of her.

Her feelings swung between shrinking fear of *what* was being lowered into that space of disturbed earth, and the dim, fruitful half-dreams of the previous night. Sarah's loud sobbing, and the awful words spoken by the clergyman drifted past her unheard.

'Juliet! Don't let me catch you putting plastic forget-me-nots on my stone when I'm dead,' Frank said, as they left the churchyard when it was over. 'Beech leaves will suit me nicely, thank you.'

He pointed to a violently blue cluster on a nearby stone, and Mrs Massey, glad of a chance of a possibly entertaining argument, said: 'Really, Frank.'

'The colours are filthy and the idea's worse, eh, Juliet?'

'Pardon?' She turned, listlessly.

'Ah, she's thinking about this afternoon, aren't you, Juliet?' (Mrs Massey was certainly thinking about it.) 'You need not be ashamed, my dear, and it isn't heartless – dear old Addy would have understood. Your whole future may depend upon it.'

Juliet did not hear the remark, as she scrambled into the car behind Frank. She glanced with relief at his calm face. He would look after her.

Clemence was thinking, despondently, how badly her grand-mother and Frank 'got on'. It was another obstacle in the way of her ever getting her heart's desire. *I'm developing into a typical apprehensive old maid*, she thought.

The procession turned in through the gates of Hightower, where Antonio now stood sentinal, in black jacket and with exactly the correct expression of dignified regret on his face.

In ten minutes the party was seated at the cold luncheon set out by the Spaniards, to which, on Frank's instructions, had been added champagne.

'It seems . . . rather heartless,' Phyllis Barrow observed, sipping affectedly. 'More like a celebration.'

'Addy will be pleased,' Frank snapped, and his use of the present tense aroused such reflections among the mourners that no more was heard from Phyllis.

About half-past three, when the elders had rested, and Frank and Clemence had strolled round the garden (Frank deploring the absence of useful weeds, and Clemence dolefully adding, in secret, her own approval of weedlessness to her list of the Obstacles), young Mr Chesney arrived, the son of that old Mr Chesney who had been the Pennecuicks' lawyer for forty years, and deputizing for his father. The party drifted, from various parts of the house, into the library.

'Do you think, Mr Chesney . . . er . . . the servants . . . Our dear friend gave me to understand, on one occasion, that she had "remembered" them. Do you think that they should be present?'

Mr Chesney having answered cheerfully that that depended upon what Mr Pennecuick thought about it, Mrs Massey asserted her position by glancing fretfully about her and demanding: '*Now* where is that girl?'

Here Juliet came hurrying in, with a cross, pale face and a compass between her teeth, both hands being full of books and sheets of paper.

Mrs Massey made a gesture indicating despair, as she turned to Mr Chesney. 'Mr Chesney, this is Juliet Slater.'

She left the statement unadorned, and indeed Mr Chesney had been briefed by his father about the teenager.

'How do you do?'

'Hullo.'

Juliet's smile and articulation were restricted by the compass, and Mrs Massey struck in sharply: 'Put those things down *at once*, please, *here*,' and she indicated a side table.

'Oh all right – just thought I'd fill up time if there was any arguin'—'

'We don't think there will be, do we, Chesney?' Frank said good-naturedly as the company seated itself. It would do no harm to warn the Barrows that he, the chief heir, took it for granted that there would not be.

Young Mr Chesney smiled, and said that he hoped not.

Juliet slid into her place only half aware of what was going on. The scant two hours since lunch had been 'spent' by her indeed, and royally. A new line of thought had opened itself, leading to regions hitherto unexplored, and her eyes were shining with an excitement that Phyllis Barrow thought of as *disgusting*. Clemence, noticing it, felt some disappointment on Frank's behalf. Was it greed? If it was, his attempts to humanize his protegée had succeeded only too well.

Mrs Massey was enjoying the fact that Juliet was 'glaring' out of the window at the vast white clouds massed in the summer sky. Really, the girl looked hardly sane; excitement over the will must have temporarily unbalanced her.

The servants were present; Frank had invited them into the room with a friendly smile, which Mrs Massey had modified by indicating that they should stand ranged in decent order by the door, where there were no chairs. Such small triumphs made the juice of Mrs Massey's life.

Mr Chesney's agreeable young voice broke the attentive silence. The sun shone between the noble clouds onto the dark colours and the worn, lined, ordinary faces – ordinary all, except one.

The bulk of the estate, young Mr Chesney began, was left to the deceased's great-nephew, Mr Francis Pennecuick; it amounted to some three hundred and forty thousand pounds. Of this sum, over thirty thousand pounds had been set aside for legacies, of which the largest, twenty thousand pounds, went to the deceased's 'beloved adopted daughter, Juliet Slater'.

Mrs Dorothy Massey, of Rose Cottage, Wanby, Herts; Miss Clemence Massey of the same address; and Dr Edward Masters of Beech House, Wanby, each received one thousand pounds. And 'my dear faithful old friend Sarah (Mrs Bason) eight thousand pounds'.

(Mr Chesney felt that a quaver in his voice would have been appropriate here, but could feel nothing but an un-legal envy of the old housekeeper, because he himself was hagridden by a mortgage.)

'A hundred pounds each to . . .' and here followed the full names of each of the Spanish servants, which Miss Pennecuick had memorized, written out, and given to old Mr Chesney on his last visit to her; these legacies were given in codicil.

When he had concluded, in a silence that was noticeable, he laid the will before him on the table and sat down, keeping his gaze fixed upon the document. *Give them time to get their faces in order.*

He looked up.

Phyllis Barrow said instantly: 'We knew that we were unlikely to benefit from Cousin Adelaide's will. But we should of course like to have some small personal memento of her. Isn't there any jewellery?' ending the sentence rather faster than she liked, but unable to repress her eagerness.

Clemence was gently patting the weeping Sarah's shoulder.

'There is indeed a long list of personal bequests.' Mr Chesney tapped some sheets of foolscap.

'Put everyone out of their misery,' muttered old Mr Barrow.

'Well – yes.' Mr Chesney sent him a properly proportioned smile. 'My congratulations, Mr Pennecuick,' to Frank, who nodded absently and said: 'Who are the executors?'

'I was coming to that. Mrs Massey is sole executrix. My client told me she felt her old friend would not find the duties involved fatiguing, but might even – er – rather enjoy them.'

'Quite right. So I shall,' Dolly said briskly. 'If you'll let me have that list, Mr Chesney. Thank you.' Then she whispered to Sarah that she could tell the servants to bring tea to the drawing-room, and Clemence led Sarah, still wiping her eyes, to the door.

Mr Chesney was eager to be off. No thank you, Mrs Massey, he would not stay to tea. He decided that the house was certainly an interesting specimen mummified in the Thirties, the girl looked odd, even unusual, and he hoped the firm might retain the management of the Pennecuick affairs; nevertheless, he could hardly wait to get back to Lucy and the children and his garden and the mortgage and the dogs.

In the drawing-room, the party was drinking tea and dissecting the afternoon's announcements, after a polite interval, of course, during which the weather was introduced.

Everyone studied Juliet, stealthily, but avidly; everyone essayed little remarks, intended to convey kindly interest in her future and a complete lack of envy. At last, when the ladies (with the exception of Clemence) had ceased lying, old Mr Barrow said: 'And what are you going to do with your money, young lady?'

He had been eating his way, with gusto, through a plateful of hot tea cakes. *Tea cakes! It must be forty years since anyone had bothered to send up the little hot buttery things for his delectation.*

Juliet looked up absently and muttered, 'Oh – I can't say yet.'

But Frank said with decision: 'University is the place for her. Isn't it, Juliet?'

'S'pose so.'

'Very wise,' said Mr Barrow, whose income, provided by a small fortune he had made at forty, had been devoted to padding him round with every comfort purchasable on this planet. 'Where do you think of going?'

Silence. The May wind sailed past the windows.

'Cambridge, I s'pose,' she said at last. 'They're best for maths.'

'Whew! Flyin' high, aren't you? You'll have to work damned hard if you want to get in there.'

'Juliet will get her place all right,' said Frank. 'The problem is what's to be done with her until she goes up in probably a year's time.'

Clemence looked at him steadily. Yes, his chief interest (next to Edible Grasses) was now Juliet Slater. *I'm sick and tired of waiting.*

'Can't I stay on here?' Juliet asked. Her quiet room and her table were calling, and the theory that had danced in her mind before she came downstairs was beginning to throb again, with an almost painful force.

'Hardly, dear.' Frank brought out the last word clearly, and stealthy glances were exchanged. 'The servants will be going back to Spain, and I shall probably sell the house to some institution. Or I might just pull it down and put the land under cultivation.'

'Or turn it into a country club,' Clemence said rather shrilly. And as he glanced at her in surprise, her grandmother exclaimed:

'*What* a good idea! Bring some life into this very dreary part of the world.'

Mr Barrow, having eaten most of the tea cakes and a thick slice of sponge cake, glanced at the clock and said that they must be going. (It was *Kojak* this evening.)

There was a general setting aside of cups, and everybody rose.

The warm wind pressed against the windows, and the haunting theory danced its stately pavane in Juliet's head as she almost ran out of the room.

# 17

'Grandmamma,' in a half whisper, 'ask Edward to drive. Please.'

'Oh dear – must I? You know he hates driving and that makes him nervous, and if there's anything that does frighten me—'

'*Please.* I – want a word with Frank. He and I will walk.'

Mrs Massey, glancing down to ascertain that her ample grey folds were in order, noticed that Clemence's hands were clenched at her sides. Most unusual. Poor child.

'Very well, dear,' she said and advanced upon Dr Masters. 'Clem doesn't feel quite up to the mark. So will you be a dear, Edward . . . ?'

Dr Masters, no better pleased than she, made himself be a dear, and off the pair went.

'Frank, walk me home, will you? I feel a bit – I don't know – queasy, and I need exercise.'

'Of course. I thought you sounded on edge. Need an arm or anything?'

She shook her head, not looking at him.

'Right. I won't be a minute. Must just speak to the servants.'

She stood, waiting: as she had waited since she was fourteen. Addy's death, unloved, unmated, childless, had been the last straw. Must she, Clemence Massey, that nice woman who's been with Dr Masters for years, die some fifty years on, perhaps, in the same way? And the long rays of evening sunlight, and all the brilliant, throbbing spring life around her, even the scent of hawthorn, increased her pain. She had no idea what she was going to do or say. But say or do something she must.

In ten minutes they were walking down the drive.

'Don't let's hurry, shall we?' she said, as Frank shut the little door after them, having smilingly waved back Antonio, who had accompanied them, beaming. 'It's such a – lovely evening.' She gulped.

'Clem, dear, what is the matter? Has the funeral upset you?' Frank looked concernedly into her face, unbecomingly flushed.

'Of course it has,' she almost burst out. 'Someone dying like that – poor Addy – with no one to love her – or – anything.'

He was silent for a moment, surprised and a little embarrassed. Then he said: 'Does that matter so much? I don't think – that side of life – troubled her much. She had all the money and comfort she wanted – friends, travel (when she was younger). I shouldn't have said she was that kind of woman.'

'What kind of woman?' It was a snap, and an angry one, and she turned to glare – yes, it was a glare – at him.

'Well, the kind to whom love and marriage mean a great deal.'

'Oh Frank! They meant *everything*, poor, poor Addy. And *all* women are that kind of woman. If they aren't, they aren't women,' she ended rather wildly.

'There are so many different kinds of love, Clem.'

'Addy didn't have *any* kind of love. She made me think of a – a flowering branch that's never lost its petals or formed any fruit. Wasted.'

'Well, that's enlarging the question considerably, to say her life was wasted. I like your comparison with the branch. I didn't know you were a poet, Clem,' teasingly, and with the object of lightening the atmosphere a little.

'Oh why must men always *generalize*?' was the angry and surprising answer, almost a cry. 'And I'm *not* a poet, I'm—' She choked the words back. 'Oh, never mind *what* I am – let's walk a bit faster, shall we?' and for the remaining twenty minutes or so, going at a pace almost as swift as Juliet's, they were silent.

Clemence felt no better; rather worse. It was as if she had within her a miniature volcano of some indefinable kind, which had yet to erupt.

'Come in for a drink?' he suggested, when, hardly realizing where she was going, she had accompanied him across the meadow to the doorstep of the almost completed Cowshed.

'Oh – all right. Thanks. I will.

He opened the door into the long, low, austere living-room, and she sank uninvited into a comfortable old chair and sat staring at nothing. The place smelled slightly of raw putty, which made her feel sick.

'Frank,' she said in a loud, harsh tone, as he was crossing the room to the cupboard where he kept his homebrews, 'can I have an ordinary drink, please? Not that . . . You do keep some, I know.'

'Of course. For the unregenerate, I do – yes,' he grinned.

He brought up one of the low tables which he had made himself during his scanty moments of leisure, and arranged glasses on it and drew up a chair opposite her, a glass of dandelion wine in his hand. Staring somewhere over her shoulder, he had plainly gone off into thoughts of something deeply interesting to himself.

Clemence angrily took a large gulp of whisky.

She usually drank little, and had today eaten sparsely because she had been so upset. The whisky rushed joyously straight up into her head, and she was instantaneously, blissfully drunk.

He did not notice the changed expression in her eyes; nor did he lift his glass in the usual salute to the years of their shared childhood. She began to feel a strong wish to talk, to bubble out her longings and her pain, and her lips parted slowly, of their own volition, in a long sigh that was poised, like a breaking wave, over a rush of words that were yet to come.

He looked across at her. 'I'm wondering,' he began, 'about Juliet— What?'

'Nothing.' (In fact, it had been a furious murmur – 'Blast Juliet.')

'You see,' he leant forward, his thin face and large eyes alight with eagerness, 'I feel she's my treasure, my trust. I'm pretty certain she's a mathematical genius in the range of Keppler or Einstein, quite incapable of making a living by teaching or anything of that sort. She needs unlimited solitude and privacy to let her powers develop. She can't stay at Hightower. She can't – and wouldn't anyway – go back to her parents. What I'd like to do is to have her here with me, and give her complete freedom for the next year and a half – but I suppose there'd be gossip.'

'Yesh.' Clemence held her glass, admiringly, up to the light, fuzzily smiling, 'There would. Be gossip.'

'And when she does make a name for herself – and I believe it'll be a very big one – it would be tiresome for her to have had . . . well . . . a shady-sounding adolescence. Added to her being a woman. What?'

Clemence had muttered something else and now was nodding; she had meant to shake her head with decision, but somehow the gesture reversed itself.

'Any hint of sex interest . . . I simply cannot face inviting some unknown female, however suitable, to come here as companion for the months before Juliet goes up. I can't face it, I'd murder the unfortunate creature. So what's to be done?' He paused. 'I simply do not know.'

'You could marry me,' Clemence said.

His glass fell to the floor.

She nodded – sagely. 'Marry me. Alwaysh wanted to marry you, since I was seventeen. I could see to Juliet and I want shome children. Lotsh of children. We get on so well, you see. Alwaysh have.'

There he sat, gaping, a pool of dandelion wine at his feet, and the smashed glass glittering. The silence lasted just long enough for reality to make its way up to the edge of the alcoholic liberty in which Clemence was floating.

She was on the brink of realizing what she had done, and if she had continued to sit, leaning back comfortably and gazing at him with that glazed, silly smile, and gently waving her glass at him, perhaps convention and common sense and bachelor habits might have asserted themselves.

But suddenly she gulped, and set her glass down with care on the table and covered her contorted face with both hands, and burst into tears, crying loudly like a child.

'Clem! Love!' Frank scrambled across the six feet separating them and took her awkwardly into his arms (with none of the

sensuous reverence with which he used to take Deirdre or
Ottolie). 'Don't – don't cry – it's marvellous – a marvellous
idea – of course, that's the solution. Only a fool like me wouldn't
have thought of it before. Of course we'll get married. Brilliant
girl – there, there,' and he attempted a soothing rocking, which
failed because she was lying back in the chair. 'Don't cry—'
A series of kisses were deposited all over her wet face as he
pulled down her hands. 'Here, have some more whisky—' He
looked distractedly over his shoulder for the bottle.

*Clemence*! He felt as if the roof had fallen in.

Then he was visited by one of those angels who bestow
strokes of genius upon ordinary people; who inspire the
sentences that heal wounds, and modestly, with simple means,
shape lives. He drew back a little, still clasping her loosely,
and said, the angel prompting him to a doubtful tone: 'You did
mean it, didn't you, my love?'

'Of course I meant it, you idiot,' she said, between sobs.
'Been meaning it for agesh, only you kept falling in love with
all thoshe—'

'No more,' he assured her earnestly. 'That really is over.
My poor Clem,' kissing her tenderly, 'you must have been so
miserable. My jewel of a best friend.'

She looked up at him, her face lacking even its usual ordinary
pleasant attractions because it was so ravaged and tear-stained.

'But you don't love me, do you?'

*Don't hesitate*, commanded the angel, in as near a hiss as an
angel can get.

'Of course I love you. In the best, most lasting way of all. As
one loves a wife. I'll love you more, too, when we're married.
You wait.'

He ventured a smile, and Clemence sat up and produced a handkerchief. Reality returned.

Suddenly, she felt more than usually sober. And all those slightly dreary but necessary spirits which had guided her since she had decided she wanted to marry Frank, stood before her, and 'The Smile of Reason' was gone from the faces of Control, Common Sense, Prudence, and Planning. Those faces were all a yard long; and their owners were enquiring in one dismal chorus, 'Clemence Massey, *what* have you *done*?'

'I think it might work,' she said shakily, after some nose-blowing which did not add Romance to the occasion.

He stood up, towering over her, looking down at her with gentle eyes. 'I get my best friend for life. You get what – you seem to want. And Juliet gets protection for her genius. Perfect.'

Juliet.

Clemence was now well afloat on the tide of reaction that had replaced the blissful alcoholic one, and she heard the dismal chorus of her inward mentors change to a warning note.

*Oh yes*, they were saying, *it will work if you don't drop Us, and don't protest about herb wines or no carpets, or, most of all, that ghastly little Juliet. It'll work all right. And work is the word*, they added coldly. *You drop Us, my girl, and see what happens.*

Clemence lay back in her chair, feeling dazed, and there was silence in the room. She was very aware of that smell of putty. Perhaps that was why she felt sick?

Frank had gone off into a stare, his eyes fixed on a wooden spoon which came from Indonesia and was hanging on the wall, for he had already begun to install his possessions. A soft sound broke into his reverie.

'Why are you giggling, love?' He turned smiling to her, beginning to laugh too.

'I was thinking – no one but you would sit staring at a spoon when you've just been proposed to.'

'Spoon – nice old Victorian word – most appropriate,' and he went over to her and began kissing her.

'You don't like being kissed, do you?' he said anxiously, in a moment, drawing back.

And Clemence, still suffering the effects of whisky and putty, burst out: 'How can you *expect* me to like it, when I'm so tired, and it's all so, oh, *do* let me go home to Grandmamma!'

Both were laughing as they went out of the Cowshed, but her laughter was not free from hysteria.

The next morning at six o'clock, an hour which she preferred to pretend did not exist, Mrs Massey, dimly dreaming, heard two loud bangs and, with confused and indignant thoughts of the IRA, sat up in bed. Her snowy curls were crowned by a cap with lilac and white bows and her night attire was unsuitable and gallant.

She at once realized, as the bangs were repeated on a miniature scale, that they had been magnified the first time (in the peculiar way that light sleep does magnify sounds) from the noise made by three small stones thrown against her window. A fourth one tinkled against the pane as she sat up.

She glanced at her watch on the bedside table, in the full sunlight of the first day of June, and having drawn on an equally unsuitable and gallant dressing-gown, she marched across to the window, vigorously opened it and peered down into the dewy little garden.

'Frank! What on earth—?'

'I've come to breakfast.'

'We don't breakfast until eight.'

'Oh – well – I'll wait. Is Clem there – awake, I mean?'

'Of course she's *here*, and probably awake by now, too, with us bellowing at each other—'

'Can I see her?'

'I suppose so – she was rather seedy and peculiar when she got in last night. She went straight up to bed. If it had been anyone but Clem I'd say she had been drinking.'

'Didn't she tell you?'

'Tell me what? (For heaven's sake come in, if you're coming. I'm freezing.)'

The air was white with drifting pear blossom.

'We're going to be married. We got engaged last night. I'm taking her over to St Alberics this morning to get the ring.'

'My *dear* boy! How perfectly delightful! I *couldn't* be more pleased! Come in, come in, I'll wake her up.' *A generous allowance, at least. Quite thousand a year, if not more . . .*

'Grandmamma, what *is* going on?'

Clemence, rosy from deep sleep, her brown curls in a Rossetti cloud they seldom got the chance to display, appeared at the door, knotting the girdle of her housecoat. She looked, as she leant from the window to smile down at her betrothed, for the first time in her life, beautiful.

Frank blew her a kiss, and repeated that he had come to breakfast.

'I'll get dressed,' Clemence said and retreated, feeling solidly and bread-and-buttery happy. *It's going to work,* she thought as she brushed her hair and put on one of her sensible dresses.

Mrs Massey's aim in life was to present to the world the image of a perfectly behaved, gracious and tactful being; but she was not so tactful as to suggest that she should breakfast in bed. There would be lots of interesting things to hear, and she would enjoy seeing dear Clem looking so happy.

Dear Clem looked shy and rather glum. *I was radiant, I remember, when James proposed; quite radiant; everyone said so,* thought Mrs Massey, in the intervals of calculating how much a year she could count on from Frank after the wedding. *Such a pity the child hasn't a more expressive face.*

The conversation was about practical affairs, and hardly touched upon the future, until a certain name was mentioned and Frank spoke of 'semi-adoption'.

'Juliet?' exclaimed Mrs Massey, more sharply than she intended. 'You're surely not thinking—'

'She's going to live with us, isn't she, Frank?' Clemence said bravely. This was what she feared most, and she thought it best to get the statement of her fear over.

'*Live* with you? Are you serious?' Mrs Massey put down an egg spoon with deliberation. 'Do you mean to tell me – *is* she serious?' looking at Frank.

'Perfectly,' he answered coolly. 'It was Juliet – in a way – who made me ask Clem to marry me.'

Clemence darted him a look bright with love.

'It was *Juliet* – what *are* you—? Have you both taken leave of your senses?'

Mrs Massey fumbled in her bag for her spectacles, which she only put on in rare moments of agitation. 'You'd better tell me exactly what happened.'

*That we won't,* said two pairs of eyes, exchanging glances.

'It's perfectly simple, Grandmamma. Frank was worried about what's going to happen to Juliet. She's . . . so brilliant and so odd. We feel someone has to look after her.'

'She has a perfectly good mother, from what I hear, and twenty thousand pounds – what else does she want?'

'Love,' Frank said, and Mrs Massey made a sound as near to a sniff as a perfectly behaved, gracious and tactful being can produce.

'Does she, indeed. Well with no looks and no figure and no manners, she isn't likely to get it.'

Frank considered explaining that he had not meant that kind of love, but decided that no explanation of his could satisfy Mrs Massey's complete incomprehension, while Clemence felt uneasily that her grandmother was only taking the common-sense view.

'We shall have to see how it works out,' Frank said dismissively. 'Certainly, it's settled. She's coming to us. So there's no point in discussing it, is there – Grandmamma?' He smiled at the self-willed, pretty old face, and hurried on before she had time to speak. 'Any ideas about the ring, dear?' to Clemence.

'Oh . . . well, I'd like to go to that shop in the cathedral precinct that sells old jewellery. I'd like a Victorian one, I think, if we can find it.'

'Of course – I'd like that too. How soon can you be ready?'

'Oh – twenty minutes – but it's only half-past seven. The shops won't be open.'

'We'll have a little tour round the lanes – I'll pick you up at eight. Goodbye for now, love. Goodbye, Grandmamma,' with a mischievous smile.

He was gone and Mrs Massey instantly leant towards Clemence with drama: 'My dear! Of course you aren't serious? You'll talk him out of it.'

'Indeed I shan't, Grandmamma. If I try, I'll talk myself out of marrying him.'

'But I never *heard* of anything so – so insane. It isn't even as if she were an ordinary pretty girl who was sure to marry. You'll be lumbered with her for life. Suppose he falls in love with her?'

'Oh *Grandmamma . . .*'

'Or she with him, which would be worse. She's such a cunning little creature . . .'

'Oh, not cunning. Half the time she isn't thinking about what she's doing, I'm sure.'

'Then she's half dotty, which is worse. Really, my poor Clem, I do beg you to think very, very seriously before you take her on. It may ruin your entire married life.'

Clemence suddenly tired of her grandmother's company. She stood up, and saying: 'I must go and telephone Edward,' went out of the room. Mingled with her feeling of solid content, there was an increasing determination not to let anything – shame, embarrassment, or Grandmamma's interfering – not *anything* spoil her happiness.

And especially not Juliet. Oh never, never Juliet.

## 18

Juliet slept.

The death of Miss Pennecuick, the utterance of that clearly articulated and clearly heard sentence, the funeral, and the announcement of her own inheritance, had drawn nervous energy even from her.

She had slept deeply for nine hours, without stirring, lying on her back amid unruffled bedclothes and outspread hair, and now the rays of the early June sun bathed her in their full light, and she began to dream.

She was moving swiftly through a vast forest of immensely tall trees, drifting effortlessly past massive trunks, visible in a remote filtered light. There was no undergrowth, only an endless carpet of dully tinted leaves that swirled up in clouds about her feet as she went; and sometimes, between the unchanging vista of silvery holes, she caught a glimpse of low hills of a tender blue, giving an impression of heat. Occasionally, across her path, there drifted slowly down a ghostly leaf.

The place seemed beautiful to her; she was almost content to be there, alone, and moving through the dim silence. Yet something was lacking. Ah, *the question* was still there: form-less in her dream, yet moving beside and within her, asking, demanding. And how could she feel fully content, and find the forest completely beautiful, while that continued to go with her?

She sighed, and looked around at the ghostly trees and down at the delicate leaf shapes rising about her feet, and then away at the hills that seemed – like all hills except the great mountains – to beckon. At last she looked upward. And the leaves on those majestic trees were dead; skeletons, pale and transparent against the pale sky, sapless and colourless and dead.

She cried out, and woke with the tears streaming down.

Her tears were not accompanied by any feeling of sorrow. She sat up and wiped them away with the sheet, and wondered why she should be crying, and thought: *What a funny dream.*

She ran downstairs ten minutes later, feeling hungry. The dream had faded, its original strength depleted into a memory. The dining-room was empty, and no places were set. Juliet, irritated at this break with custom, hurried to the kitchen. The house was silent.

Pilar was there with Sarah, sitting at the table. Sarah was holding a copy of the *Daily Mirror*, and scolding Pilar. 'Hullo, Juliet. Enjoyed your lie-in?' she said spitefully.

'Can I have my breakfast, please,' to Pilar.

'What you like? Weetabix? Or sausage?' enquired Pilar, lazy voiced and not moving. A more imaginative spectator than Juliet would have felt that the machinery organizing the big house had run down almost to a stop.

'Sausage'll do me.'

Suddenly she wanted a sausage as she seldom wanted food: a brown, tasty sausage, shining with the fat it had exuded in the pan. The thought of it successfully banished the last of another thought – those skeletal leaves outlined against the dead sky.

'I fix you two. I think you might want. They are in the oven. Keep them hot. Because I think you hungry after all the kerfuffle yesterday.'

Pilar got up unhurriedly and crossed to the Aga.

'All the what?' asked Juliet.

'Ought to be ashamed, calling Miss Adelaide's funeral by a low word,' said Sarah.

'Isn't a low word. It means a disturbance. Maria's boyfriend teaches it to me. He is university student.' Pilar handed Juliet two sausages on a warmed plate.

Juliet paused to pour tea from a new-fangled pot which retained its heat, from which Sarah and Pilar had evidently been helping themselves. She snatched up a tray from the dresser, loaded it, and was at the door when a sound came out of the kitchen. It was a loud sob. Sarah was saying something unintelligible into the hands covering her face. Pilar made to go to her.

'Oh leave her alone – she's got to get used to it,' said Juliet over her shoulder. 'Where's the others?'

'They sit in our rooms. I come to sit wiz her because she is sad. I sink,' Pilar lowered her voice, 'she be the next one to go. These old ones, they get a bad shock, and they die soon. There was Senora Elvirez in our village, I remember—'

'Yes, well, cheerio.' And Juliet was gone.

She ate her breakfast greedily, and when she had sucked down the last of the strong tea, put her elbows on the table and sat staring at the sun-rays driving in between the half-drawn curtains.

*The house's stopped like – like some clock*, thought Juliet, with uncharacteristic fancifulness. *I might phone Mum . . .*

Her unconscious wish for human company was satisfied by the distant sound of a car, and, after a pause, voices in the hall. The door opened. 'Hullo,' said Frank, coming in followed by Clemence, who went straight across to the windows and drew back the curtains.

'Oh – hullo. Hullo,' said Juliet to Clemence, who turned, nodded and smiled. 'I say, what's going to happen? I mean, am I staying here, or what?'

'That's exactly what I've come to see about,' Frank said.

(*And done me out of our little tour round the lanes. Here it begins*, Clemence thought.)

'You see, Miss Massey and I are going to be married.'

'Oh. Congratulations and all that . . . That's what they say, isn't it?'

'That, as you put it, is what they say, and thank you, Juliet.' (A silent smile from Clemence.) 'No, of course you aren't staying here, and I take it that you don't want to go home?'

'No fear,' emphatically.

'The servants will be off any time now – and I must see about a caretaker.'

'Won't that old – won't Sarah stay? Caretake, I mean.'

'Sarah has money now. Anyway, she's too old, and she would be frightened.'

'I could stay with her.' Juliet leant forward amidst the remnants of her breakfast. 'Oh, come on,' as Frank shook his head. 'Why can't I? It's quiet, and there'd be no one to bother me.'

'You would have to shop for yourself, and probably cook and Sarah would certainly "bother" you,' Clemence put in quietly. 'To say nothing of loneliness, and possibly vandals.'

'There's that chippy down at Leete, I could eat there, and who's afraid of vandals?'

Frank shook his head, and glanced at the clock.

'When are you getting married?' Juliet demanded suddenly.

'In July – and there's a great deal to do first. Why do you ask?' he said.

'Cos – I was thinkin' – p'raps . . .' The thin voice faltered and she looked down at the table. 'P'raps I could – you know. I got all this money from Auntie, haven't I? I could pay you something per week and stay with you – live in your house, I mean. We get on all right, don't we?'

*Well, thank the Lord*, Frank offered up silently. *Could anything have come about more simply?* And that 'We get on all right, don't we?' touched him.

'That's a splendid idea, isn't it?' to Clemence, who said with what she felt was an overdone heartiness that it was 'just the job', adding that Juliet could stay with herself and her grand-mother until the wedding.

'Your gran won't like that. I get on her wick.'

'Yes, I think you do, a little,' Clemence admitted. 'But my grandmother is kind as well as sensible, you know, and I'm sure you can put up with each other for a couple of months.'

'S'pose so. Can I have a room to myself?'

'Oh yes. There's a nice little spare room overlooking the garden.'

'That's all right, then. And – p'raps she'd like me to pay you a bit, too?'

'Oh, all that can be arranged later.'

'I must go and tackle Sarah,' said Frank and went hastily out of the room.

The two who were left remained in silence.

Clemence was thinking that Frank had set out with her to buy her ring and ended up at Hightower arranging life for Juliet and old Sarah.

Juliet's mind drifted back into its usual state. The actual world was once more shut out: she knew where she would be for the next two months, and the only snag would be that old cow, Mrs M. Well, she could always get away to her room. Overlooking the garden, that would be all right. There'd be trees, perhaps. There came another vivid vision of those dead leaves, silhouetted against the sombre sky.

Frank returned, and hovered at the door, plainly in need of self-expression.

'Foreigners,' he said, 'foreigners – I know all that's said about English xenophobia. But really, one has only to try getting anything settled with a group of them, and one understands the prejudice. The fuss! And the emotion!'

Clemence was laughing.

'They haven't even *started* packing. The women seem to think it's obligatory to cry every five minutes. The men sulk. I must find Sarah.'

'Can't you leave her until tomorrow?' (*My day off is being wasted.*)

'Oh I may as well do her, while I'm here. Then we'll go straight on to lunch – at a proper place,' smiling at her. 'Sarah won't take ten minutes.'

He was off. Juliet, with a silent gesture of farewell, disappeared; and Clemence was left to rest in the window seat and reflect that it was not every young woman who would have the courage to 'take on' Frank Pennecuick.

Frank found Sarah muttering angrily, still tear-stained, and resolved on extracting the last drops of dignity and drama out of her departure from the house where she had lived for fifty years.

It took him nearly an hour to get her to accept the fact that she would live with her sister in Ware, and leave Hightower to be made over to some institution, preferably connected with agriculture or, better still, research into Frank's Edible Grasses. 'We all know you're fond of weeds, Mr Frank, but to think of grass on the dining-room table what I kept so's you could see your face in it.'

'The table won't be here, Sarah. The furniture will be sold—'

'Oh Mr Frank, your great-aunt's table!'

Then he had to telephone a neighbour of Sarah's sister at Ware, and announce her arrival.

He put his head round the dining-room door; Clemence was still in the window seat where he had left her.

In the irritability caused by the footlings of the past hour, it occurred to him that she might have employed the time in sorting Aunt Addy's clothes for bestowal on Oxfam, Help the Aged, and Action in Distress. Then he noticed her uncharacteristically dreamy expression and thought, *Bless her, I suppose she's happy. And so am I, of course, if only one could get on with things. Of course I'm happy.*

'Thank God that's over,' he said. 'Now for lunch and our rings.'

'Oh – are you having one too?'

She slid off the seat with grace and came smiling across the room. She neither wanted to hear what had been happening nor to ask a few soothing questions. She had been wondering how many children they would have, and thinking, *Dammit, this is my day.*

'I am. It's one of the things I believe in, for chaps; fairer on the single girls too.'

Clemence was a little dismayed to hear that there would be any single girls, but did not comment, and, on hearing that they were to lunch at a nearby roadhouse famous for its food and pretty to look at, her spirits rose.

'Most of the stuff'll be poison,' he said, as they drove away in her car, 'but I'll find something . . . even I can't feel exultant on carrot juice.'

'Do you feel exultant?'

'Very, my dear.' He drew a finger gently down the cheek nearest to him and she shivered enjoyably.

'Frank,' she said in a moment.

'What?' rousing himself from what, she was certain, was *not* a speculation about how many children they might have.

'We don't want to talk business over lunch. Can I just hear what's going to be done to your house if three people are going to live in it?'

'Oh – Juliet will have her own house. We don't want her around all the time – we'll want to be by ourselves.' Clemence glowed. 'I'll get permission to add a bathroom and a loo to that perfectly sound shed where I keep all my tools and do my carpentry, and she can live there – it's only two hundred yards away at the end of the meadow by the hedge.'

'Not even meals with us?'

'Not unless she's invited. I'll fit her up a simple cooker.'

*This*, thought his betrothed, accelerating cheerfully, *is too good to be true.*

She heard him murmur, as she went ahead of him into the Trattoria del Santo Alberic, 'She'll like that – a house of her own.'

# 19

Juliet did not see the departure of the Spaniards on the following day; she was to meet Clemence at the crossroads at twelve and be driven to the Masseys' cottage, and she left Hightower at eleven, suitcase in hand, and missed the tears, lamentations, cursings and forebodings as the five climbed into the car grandly hired by Antonio, conscious of their having between them five hundred pounds.

Sarah, whose departure for Ware had been postponed until today, began to cry, and told Pilar she was a good girl. She promised to send cards to them all at Christmas.

'Bye-bye,' they all shrieked as the car moved away, and Pilar added in a tearful scream, "Ave 'appy days.'

'Fat chance of that,' murmured Sarah, 'I never did get on with Lucy.' She turned back into the hall and sat down beside her luggage. Her nephew would be here in half an hour to drive her to Ware.

And Mr Frank, when he came this afternoon, would find everything in order; all doors locked, all keys on the hall table. She wished that he had granted her wish to go round the place with him for the last time (her tears welled again) but there you were, *He was the master now, and Miss Addy gone. She had never thought that there Juliet would say goodbye to her – no manners, and only to be expected. Oh well, I'll be over for the wedding.*

In the great shadowy hall, silence and emptiness were beginning stealthily to impose their reign. Sarah's lids drooped. *That was nice of Pilar, saying that* . . . Sarah dozed.

'*Don't* bolt your food like that, my dear, when once indigestion does set in, it is very difficult to cure.'

'Can't be helped, Grandmamma. Edward wants me back at one sharp. Mr Shadwell's coming at two.'

'And why can't that chit make her own way here? It's only five miles. Now you've got hiccoughs.'

'Sorry.' Clemence was pulling on her blue linen coat.

'I suppose she'll get me my tea,' discontentedly. 'If she isn't paying anything she might do *something* to earn her keep.'

'Oh Grandmamma!'

Clemence turned back from the door and knelt beside her grandmother, looking up into the pretty and discontented old face. 'I'm so happy. Won't you try to put up with her for two months? I've got to—' She swallowed, and Mrs Massey pounced.

'Yes, my poor dear, you've got to put up with her for life. Run along, of course I can cope with her. I'm just a cross old woman and I can get my own tea . . . And you never know, she may fall off a bridge,' she ended with a wicked chuckle.

Clemence hugged her briefly and hurried away, feeling strongly that Juliet was not the sort that fell off bridges.

*Oh good, there's a proper table*, was Juliet's first thought as she surveyed her new room. It was smaller than the one at

Hightower, but she liked its sparse, choice furnishings, and the window looked onto a small garden glowing with flowers and ending in trees that screened some old cottages.

When she was seated at the table, her books before her, she looked out at the brilliant yellow-green leaves with a feeling of satisfaction: that tap at the door which had disturbed her solitude at Hightower need not be anticipated here, because Mrs Massey was too old and fat to get up the stairs that easy, and probably wouldn't try, and Miss Massey was out at work all day.

She sat, hour after hour. The shadows began to stretch into the endlessness of a June dusk; her eyes were sometimes on the delicate mass of symbols on the page before her, sometimes her gaze wandered among the leaves.

'Juliet! Aren't you starving?' Clemence opened the door, without the feared tap. 'We're just going to have supper. It's nearly half-past seven.'

'Is it? I never noticed.'

'Another time, if you get hungry, just rummage in the larder. It's all ready if you'll come down.'

Clemence went downstairs looking at her ring, which was gold, and made in the shape of two clasped hands, one with a frill at the wrist and one with a man's cuff. They held an impressively sized diamond.

Frank had chosen a plain, heavy signet in the same metal. To look at the ring soothed her feelings, which were still sore at being told that she would have to arrange the details of her own wedding.

'My dearest girl, I'm very sorry but I'll have to ask you to do everything . . . I've got to get rid of Hightower, or it will hang over us like a thunderstorm—'

'Couldn't you leave that until after we're married?'

'I could. But that would mean our first weeks together would be continually interrupted, and we don't want that, do we? My mind' – and he smiled – 'will be on other things . . . and there'll be Juliet's place at Cambridge to fix up, too.'

In her less optimistic moments, Clemence saw Juliet, immensely distinguished in some unimaginable way, but still unable to organize an ordinary workaday life, still living with the Pennecuicks when she was seventy.

'But you'll come with me to see Aiden, won't you?' she said. The Reverend Aiden Blount was vicar of St Mary's, at Wanby, where they were to be married. He had been there for nearly thirty years and had known them both since they were children. This gave a comfortable feeling to the proceedings, and he would also be prepared for any oddities in Frank's attitude towards the ceremony. 'Even he,' Clemence could not help adding, 'might wonder a bit if I turned up for the interview without a bridegroom.'

'I'll be there all right on the day, dear, don't worry. And I'll write to Edmund asking him to be best man.'

'Oh. What . . . what a good idea.'

Edmund Spencer was that friend of Frank's already referred to as an eccentric and a minor poet.

With the supporting framework of Hightower's daily routine removed, Juliet relapsed into a kind of concentrated dream; forgot to eat, sat up all night, spoke to her housemates only when she remembered to.

Mrs Massey would have relished a wedding with two hundred guests, six bridesmaids and a matron of honour. Clemence, when her grandmother had cautiously hinted at the joys of such a ceremony, had only said rather distractedly:

'Grandmamma, so long as I have a white dress and there's enough to eat and Edmund doesn't lose the ring – is he ever going to answer Frank's letter, do you think? – I don't care what happens. I can never get at Frank nowadays.' (This was in mid-July: the wedding was fixed for the thirtieth.)

'Oh why? Is he so wrapped up in—?' glancing ceilingwards, beyond which Juliet was presumably seated at her work-table.

'Grandmamma, you know he hardly ever sees her except when I'm there too. No, he's so busy interviewing the AIEG—'

'All those initials, so confusing . . .'

'Association for the Investigation of Edible Grasses—'

'Oh, those cranks.'

'He hardly gets a minute to himself, much less to talk to Juliet – or even me.'

'Is he going to hire a proper suit, is what I want to know.'

'Oh I don't know, Grandmamma, that's a detail.'

'Quite an important one, if you're going to wear white.'

'He said – he's got a brown velvet suit—'

'*Brown velvet?*'

'—that he's hardly worn.' Clemence, remembering that the suit had been made to please Ottolie, stumbled over the words. 'And Moss Bros clothes don't suit him.'

'Well, yes, I suppose brown velvet might look all right – we must just hope the Press and TV don't turn up.'

'Why on earth should they? We aren't anybody.'

'Oh – local rich man choosing to live in converted cowshed. That kind of thing.'

'That would be' – a pause – 'the last straw.' There were a good many straws on Clemence's back. The conversion of the carpentry shed into a house for Juliet had devolved upon her, with its interviews with painters and builders, and with the writing of letters to local councils. And, although she had her grandmother's assistance in shopping for the few contemporary gadgets Frank would consent to their possessing, this was not as enjoyable as it might have been. Mrs Massey suggested purchasing every toy of civilization that was on offer, while Clemence had to state, over and over again, 'Frank doesn't want us to have that.'

No washing-up machine (up flew two small black-gloved hands in dismay); no deep-freezer. *He says, what do we want with a deep-freezer? We're only fifteen miles from adequate shops, and I have a car, and he has a bicycle.* No electric polisher. *We both have all our arms and legs, my love.* No electric blanket. *We have each other.* No devices for grating, crushing or peeling vegetables; none for mixing cakes.

'Doesn't he realize that you'll be worn out, my poor child, besides never having a moment for social life?'

'He doesn't want any social life.'

'I dare say not. But you do, don't you?'

'Oh, Grandmamma . . . I don't know. I just live from day to day.'

Mrs Massey gave a disapproving sniff, and the choosing, the arguing and rejecting went remorselessly on. I-can-always-buy-one-when-the-children-come became Clemence's secret vow as gadget after gadget had to be refused.

No carpets.

But here she struck.

'Frank, that place isn't going to be warm enough even with thick matting – for babies. The air will still be too cold, and I shan't feel like staggering out into the snow to buy carpets.'

'Well, all right, but don't let's put the beastly germ-infested things down until the baby's actually here. Buy 'em now and put 'em in store.'

'Yes, dear.' Adding in a gloating, creamy voice that slightly alarmed him, 'Nursing mothers mustn't be worried.'

A fleeting shadow, a hazy half-glimpsed vision, passed over his mind: himself gasping for life under a swarm of very small children. But he dismissed it. Clem was so sensible. Surely. Surely . . . ?

Purposeful and organized activity on the sensible one's part got affairs moving; and three days before his wedding Frank stood with Juliet in the long rays of a July evening, contemplating her completed house.

She was pale from what must be described as 'concentrated dreaming', and her eyes were still full of its light. With hands in the pockets of her jeans she stood peering in through the half-open door, and he knew better than to ask, 'Do you like it?'

After a long stare, she went slowly up to the door, and the shade of the mighty oak fell over her small figure as she entered her house.

She looked slowly around: the floor of the long, low-ceilinged place was covered by thick, pale-yellow Japanese matting in a design of whorls and bars; the brick walls were whitewashed; a cane screen shut off one-third and hid a bed; and the oil heater was of the newest design. A sturdy table and chair and rows of bookshelves completed the furnishings. Her stare went straight to the table and she nodded suddenly; then it went to the walls, where there was one picture.

'Oh – there's . . .' Her voice died off.

'Yes – the Möbius ring from Hightower. I thought you'd like to have it.'

Juliet's feelings carried her so far as a low-voiced: 'Not half.' Then, still staring, she added: 'Could I have another window at that end,' pointing, 'so's I can see that tree?'

'Of course, I'll get that done,' he promised, feeling the strongest satisfaction.

Juliet had not yet learned to say 'Thank you.' But she had learned to admit that she wanted to see a tree. He had taught her that much.

Late that evening, as he wheeled his bicycle to stop outside his own door, he glanced across at her house and saw a light in her window, shining out into the blue dusk.

She had moved in.

The days rushed on. Thirty invitations had been sent out. It would be a company just large enough to appear cheerful. Two little distant cousins of Clemence's, still too young to be touched by liberating influences, were delighted by being appointed bridesmaids. A cake, made from strictly wholesome ingredients on Frank's instructions, was mixed and baked by one of Mrs Massey's few domesticated friends, and St Mary's was adorned, on the evening before The Day, by the ladies who always 'did' the flowers for the church – with weeds.

'Weeds, my dear, out of the hedges, and bits and pieces from that little wood where the picnickers go.'

'They won't *stay up*,' wailed the exhausted flower-arrangers, as they supervised their completed efforts at about seven that evening, 'they just *droop*. And you need *hundreds* of them to look *anything*, it's simply impossible to make a *group* or a *pattern*.

We had *armfuls* brought in by the Sunday School children –
had to pay them ten pence a *bunch*, if you please. When I was
young children picked flowers for *pleasure*. And all day it was
"Is this here all right, Miss?" in case it was poisonous. And of
*course* Wayne Palmer had to eat a berry and say it was deadly
nightshade – he *would*. And Mrs Duff Potter had to rush him
over to casualty at St Alberics General, but fortunately someone
knew the stuff doesn't fruit until October, and anyway Wayne
remembered afterwards that he spat it out. And after all the
fuss, that collection *still* doesn't look anything. Oh, I can tell
you it's been murder. Absolute *murder*.'

Whether it 'looked anything' depended upon the eyes that
looked. The dim hue of the foxgloves was repeated in the stained
glass of the little windows in the ancient church, huddled in
its yew-shaded churchyard, where birds darted in search of the
crimson berries. The pale, watery light in the church touched
to a deeper green the foliage of buttercup and ragged robin.
From the dark beams of the roof a carved face peered out here
and there, ambiguously smiling as if undecided whether to
follow God or the Devil, and the air smelled of former censings
(for the Reverend Aiden Blount was High) and the ghosts of
myriad flowers.

Massed below the blue and water-green windows were tiny
pink and white and greenish-white blossoms of which none
of the ladies, many of whom were 'keen gardeners', knew the
names; and the altar glowed with the cool emerald of leaves
and grasses, and the snow of meadowsweet.

Mrs Massey, with tart mirth, had assured a crony that she
had no intention of appearing in cheesecloth or denim; she

would wear lilac nylon over two purple petticoats and sport the smartest cap that Harrods could offer.

Her suggestion that Juliet should appear as chief bridesmaid, in order to show her gratitude for all that was being done for her, had been firmly rebuffed by Frank.

Clemence in the midst of distracted activity, explained: 'Juliet isn't the sort who has to show gratitude, Grandmamma.'

'Oh indeed. Why not, pray?'

'Because she – is – she has – oh I don't know. Unique. Look here, I really must dash.'

'*You've* caught her habit of flying off, now,' disconsolately.

'Oh Grandmamma, please don't, I'm so happy,' Clemence said absently, as she stood ticking off an item on a list.

Yes, she was – she supposed. She was sitting in the car with Dr Masters, on her way to be married to Frank, breathing the scent of her bouquet of white pinks imported from France, and beneath her attempts to remember the order of the marriage service and what she had to do, there was indeed a surprised, still, happiness.

Fifteen minutes later she saw him, tall and elegant in brown velvet, grave and familiar and kind, her best friend. She had so trained herself during the past crowded weeks to repel negative thoughts that the question crying at the door of her mind, *Is he as happy as I am?*, was heard only as a faint whisper. And the hour swept inexorably on.

Juliet was standing, poker-straight, between Mrs Massey and her own mother, the former having taken Rose under her wing and waived convention, and led her to a place among the bride's relations.

Juliet was dressed in natural shantung, with embroidery at collar and cuffs so chaste as to be hardly visible; her hat, an unbecoming girlish droop of fine straw and matching grosgrain ribbon, was of the same natural tint that she had gradually come to prefer. She had steadily resisted the efforts of Mrs Massey, who had taken her shopping, to select brighter colours. ('Then do have something *softer*, child, and more becoming. You'll look like a Rich Tea biscuit.')

The faint rustling made by thirty people in the dim, sunny light ceased; the priest stood very still, and the service started.

Juliet began by listening and looking; then her thoughts drifted away. She was aroused by a sharp poke in her ribs and 'Juliet!' from Mrs Massey, followed by a murmur from her mother on the other side: 'Julie – people are tryin' to get out.'

Juliet glanced round to see, over a brilliantly printed plump shoulder, a row of indignant faces. 'The Wedding March' was wavering out on St Mary's ancient and historic organ, and Clemence's white shape was disappearing through the door out into brilliant sunlight.

'Happy the bride what the sun shines on.' It was a shy mutter from Rose.

'I beg your pardon – oh yes. Yes, indeed, couldn't have had a better day,' Mrs Massey said graciously, resigning herself to sharing a car bound for Frank's cowshed with this person.

But dismay was almost lost in incredulity. Juliet's mother? Not a trace, not a hint, of the remotest likeness. Perhaps the father? Not here; working probably.

Working, indeed; after a scene in which he had begun by forbidding his wife to attend a ceremony got up by a lot of blasted snobs, and had ended by his giving grudging permission, with Rose in tears.

'Oh all right, then. You go, if you're so set on it. Sooner you than me.'

'It isn't that, George, but they been kind to Julie. And all that money – it looks downright ignorant not to. And that Mrs Massey did send an invite.'

'I *said*: go if you want to.' He paused at the door; it was six o'clock on a June morning, the bird was trilling to the sun, and all the room's colours glowed. 'S'pose me tea'll be ready?'

'Get along with you, you know it will.'

Mrs Slater wiped her eyes on her housecoat, and Juliet's father made a vague gesture – intended to convey forgiveness, condescension towards female weakness and farewell and went heavily out.

Rose was left to the labour of looking up a train to St Alberics (*Oh dear, have to get one of them country buses*). The difficulties of organizing a twenty-mile journey were for her almost insuperable. But a quarter of a century with George Slater had slowly drawn out, and strengthened, a largely unconscious power of will, fortified by a patience which could, when she had set her heart on something, successfully work together. She had been like a mediocre tennis player matched for years against a champion, and gradually she had learnt to hold her own. Sometimes, rarely, she won a game.

And when she alighted at St Alberics station, wearing an outsize raincoat of turquoise blue over a brightly patterned dress, and a hat composed of pink petals, and stood looking about her for that bus, there was a great car all over with white

ribbons, and a chap in uniform looking round for someone –
who turned out to be her!

She didn't half enjoy that ride to the church. And it was
Julie who had thought of the car! (*'Don't* tell your mother that
I suggested it; that would spoil the surprise,' Mrs Massey had
said.)


Juliet felt a faint sensation of pleasure at seeing her mother's
familiar form among all these strangers; and as they came out
of the church she turned to smile at her and made her second
remark since they had met:

'How's Bertie-boy?'

'Oh, he's cheeky. That's what he is. "You're cheeky," I tell him.'

Mrs Massey wondered for one incredulous moment if Bertie
were some favoured youth. But reflection convinced her that he
was more likely to be a dog, or some dreadful cat which ought
to have been put down years ago. She rustled herself into the
car. Juliet's mother looked no less dreadful than the hypothetical
cat but at least possessed some manners ('Thank you for the
invite, ever so kind of you') and also made comments on the
weather, which avoided awkward silences.

The hedges burgeoned with bright poppies, and the wheat
rippled. Frank and Clemence, hands clasped, speeding through
this miniature landscape deflowered by Man yet still as lovely
as a good dream, turned occasionally to smile at one another.

*What a funny sort of place*, was Rose's silent comment on
Frank's collection of whitewashed sheds, as the company
alighted at a gate leading into his meadows and began to file,
not without raised eyebrows, along a narrow path through
grass heavy with dew. *Looks like a lot of old barns.*

'Mr Pennecuick is a great believer in *living simply*, and not having more than he needs,' Mrs Massey, picking her way after Rose, explained. 'As I expect Juliet has told you he is a wealthy man, and there is a large house some five miles away, belonging to his late great-aunt, that could have been used for a big reception. But' – she shrugged – 'you know what men are.' She did not at all believe that Rose did. How could she, looking like that? But the fat face under that appalling hat, half turned over the thick shoulder, showed a gratifying attention.

'Fancy – I'd like to see that,' the face said shyly.

'I hear it's going to be sold to some cranky society for making us all eat boiled grass. Of course, it would have been more suitable to keep it up, but nowadays, even for a wealthy man . . .' She shrugged.

Rose was beginning to feel faint apprehension for Julie's future. Living in a lot of barns and eating boiled grass! Perhaps that twenty thousand pounds wasn't real. Yet this old lady seemed sensible enough, if she did wear a queer hat too young for her. The bride was dressed proper. But it was a funny set-up, and Rose was glad George hadn't come. She would never have heard the last of it.

And no carpets! Ten minutes later, standing by a long table laden with unfamilar foods, she thought she had never heard of such a thing. She stared slowly at the thirty animated, and mostly elderly, faces surrounding her. Several of them glanced at her curiously. She ate another of those little things: tasted of ham and cream this time and very good it was; and she wondered how ever she was to get back to that station and catch the train in time to get George's tea.

No one spoke to her. And there was Julie, standing in a corner and looking miles away, *Just as she always had from the time she was a kiddie. No more manners than a bluebottle,* her mother thought resignedly. But she also felt a faint bond of companionship with her child. *Two of us – both out of it.*

'Hullo, Mrs Slater, my wife and I are so pleased that you could come.' It was the bridegroom, coming up to her with the bride beside him. *Nice face he had, really, and her silk was real, you could tell. Ever so happy she looked, too. Ah well, let her. It didn't last long,* and Rose's eyes slowly moistened.

Clemence was getting used to this break with convention, the newly married pair circulating among the guests instead of the latter filing before them. 'I'm sorry Mr Slater couldn't come,' she said, making her manner warmer than usual because Juliet's mother was tearful.

She was a little shaken by the unexpectedly firm reply: 'Oh him. He never wants to do anything what other people do.' (*Just like someone else I know,* mused the new Mrs Pennecuick.) ''Sides, he's workin' today. This here's good stuff, Mr Pennecuick,' holding up her glass of the wine which had temporarily banished her shyness. 'Home-made, is it?'

'Yes – from parsnips – I'm glad you like it.'

'Fancy – I've seen home-made wine on the television but haven't never had it before.'

Followed a pause – filled with the cheerful screeching of that ugliest of sounds, the human voice in volume, and the smell of delicious conventional food which Frank had arranged to be served, to please his bride.

'I'm sure General Penley— Would you care to meet him?' Frank began, but Rose's shrinking away and her mutter showing him that she would not, he ended with: 'Well, perhaps if you will excuse us . . .' And the two moved away.

General Penley had got hold of Edmund Spencer. The General, red-faced and blue-eyed and typical-looking, had a shy reverance for poets; Edmund, who had at first refused Frank's invitation, had a far from shy dislike for what he thought of as blimps.

There was much to satisfy the General at young Pennecuick's wedding: food was very good; this stuff was actually drinkable; bride looked pretty and happy – but, nevertheless, there was something . . . General Penley, as not seldom, was unable to express his thoughts, but it was there all right. Peculiar, cranky, no carpet, no *comfort* . . . all those weeds in glass bottles . . .

Edmund could have told him that there were present those rarest of luxuries: beauty of light, flowers that not been tortured into blooming in the wrong season, and true love. But the mere thought of saying this to anyone present except the bridegroom sent up the corners of his long, beautiful mouth.

'You known Pennecuick long?' the General asked, looking around at the faces familiar from many a conversation about gardening or gadgets over neighbourly dinner tables.

'Yes.' Edmund's voice, always faint from nervous exhaustion, was now nearly inaudible.

'School together?'

'No. Frank was at Harrow.'

'Ah. You're not a Harrovian.'

The General was not inquisitive – he genuinely felt admiration for this titchy red-haired chap who proclaimed himself a poet, a creature whom the General had always wanted (behind his satisfaction with his military career) to be.

'Where were you, then?'

'I don't expect you've heard of it . . . sir.'

The chap's accent made the last word sound as though he were a waiter. Suit made him look rather like one too: hired probably.

'One of the lesser-known places, eh?'

'The Charles Darwin School, Luton,' Edmund invented desperately; some fifteen years of kindly interrogation by the gentry had not given him enough confidence to relate the details of an education which had ended at fourteen.

'Oh – ah – yes – never heard of it, I'm afraid – excuse me, someone over there I must talk to . . .' and the General marched away. Pity. He had hoped the chap might talk about poetry.

Those corners of Edmund's mouth turned down slightly in a bitter smile.

'Oh hullo, Mum.'

'Julie, I got to be going. That train goes at four, and you know what Dad is if his tea's not ready.'

'Oh all right.' She glanced round. 'Eddy, here's my mum wants to get to the station. You'll take her, won't you?'

Edmund looked fleetingly at Mrs Slater's bulk.

'I – don't think your mother . . . how do you do?' with a bow '. . . would be comfortable on the back of my motorcycle.'

'Oh no!' Rose exclaimed, in more than dismay.

'But the cars are waiting. If you'll come with me,' smiling, 'I'll find you a nice one.'

'All right then. Cheerio, Mum,' nodded Juliet. She had dragged off her hat and hung it on the wall above a cluster of peacock's feathers, and her freshly washed hair rayed about sallow cheeks unbecomingly flushed by parsnip wine.

'Cheerio, Julie.'

'Give my love to Bertie-bird.'

'Him! He's cheeky, that's what he is. So long, then. See you, Ju.'

'P'raps I'll send you a postcard,' Juliet smiled.

'That'll be the day,' her mother retorted, and waddled away after the little chap. He seemed all right, but she wouldn't half be glad to get home.

Julie seemed just the same, for all her new clothes and the money. Leaning back in the luxurious car, surveying the pretty country going by, Rose could not decide whether this was a comfort or not. One thing she did know: she herself was ever so lonely. But she was used to that.

At half-past three Clemence came out of Frank's austere bedroom wearing the dove-coloured suit and frilled blouse of broderie anglaise that had, in defiance of convention, been hanging for the past week in his wardrobe. Her brown curls clustered under a close cap of cream silk adorned with a single white camellia, and she looked calmly happy.

*Bless her, she's been such a good girl, earning for us both and putting up with my crotchets,* thought her grandmother (who did not really believe that she had any crotchets), *and thank heaven I need not worry about money again as long as I live.*

'So odd,' many of the guests were muttering. 'Not going abroad . . .'

'I know. I did suggest it, but *he* came up with some nonsense about there being quite enough new impressions to absorb without having to gape at *sights*,' Frank's new grandmother-in-law explained, not minding the oddness because it was not caused by lack of funds. 'But there you are.'

General Penley so far forgot social customs and military discipline as to grunt, and Mrs Massey felt, with gratification, that he shared her views.

There was the usual, always touching, little ceremony with the bouquet. Then the big car glided away, with Clemence's face, made charming with happiness, laughing through the window.

The only discord was provided by the two little unliberated bridesmaids, sulking in a corner because no photographs had been taken, and their prolonged drive home would cause them to miss *Star Trek*.

Edmund and Juliet stood at the door of Frank's house after the last guest had gone, with the July dusk hardly begun; silent, gazing at the elongated, lazy shadows lying across the grass damp with dew. Edmund at last observed that there was all that washing-up.

'Aren't you goin', then?' she asked, and he shook his head.

He was curious about his companion, and did not feel at ease with her, but who did he feel at ease with? Certainly not his current bed-partner.

'Didn't Frank tell you? I'm staying here for the week while they're away.'

'Never said a thing. Where they goin', then?'

'To my cottage on the Essex border. It's near Bury St Edmunds.'

'Have I got to cook for you?' Juliet demanded angrily, and he laughed.

'I probably cook a damn sight better than you do, and I'm used to looking after myself, and I prefer it.'

She began to move away, saying over her shoulder: 'That's all right then. S'pose you wouldn't like to do the washing-up as well?' with a gleam of mischief towards the small red-haired man standing on Frank's threshold.

'I'll do it tomorrow,' he said mildly. 'Goodnight. See you when I do.'

She was already halfway across the long-grassed, buttercup-spangled meadow and did not reply. But as she opened her own door, and at once the waves of the strange seas of thought began to sound within her, her last thought was: *We'll get on all right, him and me.*

# 20

Juliet and Edmund existed amiably enough by the simple method of each doing what they liked, without consulting the other.

Edmund, mindful of certain instructions from Frank about the care of this unique creature, did venture once to tap on her door and call, 'Juliet, how long since you ate?' to be rebuffed with an absent-sounding snarl: 'I'm all right. Got some cheese. And watercress.'

However, on the evening of the day on which he had thus been rebuffed, she appeared at the door of the Cowshed.

'Got any supper? . . . Hullo.'

'Oh, hullo. Yes, of course, stew. Just ready. Come on in.'

'I got up, see,' explained Juliet, as she seated herself, rather carefully, at the table, 'and me legs give way and down I went. Me head felt funny, too.'

'Starvation,' he muttered, ladling out mutton and dumplings.

She pulled up her jeans and revealed a thin leg, faintly sheened with hair and showing a long scratch, seeping blood. 'Done that on me biscuit tin.'

'Your what? You'll need some TCP,' he said, paling. (He had been known to faint at the sight of blood.)

'I'll finish this first,' voraciously eating. 'Me biscuit tin what I keep me notes in.'

'Oh.'

The meal continued in silence.

Edmund felt that he should have been aware, as a healthy youngish male, of their isolation in the midst of the flower-starred fields; in fact he felt nothing but a sense of how odd she was, and a bored impulse about telling her to eat sensibly in order to keep up strength for her 'work'.

Glancing at her from under his long reddish eyelashes, he wondered if she were slightly dotty. Was the 'work' the obsession of a mentally deficient?

On the fifth day of the Pennecuick honeymoon, Juliet retched on coming in to supper for only the second time. Edmund turned from Frank's small iron range, where he was putting the final touches to a ratatouille, and snapped:

'You are— It's just bloody selfishness.'

Juliet stared.

'How j'oo mean?' she said at last, sitting down as she absently retched again, and still staring at him.

'Being such a nuisance.' He poured the rich mess into her soup plate. 'Starving yourself until you're sick with hunger, worrying me and—'

'Who wants you to worry?' Her eyes, those of a hungry child, were now on the food.

'God knows I don't want to, but Frank asked me to keep an eye on you.'

'I never used to feel sick, like, when I was hungry,' she said, with her mouth full.

'It's probably because your health is better. Your body got used to regular meals at Hightower.'

The word 'body' sent him off into a fantasy about kissing her. He felt not the faintest impulse to do anything of the sort, but he did wonder what effect it would have. Suddenly he laughed.

'What's funny?' She did not look up from her plate.

'Do you *ever* think about whether you're inconveniencing or hurting other people?'

'Why should I?'

'Thanks – at least now we know where we are. By the way, what is it that you *do* think about?'

Juliet was half full of excellent food, and a little drunk in consequence: fullness, after prolonged deprivation, can produce this effect. She fixed on him her extraordinary eyes, and said with as much earnestness as her flat tones could convey: 'Coincidence.'

He was disappointed. He half expected, after old Frank's enthusiastic talk, some exotic revelation of the science-fiction type.

'Do you mean to say you sit there all day and half the night chewing over that? Coincidence like when people say "What a coincidence!"?'

'Course not,' with an impatient shake of her head. 'That's ordinary, everybody does that. What I think about is . . . why?'

She bent over her food again, eyelids lowered, knife and fork moving inelegantly.

'"*Why?*" But how do you mean? A coincidence is just a coincidence.'

She shook her head.

He made his tone gentler, as he said: 'Do tell me. I'm really interested.'

'Why they happen, I mean.' She put her knife and fork together and stood up. 'Maths comes into it, and geometry, but a lot more than that. Thanks, I feel better now, that was good. I have to – to get into a kind of – a way of thinkin', see. That's why I forget to eat.'

'So it's mathematical problems you work on all day?'

She shook her head. 'Not really working them out – I kind of see the answers straight off.'

'You *what*?'

'Look, I'm busy on something now – can't spare the time to explain, and you wouldn't understand anyway – cheerio,' and she was gone.

He glanced gloomily at the washing-up. It was a beautiful evening: the dandelions had changed from broad feathery discs to dark pointed buds, the shadows spread languidly from great elm and tiny spearhead of grass. He wandered out into the fading light, wondering vaguely how the honeymooners were faring – in three days they would be home.

Edmund's own cottage had been a complete surprise, left to him by an ungracious uncle whose comment on Edmund's poetry had always been, 'That boy will never make a ha'penny out of his scribbling.'

Edmund went there infrequently; he loved it, and the landscape of low undulating hills and fields of dark purple or corn gold in which it was set. But he could not write poetry there: the Suffolk sky was too vast; the beauty laid on him too gentle a silencing hand. He found it impossible to live in the midst of poetry and also write it, and was always pleased to return to his dingy bed-sitting room in a Luton backstreet. There, he could write poetry as he wanted.

He made little money, but it was more than the ha'penny referred to by his benefactor, and his tastes, though difficult to satisfy in an age which lauded simplicity while making it increasingly difficult and expensive to attain, were simple. As a poet, reviewers bracketed him with Charles Causley. He avoided the society of literary people.

On the morning of the return of the honeymooners, Edmund was up at five and out in the meadows, picking handfuls of buttercups and varied grasses to fill one of Frank's big red clay jars. He lit a fire which he banked down, made a stew of meat, herbs and assorted vegetables, and, having set it to simmer, printed WELCOME HOME on a sheet of paper, spread it conspicuously on the hand-woven hearthrug, looked with satisfaction about the long, light, bare, charming room, and got on his motorcycle and chugged away to the dingy Luton bed-sitter.

Glancing at Juliet's house as he passed, he saw through its low window a fair head pillowed on two arms, resting on the table amidst books. *Up all night*, he reflected; *thank goodness I'm quit of her*, and rode lightheartedly on.

He would be glad to be alone again. He had avoided with a snail-like shrinking those cries of 'Here you are, then!' and 'Well, what was the weather like?' with which normal people greet returning travellers. Frank, he remembered, had once told him that his, Edmund's, idea of perfect enjoyment was sitting alone on a tombstone by moonlight, and there had been enough truth in the remark to make him laugh.

Juliet woke about seven, aroused by the scraping of a starling's wings against the window. Yawning, she stumbled across the room, crumbling bread as she went, and opened her house to the bird, which was a regular visitor. While it was pecking superciliously at the scatterings on her doorstep, she thought, *Oh Lord, she's coming back today.*

With Frank, she now felt as unconscious and comfortable as she did with her hooded cape or her books; but there was a quality of natural practicality in Clemence that disturbed her.

About half-past three that afternoon, a taxi deposited its occupants at the gate leading into Frank's meadows, and he and Clemence, carrying suitcases, came across the new grass and marguerites, and set down their baggage in front of the Cowshed.

Frank showed a tendency to go off immediately to his vegetable patch, but checked himself, and returned smiling to his bride, advancing upon her with outstretched arms.

'Come on . . . over the threshold.'

He held her closely as, in two strides, he set her down over the doorstep.

'There. Didn't think I could do that, did you?'

'I hoped you would – though everybody does seem to make a joke of it – but I didn't think – you're so slim . . .'

'Sounds prettier than "skinny". You forget, my love, that I spend hours digging.' He rolled up his sleeve, displaying impressive muscles. 'There – look at that.'

Clemence laughed, looking approvingly around her, and then, rather avidly, at the stack of parcels large and small in a far corner. The wedding presents!

'Ha!' he said, and peered into the casserole, where a barely moving reddish surface was just sheened by delicate fat. 'Good for Edmund – his manners are on the inside, unlike most people's, which are on the outside. Leave the cases, dear – I'm going to inspect my vegetables.'

He was off; and, sighing with contentment, she ventured to cross the room and open one of the smaller parcels.

She was packing a basket to take tea into the meadow, when a shadow fell across the open door and a flat voice said:

'Hullo. Can I— Will it be OK if I have tea with you?'

She turned. Juliet stood there, holding out – horrors! – a wild orchid of a rare type growing only in three or four places in England. Frank would *explode* – it was marked with an asterisk on the list of plants forbidden to be gathered.

'Found it in that wood over there,' jerking her head. 'There was only one. It's – pretty, isn't it?' doubtfully.

In fact, it was strange and ominous-looking rather than pretty. But Clemence's one thought was to get the thing out of sight before Frank appeared from his inspection of the vegetables, and she almost snatched it.

'It's beautiful,' heartily, 'and thank you very much from us both – I'll put it in water, in the bedroom. Of course, we were expecting you,' hurrying off with the precious object, which she shoved into a drawer, thinking, *Blow everything.* 'And get out a pot of jam, will you?'

'What sort?' called Juliet, standing before the rows of comely jars.

'Oh strawberry – that's the best, don't you think? And,' Clemence hurried back into the living-room and thrust the tea basket at her, 'be a dear and carry that for me.'

They went out into the westering sunlight, and saw Frank coming towards them with his scythe over his shoulder.

'Let's have it under my tree,' Juliet called. 'There's cow muck, but we can put those big leaves over it,' kicking at a dock plant as she passed.

'The authentic rustic scene is a blend of the idyllic and the coarse,' said Frank, bending to kiss his wife. 'There . . . I shall do that every time.'

She said, 'You are an ass,' and laughed, but she experienced a calm, deep happiness.

The sun went down; the afterglow lingered; back at the house Frank worked over some excruciatingly boring-looking figures supplied by the AIEG, and Clemence, having stolen away to destroy the already fading orchid, began to unpack another wedding present.

The air was very still. The fire in the massive range gave out its barely noticeable heat; a cricket obligingly chirped, and some miles away on the St Alberics road car headlights probed the soft sky, while their noise offended the ancient country silence, yet left it, after their unhappy passing, unstained. And Juliet had vanished after tea; her light burned steadily at the other end of the Big Meadow.

'Well,' Frank said at last, looking up from his work with an air of finality, 'something's been achieved.'

'Going well, is it?' Clemence asked, being the good-wife-interested-in-husband's-boring-business, and he laughed.

'I didn't mean the AIEG – I meant Juliet asking us to have tea under her oak.'

'Oh, that . . . Yes, it was nice of her.'

'In anybody – ordinary – it wouldn't have been worth remembering. But from her, it was a distinct step forward. I'm very pleased – and very happy,' glancing round him. 'God, I am turning into an old pussy cat. Is there any cheese?'

There came an afternoon some weeks later when he returned exulting from his interviews with experts at Hightower.

'It's on,' he shouted to his wife, striding across the meadow. 'We're keeping the house and running it as a centre for the AIEG . . . A grant from the Min. of Ag., a goodish bit from the Soil Society raised by that appeal, lots of fifty pieces from the Friends of the Earth (bless their mostly young hearts). We're in business. We've just been going through the finances.'

Clemence, at the front door in her cooking apron, nearly exclaimed, 'Oh Frank!' in dismay. Hightower, with its land, had been valued at £500,000. It was true that they had plenty of money, but what were the hypothetical children going to say when they were twenty about this throwing away (for so she regarded it) of potential riches?

She said nothing.

'It's the best thing,' he argued, feeling a disappointed quality in the air. 'The place might hang about for months waiting to be sold and there's so much to be done, here and with the AIEG . . . Now they can use the money we've collected and start in a rent-free place . . . Besides, I know the soil round here like the back of my hand.'

'Wouldn't the money you got for Hightower have been enough to start the AIEG?'

'Perhaps. But there would be all the bother of finding a suitable place. No, this is a splendid solution. By the way, I shall be off to Canada next week.' He emerged from the cloakroom, flapping his hands vigorously.

'Frank! Don't do that, it looks really dotty. *What* did you say?'

'Saves towel-wear,' he grinned. 'Besides, the Romans always did it—'

'No they didn't. They had hot air. *What* about Canada?'

'To investigate that four thousand square miles of scrub in the north-west – irrigation and fertilizing possibilities. A bunch of experts is going. Wives too – you can come. But I warn you, it will be no expense-account picnic.'

'Who'd look after Juliet?' Clemence said grimly, seating herself before the teapot. 'No, don't say she could look after herself – she'd starve to death.'

'Yes – I hadn't forgotten her. I was going to think about that later. But wouldn't you like to come, darling?'

'I'd like to be with you, of course.'

'I don't expect you'd see much of me – I shall be flying all over the place, taking soil samples.'

'And I'd be a bit bored and lonely . . . No, I think I won't come.'

'Oh. Don't you want to be with me?'

'Of course I want to be with you, you great goat, but we can't have everything in this world,' she said demurely. After years of living almost beside him with the notion of marriage always in her head and never in his, there was certainly satisfaction in seeing him a little piqued at her decision.

# 21

When Frank came back from Canada, he set about organizing a place for Juliet at Cambridge.

He chose the Margaret Fuller Foundation, an American college that was the newest and glossiest addition to the cluster of ancient beauties gathered beside the Cam.

The building was the design of a Californian architect, and based upon the lines of a condor in flight; the effort of producing buildable plans, in which weight was married to airiness, had sent him mad at the beginning of what could have been a career as notable as that of Frank Lloyd Wright, but as the college was strongly imbued with the doctrines of the Women's Liberation Movement, his fate was seldom mentioned except as illustrating the inherent weakness of the male.

The staff tended towards youth. Flying hair, unconfined busts and large mouths – all displayed with intimidating arrogance and almost perpetual anger. They laughed a good deal, loudly and sneeringly. The old male dons at the old colleges shook their heads on encountering these Amazons, and made unanswerable statements about biological facts; and very old Dr Amory, PhD and goodness knows what else, called them the Bacchae and quoted Tennyson – 'Let them rave, let them rave.'

Frank did not notice the liberation flavour; what attracted him to the Margaret Fuller Foundation was the fact that it had produced, during its brief existence, four Double Firsts in Atomic Physics, while its Principal, Mrs Saltounstall, was currently engaged in discussions with the university's governing body about a new prize – for women only, and for some scientific subject. 'There is absolutely no doubt at all,' she emphasized in her soft, accentless voice, 'that the old theory that women cannot excel at the more, shall we say, objective disciplines, is extinct. And I am particularly anxious that the Foundation should draw in girls from the working class who have taken high numbers of A levels in the British comprehensive schools.'

Only once, during the train journey with Frank, did Juliet awake out of her thoughts to watch a bird glimpsed for a moment through the window.

'There's a bird keepin' still in the air. Never saw that before.'

'It's a hawk, I expect – yes,' as the train carried them on. 'Did you notice the tiny head?'

She shook her own. 'Only noticed it was keeping still, like.'

'Hovering, it's called.'

She said no more and some minutes later the train drew into Cambridge.

Juliet did not notice Cambridge: the pale, austere classicism of the colleges and the lawns of richest green spread before them, and the shadows that added to their grace – all passed her by.

'You comin' along with me?' she asked Frank as they emerged from a superior restaurant, fortified by a good lunch and an excellent champagne.

'Good heavens, no. You aren't a child or wrong in the head. Why? Nervous?'

A pause.

'Not exactly nervous, I'm not. This woman I'm going to see – what did you say her name is? She the head?'

'Juliet! I *told* you all that only an hour ago.'

'I know,' smiling dazedly up at him, 'but me head feels funny.'

'That's champagne,' he said resignedly. 'Perhaps it wasn't a very good idea.'

'Don't you believe it, it was smashing,' said his embryo Einstein reassuringly. 'How do I get there?'

'Her name is Mrs Saltounstall—'

'What a mouthful,' Juliet interrupted predictably.

'And mind you get it right. It's the most aristocratic name in America – *Sal-toun-stall*. And you go past those lights,' pointing to the traffic signals, 'and down that long road where the trees are. Then first left, and there it is.'

'First left, how'll I know which it is?'

'Because it's as big as the Crystal Palace,' he snapped. '(Oh no, you wouldn't remember that.) It's huge and a funny shape and it's mostly glass. And now get along, you mustn't be late. Good luck.'

'All right – keep your cool,' and with a careless wave, she was off. 'See you four o'clock at the station,' over her shoulder.

Frank went off to sit overlooking the River Cam on the Backs to regain his cool.

Juliet idled on. She was wearing one of the neutral-coloured dresses she affected and her hair caught the sunlight. One or two tourists glanced at her with interest.

There had fallen upon her, helped by the champagne, one of those states which she knew well, in which the real world seemed unreal and as if seen through a sheet of glass. And as she moved slowly through the lively crowds, there grew with it another sensation, one that was not familiar; as if her longing to find the secret governing the law of coincidence had become – not visible – but *present* in these ancient buildings and streets; as if all her passion to learn and Learning itself were floating like some spicy fragrance in the air.

It's better than the champagne, she thought dreamily, and then there was a flashing dazzle before her eyes and the fragrance had vanished, and that great glass building must be the college. It had many little windows indicating students' quarters, so small as to be not unlike the cells of nuns four hundred years ago, and a wonderful swoop of roof and walls, suggesting the wings of a mighty bird.

The Principal's room, being paid for by American millionaires, did not suggest nuns. It was furnished and coloured, though Juliet did not notice, with what may best be described as crushing modesty. The carpet, the few ornaments, were all but priceless, in terms of money; sweet-scented woods, porcelain thin as flower petals, the pink and yellow and magenta of

Korean art, were blended into a startling harmony. All this made a setting for the small white-haired woman seated at a desk.

Could Frank have seen Mrs Saltounstall enthroned, he would have remembered the American pioneer scholars who studied their Latin in wooden huts by candlelight while the wolves howled outside, and he would have said that Learning needed none of these mock-modest trappings.

Mrs Saltounstall looked with a pleasant smile towards Juliet, advancing down the forty-foot room.

'Miss Slater. Good afternoon. Sit down, please. That's right.' Blue, narrow eyes beneath the drooped eyelids raked Miss Slater like searchlights.

*Not nervous. Oh, anything but,* and Mrs Saltounstall experienced a familiar irritation. How she disliked girl 'characters' with a tendency to assert themselves! All that mattered was working, getting a First, and adding prestige to the Foundation. *Odd appearance, too. But we'll see.*

'Now, Miss Slater. You have five A levels and were at the Hawley Road Comprehensive School in North London. Why do you want to come to Cambridge?' Her tone had changed; she shot the question.

'I don't want to, not reelly,' answered, unhesitatingly, a flat voice with cockney vowels. 'I'd sooner work out what I got to think out by myself. But Mr Pennecuick, that's my guardian, he said at Cambridge there's people who'll *listen* when you tell them what you try to explain – you see, at the comp' – she leant forward slightly – 'they were ever-lasting on about exams.' She came to a stop.

'And so shall we be here. If you get a place,' Mrs Saltounstall answered her. 'Make no mistake.'

Juliet stared at her, rather desperately.

'But can't you help me? 'Cos if you can't, I don't want a place. Let some other girl have it what does.'

'If you tell me what it is you are working on, we shall – progress,' Mrs Saltounstall said. She was slightly off-course. The girl had many of the marks of the adolescent exhibitionist, but there was another quality, hard to define even for this expert, which precluded the verdict.

'I want . . .' pause, and a struggle reflected in the sallow face. 'I want to find out what makes coincidences.'

'Indeed. Well, no doubt you know that Arthur Koestler and Sir Alister Hardy, who is working at Oxford, have both written on the subject?'

'I read *The Roots of Coincidence* – it didn't get anywhere,' Juliet said rapidly. 'It had a lot of interesting ideas but it never *got* anywhere. See – what *I* want to make is a – a theory of coincidence, and a law. Like the Second Law of Thermodynamics. That's why I – would like to come here. On second thoughts,' she added.

Mrs Saltounstall allowed herself a faint smile.

'Well, you have your remarkable A levels. As for your law of coincidence, we will see if our Atomic Physics don can help.'

She paused, and picked up the internal phone to call the secretary. 'We cannot have you up here for three years, floundering about in theories of coincidence, you know.'

There was a silence. Through a long window Juliet saw the broad silver of the river.

'If I . . . get a place . . . will I have to do things?' she demanded suddenly.

'You will certainly be offered a full programme—'

'Mr Pennecuick, my guardian,' Juliet interrupted, 'he said there'll be a lot of theatre societies and playing hockey and all that. I won't have to do any of that, will I? Because I don't want to.'

Mrs Saltounstall was meditating a little lecture on the necessity of some relaxation when the Atomic Physics don was ushered in by the secretary.

Mrs Saltounstall turned to her.

'Miss Lipson, this is Juliet Slater, who is applying for a place here. Can you spare twenty minutes? You can both sit in that corner,' indicating a darkish nook and a bamboo sofa beneath a great shrub of rose geranium.

Miss Lipson, an Englishwoman and an honours graduate of Cambridge, was accustomed to what she thought of as 'American ways' at the Margaret Fuller. She picked up Juliet with a cool green eye and led her to the sofa, to which she pointed with a long white finger. She had seated herself, and was parting delicate pale lips to speak, when Juliet leant forward and began, rather loudly:

'J'oo know anything about coincidence?'

'What do you mean?' Miss Lipson asked, a little tartly, but interested by the face leaning towards her and deciding that the principal would not have asked her here to give her time to a time-waster.

Within half a minute of Juliet's explaining, so far as she could, what she did mean, the two young women were talking together in a language that only a few people in the world could have understood.

The languid educated voice and the flat cockney one flowed on: answering, questioning, correcting, until the speakers came up against some mathematical law standing solidly in the path of the conclusion they had reached; now running down some algebraic highway or geometric lane leading nowhere, now soaring amidst Boole and the New Physics. But always returning, in grotesque contrast to the eremitic terms in which they talked, to small examples; little domestic or everyday incidents in the actual world that was seemingly spread outside the airy spider-work fabric of unbreakable law amidst which their talk had been climbing.

'Have you come to any conclusions?' Mrs Saltounstall had walked down the length of the room and was standing over them.

Miss Lipson got up gracefully and Juliet did the same without the grace.

'I think there may be something in what Miss Slater has been saying—'

'She *understands*!' Juliet cut in loudly. 'First person what ever has, what I've met.' (Her grammar went headlong.) 'So if there's any more here like you, Miss,' turning to Miss Lipson, 'I'd like to come.'

Mrs Saltounstall said, 'You may go now, Miss Slater. You will hear our decision after you have sat the entrance examination. Miss Lipson, would you kindly stay for a moment?'

The secretary led Juliet to the door.

The principal sat down at her desk and, indicating that Miss Lipson should take a chair, looked at her enquiringly.

'A remarkable grasp of every branch of mathematics, including much of the higher branches which she has taught herself during the last year. Remarkable. I have not met it before except in very advanced mathematicians. She is up to anything we could teach her here.'

The slow voice had been austere, but the gaunt cheeks were faintly flushed.

## 22

'There was a woman there. She understood!' Juliet burst out, hurrying up to Frank at the agreed meeting place on Cambridge station. 'I talked to her, nearly an hour must have been, and she—'

'Get in – get in – you nearly missed it. Where *have* you been?'

'Sittin' in one of the little parks. Thinkin' . . . Why've I got to take their old exam?' settling herself in a corner seat as the flat fields began to rush by. 'I don't want all that history stuff.'

'Well,' he said, foreseeing much toil ahead, 'the examination is only weeks away. We'll just have to work in shifts and sit up all night—'

'You can't help me with me science subjects. None of you'd understand.'

'No, but Edmund and I can help you with your English, Clemence with your history. Er – won't you need to revise your scientific subjects at all?'

'No,' was the simple answer, and she turned to watch the country flashing past, saying no more until they alighted to change at Norwich.

*

'Well – how did it go?' Clemence asked, when Juliet had hurried across to her house and shut herself in.

'Oh – well, I think – I didn't get much out of her – you know she's almost inarticulate.'

'Yes,' Clemence said, thinking how much worse Juliet would have been if she were articulate.

He glanced at her sharply. 'Have you been crying?'

'Well, yes, a bit. It's nothing, dear, only something Grandmamma said. It doesn't matter.'

'Well, come here and be cuddled and tell me all about it.'

It transpired that Mrs Massey, settled by Frank with a comfortable income and a new flat in town, three new caps of striking design and some very expensive scent, had launched on her granddaughter a lecture on the unwisdom of parenthood.

All the views of over-population she had picked up from the radio and television – all of which disguised her own very strong dislike of the prospect of becoming a great-grandmother instead of living in unruffled comfort and gaiety – were brought out and stated with solemnity.

'Well,' said Frank at the end of the recital, 'we must see what can be done.'

Frank and Clemence, working separately and each for an hour at a time, hauled Juliet (there is no other word for their labours) through English history from Aethelred the Unready to Elizabeth II, finding her flawless on dates and bored with anything to do with people or the imagination.

Edmund, returning so soon with reluctance from his lair, applied himself conscientiously to dragging her through a resurrection of what she had, presumably, learnt about English

literature at the comprehensive. Edmund's ear for vowel and
consonant was exquisite, and he faced a pupil neither capable of
hearing that 'With radiant feet the tissued clouds down steering'
was a beautiful line, nor of understanding when he explained
why. She committed that ultimate sin against the poetic Holy
Ghost by asking, 'Why can't they say it so's you can understand?'

'Don't you like any of it, Juliet?' he demanded, pale with
hidden irritation.

'That bit about trees I like,' she said haltingly – '"branch-
charmed by the earnest stars" – what's that mean, "branch"?
That's what trees have.'

'What?' He had gone off into an angry reverie – such a
waste of *time*!

'"Branch-charmed by the earnest stars." I like it. What's
it mean?'

'I'm damned if I know – *precisely*,' he said at last. 'It's an
example of what I call poetic obscurity in the good sense. Who
wrote it? (I know, but you tell me.)'

'John Keats, 1795 to 1821,' came the unhesitating answer.
But when he tried her with Eliot's 'In which sad light a carved
dolphin swam', with its final superb, ponderous, Anglo-Saxon-
suggesting past participle, he met with, 'They say dolphins
have got intelligence,' and gave up.

'We'll just have to pray she doesn't get plucked on *aesthetic
appreciation*,' he said gloomily to Frank, who was thinking with
satisfaction about the trees and the dolphins.

On the day before the examination Clemence said casually to her
husband that she did not feel up to escorting Juliet to Cambridge.

'Not ill, are you, dear?'

'Oh no, just not up to it.'

'And I've got this meeting . . . It'll have to be Edmund.'

'Can't she go alone?' Clemence looked up at him with a calm expression; she was lying back in a long chair in the sunlight. The hour was just after breakfast, and from within came the reassuring muted sounds of a 'daily woman' clearing up. 'She isn't a child,' she added.

(Here it was; the first argument over Juliet. Mild, indeed, but an argument.)

'I know, but she might want to blow off steam to someone.'

'*Juliet*? Blow off *steam*?' Clemence tried to maintain the calm expression.

'Clem' – he hesitated – 'I hoped you were getting used to her.'

'I am used to her. I just don't feel up to going to Cambridge and back. It's very hot. And – I – I don't feel like it.'

'All right then, dear. I'll see Edmund.'

*Victory*, thought his wife, as he swung off. *Hardly any trouble at all – though he did forget to kiss me . . . Perhaps he didn't forget.*

She went slowly through her morning's tasks: the telephoning and the supervising. But by lunchtime this solemn creeping about and pondering every action was swept away by a sudden feeling of hunger. She began to laugh, and finished off the afternoon at her usual pace.

Frank was met that evening by a hug and a savoury smell of cooking, but Clemence did not leave with Juliet on the following morning for Cambridge.

Edmund escorted Juliet as far as the doors of the Foundation.

Surrounded by hastening crowds of what he sourly thought of as young females who would have been better employed at the summer sales, he paused at the soaring edifice of glass and marble.

She was darting up to the entrance as he said: 'What about lunch?'

'I'll find somewhere – you enjoy yourself. See you,' and with the nearest she could come to a teasing smile she disappeared through the doors with a crowd of other would-be students. The American 'r' was loud on the dry, sunny Cambridge air.

'Good luck,' he called. She did not hear.

He sauntered down the long tree-shaded road. *And now I will enjoy myself. Beer first.*

He had the beer; and spent the rest of the day sitting on a bench in a shabby little public park opening off a backstreet of ancient houses, next to an old man feeding sparrows.

Mercifully, the old man was silent, except for a 'Good day to you,' when he shuffled away; and Edmund, having lunched off a lump of cheese and two cold sausages, found, as a bonus, that his neighbour had left behind a sizeable piece of cake which, on being tasted, was found to be excellent and served him for dessert.

He became absorbed by this small, untidy world of birds, squirrels, litter and silence; and fell into a half doze, half dream from which he was aroused by the bells of Cambridge chiming four. Hurrying through the streets still crowded with loitering tourists, he wondered, for the first time since that morning, how Juliet had 'got on'.

He was waiting by the station bookstall and beginning to feel apprehensive about her non-arrival, when she came in sight. With her was a tall girl with red hair.

'This here's Sandy,' she announced, jerking her head at her companion. 'Sandy, this is Edmund.'

Sandy said 'Hi, Edmund' with a glorious smile, and looked away towards an approaching train.

'She's been helping me,' Juliet said. 'I was walkin' along, see, saying to meself out loud, "Who the hell wrote *Paradise Lost*?" and she came up behind me.'

'And I said "Milton, you clot," ' gurgled Sandy.

'We got talkin'. She goes horse-ridin', hunting after foxes. Cruel, I call it.'

'Balls,' said Sandy cheerfully. 'Here's my train. Goodbye, Edmund,' nodding. 'Au 'voir, Juliet. See you in September.'

'If I get me place,' Juliet called, skimming along beside the moving train. 'Thanks for the help.'

'Of course you will, you dolt.' The beautiful head, which irresistibly suggested to Edmund that of some high-bred racer looking out of a horsebox, was withdrawing, when he was astounded to hear Juliet scream, as the train snatched Sandy away: 'Wish you wasn't goin', Sandy.'

'Simply *got* to go to lousy London. Bye-bye,' and she was a quarter of a mile away.

'Diana of the Uplands,' Edmund muttered.

'Pardon?'

'Nothing. It's an Edwardian picture. There's a refreshment bar on our train,' as they boarded the Norwich express which followed quickly on Sandy's train. 'We'd better make for it. I suppose you had some lunch?'

'Fergot. Want to know how I got on?' looking back at him over her shoulder as they pushed their way down the crowded corridor. 'I got me paper somewhere here,' patting herself. 'Course you won't understand the science questions.'

'Nor want to, thank you – I say, when you said thanks for the help . . . ?' They were now seated at a plastic table.

'She just told me about *Paradise Lost.* Good thing she did.'
Juliet brought out a crumpled paper from somewhere, and
pointed with a finger protruding from a hand wrapped about a
cheese roll. 'We got a Milton question. See? A fucker, isn't it?'

'I see that you have quickly picked up your girlfriend's
vocabulary,' was the dry answer. (Beautiful upper-class girls!
How he hated them.)

'I don't get you. She was all right. I think I done all right
in the English, me and her *compared notes.*' The phrase came
out a little self-consciously and Edmund suspected that it, also,
had been picked up from Sandy.

'How about another roll?' he asked, and went in search of
that and another beer.

Faces like Sandy's haunted him. His life was scattered with
such forever elusive images.

*What I need,* he thought, blundering laden back to their table,
*is some cosy puss to pick me up in her jaws and carry me off for life.*

About three weeks later, on a morning so beautiful that every
remark made against the English climate was forgotten, a letter
was handed in at the open door where the three – for once,
Juliet had joined them – were seated at breakfast.

Frank, after an inspection of the envelope, handed it to her.
She tore it open and scanned the typed page. Then she looked
up, and announced in a tone of mild satisfaction:

'I got me place.'

'And I' – Clemence announced, looking up from an untapped
egg – 'I am going to have a baby.'

# BOOK THREE

## 23

Clemence obtained her way in many things, and Frank his, in approximately an equal number. This helped towards making an unusually happy marriage.

Frank, the more imaginative of the pair, sometimes thought that the two large meadows, shut away from the outside world by their ancient thorn hedges, made, literally, a world of their own, in which he, at least, lived an ideal life.

Supported by his own fortune and that left him by his great-aunt, he could avoid most of the pressures of contemporary Western life; and his own temperament, and Clemence's absorption in their children, kept his few worries confined to their family circle and, as far as the larger scale was concerned, to the AIEG, which continued to steadily increase.

His family continued to increase, too; Clemence planned like a general before a battle and Providence apparently planned with her. Fifteen years after their wedding day, Frank sometimes felt himself surrounded by a crowd of shrill-voiced, astoundingly energetic, clear-skinned, silky haired, diminutive strangers: Hugh aged fourteen, Alice aged twelve, Edith aged ten, and Emma and Piers aged respectively eight and six. He had more than once gently hinted that five was enough, and Clemence, grown becomingly stout, had smiled dreamily.

She had had her way about children. And she had her way about the House, which she had demanded (undoubtedly it had been a demand) should be built to replace the Cowshed after the birth of Edith.

The House had ten rooms, and was built on two storeys to save everyone's legs; and it took up most of First Meadow, Second Meadow being given over to wheat, vegetables, and accommodation for a cow, a pig and chickens. Juliet's house, once a comfortable two hundred yards distant, was now at the end of Clemence's flower garden. Two of its three sheltering oaks had had to be felled, because of disease, but the largest and most impressive remained, and under it was the family's place for meals out of doors.

Each house also had its own telephone, Clemence having insisted that to share one between two houses – one where there were three small children and another where there was an absent-minded genius – would be unheard-of and dangerous.

Hertfordshire elm, Cornish slate, the best natural products from almost every county in England had been used to build the House; and its low, comfortable lines and solid beauty had so grown upon snobby Wanby that it was boasted of. Local newspapers, when occasionally referring sneeringly to the AIEG, described Frank as 'the eccentric near-millionaire'. Occasional motoring tourists, slowing down to gape at the House, were disappointed to get a glimpse of nothing more startling than, occasionally, a happy face.

There was only one shadow upon this genial glow.

Juliet.

Fifteen years had sped for her as fast as she herself had skimmed the surrounding lanes while home on vacation from the Margaret Fuller Foundation. Thick spectacles with horn rims now added to the natural disadvantages of her face; but her strange eyes, thus magnified, showed to advantage.

While on one of his frequent missions around the world attempting to persuade governments into buying into Edible Grass Ltd, Frank would reflect upon his patriarchal life. It was solid, contented and, in spite of the bitter opposition to the AIEG from the meat cartels, increasingly useful. Clem was happy, the children beautiful and promising, and his fortune, in the hands of competent advisers, had, in spite of large expenditure upon promoting Edible Grass, Ltd, increased.

But Juliet had not fulfilled her promise.

While at the Foundation, she had shown signs of doing so, passing top of her year in the Finals and, in addition, being the first graduate to win, with distinction, the prestigious new prize which Mrs Saltounstall had persuaded the governing body into instituting.

Juliet declined the offer of a research fellowship in mathematics at the Foundation with such an absent ungraciousness that it was not repeated; and indeed, her three years there had showed an application to the curriculum so intent as to seem obsessive, and some of her tutors suspected her of being unbalanced: as a member of a board of eminent academics, she might one day collapse or explode.

She had made no friends.

The beautiful and foul-mouthed Sandy had made a bet with several of her set that she would take the Weirdo out to lunch three times a term, and won it. But no embarrassed liking lay hidden behind the bet; Sandy was embarrassed only when trying to express her feeling for horses. She made the bet because the Weirdo would so obviously rather work than have lunch, and Sandy liked to torment her.

At the end of her lazy, promiscuous, laughing first year, Sandy was sent down rejoicing, and Juliet never saw her again. Her departure left a tiny fracture in Juliet's carapace. She even thought quite often of Sandy, the Honorable Elvira Roxeth.

Juliet's other fellow undergraduates meanwhile ignored her, except for the exchanges of every day. A reputation for extreme cleverness had somehow escaped and had at first surrounded her; but soon they became accustomed to it. It only expressed itself in examination results; and she herself was so odd as soon to earn her nickname.

She led what seemed to her the ideal life she had longed for since her arrival at Hightower.

She had her own little cell, as sparsely furnished as a room could be: the narrow bed, shelves round three walls overflowing with books, the Möbius ring from Hightower and a key to her door.

There was also the informed company of her tutor when she needed to discuss a difficulty, and, when she must walk, flat country lying under a vast sky. There she could glide along until dusk slowly descended, going ever further into that dreaming mood which, she now knew, was more fruitful than study.

There were also the birds.

To them she gave the scanty stream of love which Frank had coaxed from her.

These visitors to her windowsill were not encouraged at the Foundation. Had they been sparrows, blue tits, wrens, and others of the small kind, sweetly feathered in tan or russet with an occasional gleam of orange or blue, and endowed with piping voices, they might have been tolerated and their tiny droppings ignored. But the severe angles and cliff-like heights of the great building attracted stout waddling pigeons and voracious gulls with greedy yellow eyes. The Foundation was more than liberal with rules; solemnly did it recognize the myriad idiosyncracies in human nature; faithfully it went forward under the banners of Susan Sontag and Betty Friedan. But seagulls on the windowsills it was not having.

Juliet felt a vague identification with the birds and their need for a refuge far above the dwellings of human beings. She openly saved scraps from her own meals at the college table, scooping them into a paper handkerchief. Emboldened by 'encouragement', the birds would bang their beaks on Juliet's windowpanes, eyes bolting with greed and incredulous indignation, while she was vaguely aware of their summons but could not bring herself to break her train of thought or, more valuable still, the dreaming.

Afterwards, the dream retreating and the thought concluded, she would open the window, light a cigarette, and scatter their food. *I used to feel like that, as if I'd go mad if I didn't get a bit of peace. Only with them, course, it's food.*

The papers she submitted to the Science Group, the only Foundation society which she joined, were seven in the course of three years; and dealt always with one subject: coincidence.

They were written in a plain style which should have made their subject intelligible, had it not been fatally associated, in the minds of the scanty audience, with mystery and marvelling, so that, even if any conclusion had been reached at the end of each short paper, it would have received no credence.

Quite soon, the Weirdo gained a reputation for being obsessional about coincidence. She was pigeon-holed, and mildly pitied, and her papers forgotten as soon as heard.

Only Miss Lipson, who always attended Juliet's readings of her papers, treated them with respect. Miss Lipson, growing thinner and more caustic in speech as the three years passed, liked Juliet, who frequently consulted her; it was not a human liking, but the kind of attraction Miss Lipson felt for stars, or for certain contemporary music.

'Matter of fact,' Juliet said to this sole supporter, 'I'm working on a – a longer paper. I've done three pages. *The Law of Coincidence: Some Investigations and a Conclusion,* it's called.'

'Indeed,' was Miss Lipson's comment, from the big armchair where she lay back amid clouds of the tobacco smoke she was forbidden by her doctor to inhale. 'How long do you think it will take you?'

'Oh – ten years, fifteen, maybe longer,' withdrawing one hand from behind her back, where she had kept it since entering the don's study. 'I was out walking, see, and I saw this, and I thought: *That's like someone.* And then I thought: *Miss Lipson.* So it's for you.'

She held out a white flower shaped like a star, small and fragile on a noticeably long and slender stem.

Miss Lipson took the frail thing between fingers equally white and frail, and laid it, meditatively, on her desk.

'Thank you. Would you say it was a coincidence, our being alike?'

'Not *pure*,' Juliet pronounced, after thought. 'I say, don't tell anyone about my thesis, will you?'

'No.'

'Cheerio,' and Juliet was gone.

Miss Lipson picked up the flower and studied it.

'A gift from a genius,' she murmured at last. 'Oh yes.'

Juliet worked.

Slowly, a quarter of an hour at a time: on summer mornings when she absented herself from a lecture which, she had carefully calculated, she could safely cut; in the small hours when the noise of traffic was almost stilled and the bells of Cambridge made their deep declarations on the dim, chill air. She sat at her table, wrapped in the current hooded cape, hair coiled on top of her head out of the way, and slowly, oh so slowly, wrote word by word the sentences that expressed all she had vaguely felt, and had then begun over the years to prove, since childhood.

She wrote the papers for her Finals if not carelessly, with disrespectful speed; the knowledge implied in the answers demanded was not, to her, a laboriously acquired discipline, but something as familiar as her work-table or that same cape. She usually finished her papers an hour before everyone else – and sat, the recipient of resentful and incredulous glances, gazing out of the window at the waving trees.

And when the results were out, and she was top of her year, all but a few undergraduates thought: *She's welcome.* For who would want to be so brilliant, and also so plain, so thin, so uninteresting and such a weirdo?

\*

'Satisfied, love?' Clemence asked Frank at the breakfast table when the results came. Juliet had returned to her house to tend to an injured rat which she had found in a ditch and carried home, struggling, wrapped in newspaper.

He shook his head. 'She's done brilliantly, but that's no more than I expected. No . . . I'm disappointed.'

'Oh dear,' his wife said, with the merest hint of malice. 'What did you expect?'

'I don't know, quite. Something . . . astonishing.'

Clemence was again with child but, for once, not engaged in wiping or comforting the last one. The current nurse, Brigitte or Gretl, was doing that, in the nursery. Breakfast-time was reserved for Frank.

'She's not yet twenty-one,' she said, regretting the malice, and meaning to comfort.

'I realize that. But her kind has a habit of dying young. To put it sentimentally, they burn themselves out.'

He came over to kiss her. 'I'll be back – I don't know – eightish. There's a meeting.'

'I'll try to get her to choose something else than those dreary colours Grandmamma used to call "Rich Tea biscuit" for the presentation or whatever it is. When she gets her degree.'

He laughed. 'I miss your grandmother,' he said truthfully, and went out.

Mrs Massey had died precisely as she would have wished: asleep in her chair, dressed with her usual suitability and grace, and with both white hands loosely folded on her creaseless lap. This, after some five years of theatres, drives, society, and choice little dinners. Who could wish for more? Except that she could never get Alice, much less that stubborn little Edith

(*Clemence was going to have trouble with that child*) to call her
Pretty Granny.

Clemence, left alone at the table, folded the *Daily Telegraph*.
*I really must try,* she thought, *to like her* (as her thoughts ranged
over her personal riches and compared them with the dry and
dusty store of the sallow virgin a hundred yards away). *I've
got so much, and she has so little.*

She sat down abruptly, then got quickly up again. *But she
can keep her breakfast down,* she thought, hurrying from the
room.


'Wish you'd change your mind,' Juliet had said to Miss Lipson
when she looked in to say goodbye on the last day of term.
'I got me own house, I told you. You could be quiet, and have
breakfast in bed.'

'I can't, thanks all the same.' Miss Lipson looked down at
her copy of Descartes, in whose pages the star flower on the
long stem was pressed. 'I never go away. I dislike it.'

'. . . and thanks for all the help,' Juliet had added.

'No need for thanks, I enjoyed it.' She was referring to
one or two elucidations which she had given, bearing on the
mathematics, in *The Law of Coincidence: Some Investigations and a
Conclusion.* Miss Lipson added suddenly: 'Thanks, really, Juliet,
for asking me to stay and have breakfast in bed.' A faint smile
on the pale lips; three years had increased that suggestion of
a skull in the delicate head, so that it had become disturbing.
'As – as a matter of fact, I may have to go away, quite soon . . .
and that's boring enough.'

'Far?' Juliet asked absently, sliding an ivory bracelet, Frank's
present, up and down her arm.

'I don't know exactly. In fact, I don't know at all.' She began to cough, and slowly lit another cigarette. 'By the way, if you'd like to do something to please me, will you include a footnote in your thesis – when it's finally ready? Saying I was responsible for suggesting the line of thought that led to . . .' She added a sentence that perhaps twelve people in the world would have understood.

'Course I will. I'd meant to anyway.'

Miss Lipson looked down at Descartes. 'It will be my immortality. Goodbye.' She did not look up.

'Might send you a card,' Juliet said, lingering she did not know why, at the door.

'Send it soon, then.'

'Because you're going away?'

A nod of the down-bent head had been the only answer.

## 24

Line by line, word by word, Juliet added to *The Law of Coincidence*.

She walked every day, and sometimes on the long summer nights, noting the slow turning of the year from bud to falling leaf through mist and frost to bud again. It was her only recreation.

Sometimes she came in to meals when the children were present, and looked at them with less interest than if they had been small animals. They called her Juliet, and gradually, as the years mounted, the following ritual conversation developed:

'Mum, can I go to Juliet's house?' (Never 'Can I go to see Juliet?')

'You know you can't.'

'Ohwhynot?'

'Because she's busy.'

'What is she busy *for*?'

'Writing her book.'

'I want to see Ratty.'

'You know poor Ratty's *dead*, Hugh. Do find something to do.'

'That's what I *meant*.'

'Oh you want to go to his grave? Take Alice.'

'Don't want to.'

'And ask Pilar to go with you. I don't want you falling in that ditch.'

Some years after Juliet's return from Cambridge, Pilar had arrived at the Pennecuicks' – exhausted, travel-worn, almost penniless, and in tears after a fruitless visit to Hightower, 'full of busy people, who made a rudeness to me'.

Filled up with lunch and sympathy, she had unfolded a story of betrothal, sisterly jealousy, and betrayal worthy of Verdi at his Verdiest. Suddenly she had knelt at Clemence's feet and implored to work for her, 'to care for these little angels', indicating Alice and Hugh, who were making paper boats and ignoring the drama.

Clemence said that they would decide about that when Mr Frank came home, and distracted Pilar from her misfortunes by taking her on a tour of the House, which caused gasps of ingenuous admiration.

When Frank returned, he surprised Clemence by at once granting Pilar's plea, pointing out that all these Brigittes and Françoises, though nice girls, meant constant change for the children. Frank believed in deep roots, even in minor matters.

So she stayed, grew plump and merry and regained her prettiness; was loved by the children (although Edith sometimes observed ominously: 'Pilar's silly') and hunted the drama that was necessary to her nature where she could. She believed that *Mees Juliet – such a fright now she wears those glasses!* – had a secret lover. (Well, not exactly secret, for had not Pilar seen them together in the café called the Golden Pig?)

*

Arthur Robinson had left the bookshop years ago and, having been firmly fixed in the clutches of his Brenda, was now, in his early thirties, staggering under the usual male contemporary load of marriage, mortgage, child's education, car, garden, house decorating and inflation, all mixed with vague guilt and a feeling that he never knew what was going to happen next.

One evening he had recognized Juliet, hastily swallowing a cup of the Golden Pig's awful coffee, and had nervously reintroduced himself.

Juliet so seldom thought about people that the few she did think about, including Sandy and Miss Lipson, etched themselves into her memory.

She welcomed Arthur at once, with mild pleasure, and even repeated the elephant joke as she told him that he was the only boy she had ever been out with.

Arthur, on hearing this titbit, uttered a gallant masculine, 'Go on!'

"S'true. I've always been so busy. That kind of thing doesn't interest me.'

'Is that so?'

Arthur knew a second's wild wish that it did not interest him, but pulled himself back from the abyss.

'I'm married,' he said quickly – then went on: 'Have you been living here these last years? Funny I never ran into you. Remember those coincidences?' (A faint glow came to him, as he remembered being nineteen and free.)

'I was away three years, at college. And I did look out for you at the bookshop but you'd left, they said. I get all my books there, except some you can only get in London.'

'Oh . . . About coincidence, are they?' smiling. *Funny little piece. So different from Brenda.*

'I'm writing something,' Juliet said abruptly, feeling an unfamiliar wish to confide.

'Oh – a novel?' Still smiling. 'How about another coffee?'

'Thanks, but I must be getting back.' She stubbed out a cigarette. 'I still live at Leete, only now I've got my own house. No, it isn't a novel—'

'I've always felt I could write, if I had the time.' The cliché came mechanically from the sensitive lips.

'No, 't'isn't a novel,' she repeated as if he had never spoken.

*Well, they're all the same*, he thought bitterly, *however different they might seem. Never listened.*

'I never read novels,' Juliet went on. 'It's a – scientific work.'

'Oh. Above my head, I expect.'

'It's above everybody's head,' she said calmly and, having risen to go, sat down again. 'I *would* like another coffee, please. I did know one woman at the Foundation who began to understand what I'm after, but she never answered the postcard I sent. Years ago, that was – I think.'

Ordinary time, like everyday life, was vague to Juliet.

Arthur felt a curious satisfaction in finding Juliet Slater as odd as ever. She then surprised him, as she had always done, by asking: 'Do you know a book writer called Edmund Spencer? His poems, I mean. He comes to my guardian's house.'

Arthur's expression changed. 'Yes, I *do* know Edmund Spencer's work. Now *he's* a true poet.' He hesitated. 'I say, could we meet sometimes, Juliet? We could talk. About books?'

She shook her head, where the load of glittering hair was pulled up into a knob, becoming only to a face fairer than hers, and drew up the hood of her cape.

'I simply haven't the time.'

'I said *sometimes.*'

'I'll see how my work goes.' She was standing, poised for flight. 'I would like to, but . . . Tell you what – I'll meet you here on the first of every month, same time. But if I don't come, you must understand its work, and not make a fuss.'

She was gone: flitting out of the door and leaving him to pay both bills, and not seeing Pilar who was crouching, alight with excitement, behind one of the Golden Pig's unnecessary pillars.

Pilar managed to catch the same bus as the detected one.

'You 'ave been shopping?' she began sunnily, as the bus rushed away into the long June dusk.

'Course not,' Juliet said. 'You know I hate shopping. Been to a lecture.'

'Oh – is interesting, the lecture? What is about?'

'Lawrence of Arabia.'

'Oh, but that is an old film.'

'It wasn't the film. It was about how they made it.'

'Is not so interesting, that.'

'I wanted to hear about the desert.' Juliet was looking out of the window at hedges and meadows distinct in the water-clear light.

'Oh horrible! All sand.'

'They had some stones there, on show, that really came from the desert. You could touch them.'

'Interesting, the stones,' Pilar said again, glassy of eye. She was longing to add: And then you meet a friend, I think? *But Mees Juliet, she was strange, you never knew what she might do.* Instead, she asked if there was 'anything about the stars?' and Juliet thought she meant the stars in the heavens, and Pilar explained that she meant Omar Sharif and Peter O'Toole. And while this was being disentangled, the bus stopped at Wanby, and there were Clemence and Frank, looking out anxiously from Clemence's big new car.

'Something terrible is happening!' cried Pilar, leaping from the bus and hurrying across the road. 'Who is at home with the children?'

Juliet followed, almost as swiftly.

'They're here,' Clemence said, as two faces peered animatedly from a rug on the back seat. 'Get in. Children, move over.'

'It's your father, Juliet,' Frank said in a lowered tone, as they drove away. 'Your mother telephoned.'

She was silent for a moment. Then she sighed; not, he thought, from sorrow, memory or grief. It was a sigh of impatience.

She said flatly, 'I'd better go up tonight, s'pose. She'll be on her own and scared stiff.'

'You can just catch the ten o'clock, gets in at eleven-forty.'

She was silent, the arrangement having been made, and he was silent from satisfaction. There had been the impatient sigh, but no hesitation. Truly, she had progressed along the road to humanity. If the promise of genius had flickered and died, at least something else had been achieved.

Presently she asked: 'How did he go?'

'Very suddenly, your mother said. It was a stroke.'

'He'd only been retired eighteen months. Think that caused it? He always did like his job, Dad.'

'Possibly. One can't tell. Retirement comes as a shock to some people.'

She was silent again.

Pilar, huddled up close to the sleeping children, listened intently, but could detect no sobs, stifled or otherwise. *A heart of stone! No doubt she thinks of the secret lover.*

Just as the car drew up at the gate of Frank's meadows, Juliet said: 'Frank . . .'

'What, my dear?' turning to her as Clemence got out to open the gate and Pilar began awakening the sleepers.

'Do you—? She won't want to come and live with me, will she, do you think?'

'Most unlikely,' Clemence put in loudly over her shoulder as she swung the gate back. 'Your mother might try it for a week, but she'd never stand it, bless her.' Clemence got back into the car, where Alice and Hugh were demanding 'grown-up supper'.

'She's never been here longer than a day and she always said it was "funny". *He* never would come. I did *ask* him,' Juliet said, resentfully.

The car was bumping through the long second-growth grass and marguerites; the lights of the House shone through the clear dusk. Juliet looked longingly towards her own home.

'I come with you, Juliet, and help you,' Pilar said importantly. 'There will be packing.'

'Packing! I'm taking pyjamas and me toothbrush – and that's all. I'm not going for six months.' It was snapped.

*

During the first shocked hour Mrs Slater thought of something even worse than going to live with the Pennecuicks: Juliet might come to live with *her*.

She was astonished, bewildered, and very afraid of *that* on the bed in the next room. The bird, sleepy and also bewildered at his cage being left uncovered so late, sulked on his highest perch and did not respond to her coaxing.

But Juliet's arrival, just before midnight, comforted her. There were no kisses or cuddling, beyond a peck on one cheek, but Rose was used to going without kisses, and Juliet's matter-of-fact manner, though rather shocking, was soothing, *More like some doctor or nurse*; and Juliet accompanied her into the bedroom, 'to see your poor old dad', and stood, looking down at the body. The change that comes to some with death had overtaken him, and the leathery, lined face was almost unrecognizable in its calmness.

'Poor old Dad,' his daughter repeated at last. 'He didn't have long to enjoy his retirement.'

Rose sighed heavily. 'He didn't enjoy it all that much, Julie. Retirement. He missed work. Could you fancy a cup of tea?'

'I don't mind, Mum.'

Juliet slowly replaced the sheet which the ambulance man, distractedly summoned by Rose from Whittington Hospital Casualty, had decently drawn over the still-clothed body, and followed her mother into the kitchen. How small and gaudy it looked. She thought with relief of the notebook in her suitcase filled with a problem she was working on.

Rose sipped scalding tea with a faint sensation of returning comfort. She looked at Julie, sitting upright and silent and heavily spectacled opposite her like some old owl, and suddenly *knew* that whatever else she might want later when she had – had got used to things a bit – it was not to have Julie (*Well, she is my daughter, but she's always been more like some stranger*) living with her.

'I been so frightened, Julie,' she began at last, with a heavy sigh, 'though Nurse was ever so nice, and Dr Baker too, and Mrs Dickson come in, but she's got to be at the factory by half-past eight, and she must get her rest, and the kids to get off to school . . . But I was *afraid*, see, nowhere to sleep but – but in there with – with—'

Juliet leaned across and stroked the plump freckled hand lying on the table.

'And – can you stay for a bit, Julie? For – for the funeral? – Oh dear, I can't believe it.'

Juliet's face, already pale with exhaustion, grew almost greenish.

Ten years ago she would have refused to make this journey to London. Now she had come with hardly a second's hesitation. But she foresaw a future in which her peaceful life was disturbed again. Frustration, a return to the old and sullen miseries.

The next instant Juliet's cloud of apprehension lifted, sheered off into nowhere.

'Only for a few days, Julie,' her mother said, with as much tenderness in her voice as husband and daughter had left to her. 'I know you're happy where you are, workin' on your book and that, I'll be all right.'

A sudden and shocking conviction, instantly dismissed, came to Rose that she *would* be all right; what with her widow's pension, and George's pension from BR, and the money Frank sent regular from Juliet's account.

'I'll be a bit lonely,' she added, 'but I expect I'll get used to it.'

The sentence: You'll have to come and live with me, then, Mum, could not be forced through Juliet's lips. It stuck, like some huge and acidulous growth – and then, for the second time, the threat vanished.

'And I won't be comin' down there to live with you, neither,' her mother said, pouring more tea, 'so don't you think it, Julie. I know you'd have me, love—'

Juliet looked at her in surprise, and then they exchanged an odd little smile, as if each understood, and forgave.

'Fact is,' Mrs Slater said confidentially, 'it's funny down there. Funny way of living. Everyone's very kind and all that but – all that money and no carpet in the lounge, I can't get over it. Don't feel it's *right* somehow. And the food! I wonder those lovely kids look as well as they do, or how you can stand it. Parsley and that yog-stuff for your supper! No wonder you're thin. No, it would never suit me.'

Juliet smoked and sipped tea in silence, her thoughts straying to her notebook.

'Julie?'

'What, Mum?' She roused herself.

'How about – the sleeping?' Rose had paled.

'Now, Mum. Pity they couldn't take him away.'

'Oh Julie. Your dad. Doctor said it couldn't be arranged until tomorrow.'

'Well – let's see.' Juliet got up and went through to the living-room. 'There's the sofa – you can have that – and plenty of room in that chair for a little one.' (This coaxed the wateriest flicker of a smile.) 'I'll sleep there.'

'It'll be ever so uncomfortable.'

'Shan't notice. I got something I want to work out.'

At this reappearance, in such an hour, of Juliet's 'work' – that mysterious activity which had made her unlike other women's daughters, and had driven her into running away, and 'funniness', and boylessness, and, as the years passed, being an old maid – at the intrusion of this familiar devil into what should have been an occasion for intimacy and crying, Rose felt a spasm of irritation. She had to control an impulse to say: Oh, *you'll* be all right, then. Instead she muttered: 'Julie, could you go in and get my nightie? Under the pillow. Sounds silly, but I'm that afraid—'

'Course, Mum.'

They had left the light on. There lay the sheeted shape on the bed. Juliet looked down at the uncouth white bulge, then lifted the pink pillow slowly, in order not to disturb the head, and drew out the nightdress case made in the shape of a smirking puppy. She stood, staring, the case dangling from her hand.

This was the second time that she had seen death. Again, that stillness! Over the whole house; not an ordinary quiet. *It's like when there's snow*, she thought. Then she put down the gaudy case and gently lifted the sheet. For a long moment she looked down at her father. Suddenly, she bent and kissed the brow, corrugated by the working of life. As her lips touched it, something rushed up into her throat, her eyes filled, and she uttered a loud sob.

'Julie!' Her mother, half undressed, blundered into the room. 'There, there, love, have your cry-out. Do you good. Doctor said so.'

'I'm all right, Mum. Upset me for a minute, that's all.'

And she cried no more that night. But Frank would have said that she had taken a long step forward.

Two days passed with their usual mingling of incredulous grief and necessary, shocking arrangements.

Mr Slater was buried in the lower part of Highgate Cemetery, not a hundred yards from where his parents and grandparents lay, for he was a Kentish Town man and had lived there all his life. His grandfather used to tell him of the building of the great arch, spanning the country road down which the herds, driven by shouting drovers, descended to the slaughterhouses of Smithfield.

Afterwards, relations, friends and neighbours crowded into the little living-room to drink tea, eat Mr Kipling cakes, and stare at Juliet, who richly rewarded their curiosity by showing no tears and being so plain. (*Educated, was she? Much good might it do her.*) Any questioning was irritatingly quenched by the curtness, just short of rudeness, of her manner.

She moved about the crammed little room answering enquiries (how was she these days? and not married yet?) and reminders about having known her when she was a tiny girl – with smile fixed and eyes fastened, so steadily as to appear alarming, upon the enquirer's face.

Rose made up for her daughter's tearlessness by weeping throughout the gathering. This was approved as being the done thing. But Mrs Dickson observed to Mrs Barnett that it wasn't as if they had got on all that well; to which Mrs Barnett replied, 'Well, you know how it is,' and as they both did, Rose's tears were satisfactorily explained for them both.

*

When Juliet left at the end of three days, which to her had
been barely endurable, her mother went with her.

'There isn't room for you, Mum, not at my house,' Juliet
explained. 'You know that. But Clemence – Mrs Pennecuick –
she's got ever such a nice spare room, and there'll be company
for you. You'll like Pilar—'

'Some foreigner, isn't she?' Rose sniffed.

'She's Spanish, but she talks good English, and you like
children, don't you? A change'll do you good,' she ended, so
full of dismay that she could not bring herself to add: and of
course, stay on if you want to.

'It's kind of Mrs Pennecuick, but I'll only stay the weekend,
Julie. There's all the clearing up to be done at home' (a gulp)
'and 'sides, I made up me mind.' This was a sentiment which
Rose had not had a chance to express for thirty-three years.


Juliet sat up all night, working, smoking, and fruitfully dreaming,
and sometimes looking slowly around her silent house where
a rescued starling, almost recovered, dozed in his cage, and
some rhododendrons which Clemence had left for her, glowed
crimson in the shadows. Outside, in the summer stillness, the
thorn thickets were motionless in the young moon's light, and
Juliet's tortoise's head was tucked into his richly patterned shell,
and she was as happy as a creature living without the usual
springs of human happiness can be.

Her mother was seen off to London on the Monday morning
by Clemence, Juliet and the smallest children, whose half-term
at their nursery school it fortunately chanced to be.

The childen showed a flattering liking for Rose, who had
novel and, to them, attractive alternative names for dogs and

horses, and they fell as if starved upon the ice creams she insisted upon buying them.

Clemence, led by Frank, discouraged ice cream, unless made at home. But she was so relieved that Rose did not want to live at Wanby that she permitted the ice creams as a kind of thanks-offering, and smiled on the purchase of five of the most expensive to be had. Rose leant out of the carriage window and waved farewell to two small, smiling faces, licking and waving like automata.

*Little dears,* she thought, settling back into her corner seat. *There, I never waved to Julie.* And her thoughts ran guiltily on. *Poor old George . . . It don't half seem funny to be* – the word came shockingly into her mind – *free.*

## 25

Quickly, so quickly that Frank sometimes commented upon their pace, more years rushed by.

Hugh was in his first term at Cambridge and compared notes with Juliet during vacations.

Alice had declined formal education, and announced her intention of being an old-fashioned girl. 'Prehistoric, you mean,' said Edith, who was ardently feminist, and aiming at a place at the Margaret Fuller. Joshua, born four years after Piers and thereby breaking the planned two-yearly pattern, was five, and known, under protest from his elders, as Josh. Clemence was gradually, but steadily, putting on weight; Frank growing baldish; and Juliet, on her next birthday, would be thirty-eight.

She had had some small but distinguished successes in the past twenty years – the most notable a paper in *The History of Ideas: An International Quarterly Devoted to Intellectual History*, published in Pennsylvania.

Her name was becoming known in the narrow world of scholarship which yet covers the widest conceivable fields, but it was only known; it was not respected. A faint aura of 'crank' and 'obsessionist' hung about it, for every paper she submitted, however faultless in mathematical logic, dealt with the one subject; and, to other scholars, that subject belonged to the half-world of popular superstition and marvel, where accuracy had no place.

Some months before her thirty-seventh birthday, she had finished the fourth and final draft of *The Law of Coincidence: Some Investigations and a Conclusion.*

But she told no one. She was very tired. She put her pen down gently on the table beside a vase of windflowers and bluebells gathered by Emma that afternoon in the woods; slowly shut the pages of her manuscript; and let her head, with its burden of greying, thinning hair, drop onto her folded arms, and, her mind swimming with incredulous triumph and also with a kind of sorrow, fell asleep.

'I suppose, as usual, none of us will be able to make head nor tail of it,' was Edmund's comment, on hearing of the paper in *The History of Ideas.*

'I understood quite a lot. It's a kind of account of how she came to build up the theory in her book – literally, the history of an idea. Not exciting, but fairly lucid,' said Hugh.

'Isn't that thing finished yet?' demanded Edmund. He now had three more collections of poems to his name, and a firmly established favourable reputation. He was a frequent visitor to the House, and a guest at all the birthday parties. He had descended, at the age of fifty, onto the pretty bosom of a kind little shop assistant, twelve years younger than himself. He was happy in her devotion and awed admiration. Circumstances had emptied of tenants the top floor of his old quarters in Luton, and with the rent from his cottage, payment for his occasional work as a locksmith, and a small but steady income from his poetry, they lived there in that almost forgotten state, modest comfort. He would not take money from his Maida; he liked her to spend her salary on clothes and scent.

'Where is Juliet tonight?' Alice asked idly. 'Didn't I hear something about going out with Arthur? Mrs A won't like that.'

'Alice, where do you pick up all this gossip?' her mother demanded.

'People *confide* in me,' and she rolled her lovely eyes.

Frank went across to the window and drew back the curtains. 'She's back,' he announced. 'Her light's on.'

'It must have been just coffee at the Golden Pig,' from Alice. 'And it's not even ten yet. Poor old Juliet. I don't expect she's ever been to a dance in her life.'

'How is Rose?' Edmund asked. He liked Juliet's mother; they joked, on the rare occasions when they met on mutual visits to the House, about her fears of riding on his motorcycle at Clemence's wedding.

'Oh – putting on too much weight. Juliet goes up to see her every month,' Clemence said.

'Does she like being in that place?'

'I think so. She seems happy enough,' said Frank.

'I'm always so glad,' Clemence said, 'that she's had fifteen years of real enjoyment. She goes to the movies, and takes holidays at Blackpool. And all her friends . . . It was a mercy that awful man died when he did.'

'That's what you're all going to say about me,' Edmund said.

'Of course we are, old chap. But before you leave us, have some turnip wine. I'm going to,' from Frank.

'Christ,' said his friend, softly, 'doesn't the very conjunction of the words put you off? "Turnip" – solidity, stupidity – and "wine" – golden vine leaves, sunlight, gaiety, rubies . . . No, thank you, I will *not* have some turnip wine. Haven't you any whisky?'

'He keeps it for illness – oh damn, there's Josh,' and Clemence hurried from the room.

Pilar was no longer with them. At forty, she had married a St Alberics greengrocer, prosperous and uxorious, who admired her exotic prettiness and accent; and she was comfortably settled. She and her husband, Pilar weeping copiously, had attended Sarah's funeral five years ago, accompanying the family group from the House, and glowing with gratification between her tears.

Clemence found Josh already soothed by the pleasant-faced Norland nanny who had replaced Pilar. She went slowly downstairs, thinking that she would have liked to do everything for Josh herself, but with a large house to supervise, and the affairs of the other children to overlook and largely to direct (for Frank grew yearly more occupied with the AIEG), there was no time for revelling in bathing, soothing and walking Josh; barely time to read to him every night for fifteen minutes, but this Clemence insisted on.

Her conscience about Juliet was clear: she had done her very best, even to gently discouraging (and Clemence was not a gentle person) the constant smoking and the wearing until actual shabbiness of the gnomish capes in sandy tweed, and the straight stone, dun or khaki dresses.

'If only she would use lipstick,' she said once to Frank, in irritable frustration, 'not very bright, but pink – it would make such a difference. She could look really striking, if she'd only bother.'

'She's got something in her head more important than looking striking.'

Three months after Juliet had finished the fourth and final draft of *The Law of Coincidence*, her mother died. Of a stroke, and very quickly, in the expensive and comfortable private home in which Frank had maintained her on Juliet's money since the upkeep of Rose's flat had proved too much for her. Juliet was even paler than usual at the funeral, and said afterwards to Frank that she was glad she had seen her mother only a week before she 'went'.

That night, alone in her house with her books and the animals (usually injured in some way and restored to health by herself), she sat thinking about her mother's life.

The manuscript of the final draft lay on the table, carefully written in the square hand she had learnt at the comprehensive nearly thirty years ago. She lay back in the one comfortable chair in the room, letting the warmth and quiet seep into her spirit.

Her cat dozed on a mat knitted for it by Emma; Billy-bird, Bertie-bird's successor, slept in his cage under cover of one of Juliet's old sand-coloured skirts; she had adopted him when her mother had entered the home. Hrothgar, her raven, drowsily glowered on his perch.

Juliet's thoughts were vague and sad: she remembered her mother's timid affection and how she had never put herself forward in any way. *Funny* – mused Juliet – *Poor Mum* . . . She felt, for once in her life, aimless. There was nothing to do.

Her thesis was finished. Years of unceasing work, unconscious and conscious, were ended. There it lay on the table: *finished.*

She looked slowly round at the shelves filled with her books, and her eyes lingered on those dealing with natural history. It was not in her nature to look at clouds, grasses, running water, without learning how they appeared, grew, ran. Frank had seen with regret the shelves filled with works which were informative, but not imaginative.

But on glancing into them, he had noted that their authors were mostly Victorian, or of the more popular type, the facts therein related with an awe suggesting, yes, the raw material of poetry, and also the atmosphere of an age only beginning to question the existence of the one he himself thought of as the Star Maker. *I suppose*, he had mused, returning a volume on snow crystals to its place, *that's all I can hope for now. And there are the animals.*

Juliet moved restlessly; she, who was usually either so still or skimming like a bird, got up, after a moment's rather desperate staring around, and went to the drawer in her table. She opened it, and took out a square parcel shaped like a book. It was loosely folded in thick, alien-looking paper and string. She stood holding it for a moment, then slowly lifted it and breathed in a faint scent: spice, cinnamon, ginger, dry grey-green leaves nameless in the West which grew in hollows in the endless desert. The smell of the East.

## 26

Late in the afternoon of Juliet's thirty-eighth birthday, preparations were lazily beginning, in a late heatwave, for the picnic tea under her oak tree.

'It's dry, Josh. The water's all gone away.'

Nanny, wearing a bikini and wishing she had worn instead a cool white dress like those of Josh's sisters, patiently followed the little boy through the grass, long ago cropped for a second growth of hay, and the fading marguerites. He was naked but for a sunhat and sandals, and making for the ditch.

'Where has the water gone, then?'

'Oh I don't know.' Nanny fanned herself with a dock leaf. 'The sun dried it up.'

'But where has it *gone*?'

'I don't *know*, Josh, you ask Juliet, she's the bright one around here.'

'There will be mud,' he muttered hopefully, and they meandered on, until deflected by a passing butterfly.

Alice and Edith were coming out of the house carrying baskets of crockery and food; Hugh, naked as Josh but for shorts and a large Peruvian hat, followed bearing the birthday cake.

'Anything dottier than this I can't imagine,' he said. 'Everything'll melt.' He was addressing Edmund.

Maida had, as usual, refused with tightened lips and a bright little smile, to accept Clemence's warm, written invitation to the birthday party.

'Our school mag had a ravvy notice of your *Warning Water*,' said the voice of Emma behind Edmund. 'Normally Esme Skelton – she's our editor – chooses such utter blether. All brain and no music.'

'Thank you, love,' Edmund said gratefully. 'Help me get this thing spread out, will you? I'm terrified of crumpling it.' A large white cloth was part of the ritual.

'There's the postman,' called Alice, kneeling to unload her basket.

'How do you know? And who's going to fag across two fields in this?'

'Saw the van through the trees.'

'I don't expect it's anything – a hundred and fifty shopping days to Christmas, or something. Hugh! It will *melt* if you leave it there . . . here, in the shade, where there's a breeze.'

'The wasps will get it.'

'Oh blow – so they will. I'll have to ask Juliet . . .'

Emma ran across and tapped at the shut door. A chorus of chirrups and squeaks and one familiar pig-like snort were the only answer. But at that moment Juliet herself came slowly through the thorn thicket beyond the house, followed by a young black retriever, panting with long pink tongue exposed, and drooping head.

'Hullo. Hullo, Robert, poor hot boy, then – I say, is it all right if we leave the cake in your house? It'll melt if it stays outside . . . but you aren't supposed to see it.'

'The door's unlocked.'

The rule that no one entered Juliet's house without her permission had stayed unbroken for twenty years.

When Emma emerged, having paused to gossip with Claudine the hamster and Hrothgar the raven, Juliet was lying back in a rattan chair on the paved space under her tree, where the cloth was to be spread. Her eyes were shut, her face leaden. Robert was resting, with his nose across her knees.

'I say, are you all right?'

"Course,' her eyes opened. 'It's the heat.'

'Shall I get you some lemonade?'

'I don't want anything.' Her hand began slowly stroking the dog's satiny head, and Emma went away.

'You know,' she confided to Alice in an undertone as they unpacked mugs and plates, 'she only had two cards by post this morning – rather sad. One from Piers from school – he's good like that – and one from her old Arthur.'

'*Not* signed by Mrs A,' in a drawl.

'Oh Alice, don't make things out of nothing – it's so – so *female*,' Edith cut in irritably.

'Thought you were all for the female, dear sister,' in an even slower drawl.

'Not that sort. Did you see Josh's card? He painted it.'

'Juliet loved it,' Emma put in hopefully. She had once been told in a casual way, by her father, of his lifelong plan for Juliet, and, moved by the confidence, she 'kept an eye open' for any signs of humanity in their protegée.

'Oh rubbish – Juliet never loves anything. What was it? Mud, I bet.'

'Yes, all brown with a kind of green squiggle in the middle. He said it was a fish – "not dead, but very ill".'

The three laughed, looking across the meadow to Josh and Nanny, wandering near the hedge.

'Nanny looks nice in that thing,' Emma said, who made it a habit to be agreeable, and was heartily despised for it by her sisters.

'Too fat, and bikinis are vulgar too.' Alice touched her billowing lawn skirt.

'And designed to attract men—'

'We'll leave the jam till last, shall we, because of the wasps?'

Nanny and Josh were lazily approaching, Nanny having set Josh to pick buttercups; and he, satisfied that the mud had 'all gone away', contentedly pulled off the flower heads and was now intent on arranging them in the mugs.

'No, Josh. Just in that one, in the middle. People don't want to drink flowers.'

'Bees do. Drink them.'

'Here, give them to me . . .'

The languid afternoon stole on, as if Time were walking on tiptoe. Juliet had gone into her house and her door was shut. At a quarter to five, when the fire was burning well and the big brass kettle beginning to sing, Frank's bicycle drew up at the outer gate. He paused, to investigate the letterbox, then came on, with one letter and a parcel.

He was greeted with waves and faint cries.

'Do buck up, Dad, we're gasping.'

'We're *melting*.'

'Daddy, Daddy, the mud has all gone away and I put butter-cups in the mugs.'

'Hurry up and wash, darling,' from Clemence, lying in a garden chair wearing the palest of lilac dresses printed with grey flowers, chosen for her by Alice.

'I'll just give this to Juliet, and be with you,' indicating letter and parcel in the basket.

'She's in her house.'

'Seems off-colour, I thought,' Edmund muttered as Frank came up. 'I'll take that,' putting a hand on the bicycle.

'She has been for weeks – I was wondering if she oughtn't to see someone.'

'Wouldn't be any use. The spring's gone and she's running down. You'll have to face it.'

'What do you mean?' said Frank, turning at Juliet's door with letter and parcel in his hands.

Edmund shrugged. 'Exactly what I say. Most people have families, or ambitions, or sheer necessity, or a good constitution to keep them alive. She hadn't anything but that extraordinary obsession of hers, and now she's finished it – worked it out of herself – and she's . . . collapsed. As I said. The spring has run down, and she's going with it.'

'Oh nonsense. It's the heat.'

Frank glanced irritably at the things in his hands. 'Where's this from – Qu'aid? That's that extraordinary place in the desert. We wrote to them about irrigation and got something back that might have been written in the eleventh century – and the parcel's from there, too.'

'Perhaps Arthur's on a package trip and sent her a little prezzy,' said Alice, who had come floating up to peep.

Her father absently patted her shoulder, and went up to Juliet's door and rapped on the highly unsuitable pixie knocker given to her by her mother.

'Juliet! Post for you, and tea's ready.'

There followed that pause, which he associated with summoning Juliet from behind a shut door ever since he had known her.

Afterwards, he knew that those pauses would never seem the same in memory again.

The door slowly opened. She stood there, hair newly dragged into its usual knot, wearing one of what the girls called her 'sandies', but this one had a wide, delicate lace collar and her arms were bare.

'Hullo – I'm just ready.' Then she saw the parcel and letter and absolutely snatched them from him, turned and shut the door in his face.

'Mannerless Maggie,' said Alice.

Juliet stood in the hush and tempered heat and silence of her house, staring at the envelope. She was as solitary as the city of Qu'aid, in the desert where it had stood for a thousand years. She had never felt fear in her life, but she felt it now: she feared the contents of the envelope, with its row of exotic stamps, printed with silver crescents and graceful green Arabic symbols.

She shivered in the heat and said, aloud, in the flat tones that had not altered much over the years:

'I haven't got it.'

Then, slowly, she turned and took from her table a paper knife, and again slowly, with the deftness that marked all her minor actions, slit the envelope and unfolded the contents.

In her hands were two sheets of thick, creamy paper, so rich in texture as to suggest parchment, one covered in delicate red and green loops, whirls and curves, the other with ordinary typing, and in English. Hardly noting the lovely shield that headed both sheets, she rushed at the typed one:

Miss Juliet Slater:

Madam,

The Governors and Doctorate of the University of Qu'aid have the honour to inform you that your paper *The Law of Coincidence: Some Investigations and a Conclusion* has received the Avicenna Award totalling the sum of one hundred thousand pounds sterling, together with election to the Doctorate of the University.

You are instructed to attend at the University on November the fifteenth next, to receive the doctorate, bringing such of your family as may wish to be present.

Dr Abdul Kamin, Head of the Governing Body, requests me to add that he trusts you are sensible of the honour bestowed upon you.

I remain, dear Madam,

Yours sincerely,

Mark B. Audley<br>(Secretary to His Highness<br>the Emir Abdul Ahmet, UAR)

Juliet did not move. She reread the letter three times. There was no sound but the frenzied beating of a bumble bee against the slats of the venetian blinds.

There then came to her an emotion totally unfamiliar: gratitude. To Frank, and his quarter-century watch over her; to Aunt Addy whose death-bed words she had almost forgotten, whose legacy had bestowed upon her solitude and silence, and freedom to work steadily and in patience; to her mother, who had neither wanted to live with her nor insisted upon her going 'home'; to all the things which made her home: the birds and the animals, and even her great table and the bamboo and rattan chairs. All these things, living or inanimate, seemed to her in this unfamiliar exultant mood to have helped the seed within her to grow, at last, over long years, into a mighty, solidly rooted tree.

A sound, faint and regular, invaded the confused storm of feeling, and she slowly turned her head to look at the clock. She had been standing, the letter in her hand, for nearly fifteen minutes. At the same moment, there came a roar from outside: 'Josh wants tea!' followed by a hesitant rapping, and Clemence's voice: 'Juliet, are you all right?'

Juliet went slowly across the room and as slowly opened the door.

Josh instantly threw a handful of grass at her, again bellowing his desire for tea.

Clemence, after one look, put a hand on her bare arm. 'Juliet. What is it?' She had never seen Juliet's expression like this – broken up, moved, the eyes behind the enlarging lenses blazing.

Juliet silently handed her the letter, keeping the parcel in one hand, and Clemence's eyes ran down the typed sheet until her lightning perusal ended in a gasp: 'Juliet! How super! How absolutely marvellous for you – I'm *so glad* – hundreds and hundreds of congratulations . . . Oh, where's Frank. We *must* tell him.'

Then they were rushing towards the group gathered around fire and kettle, all staring in some alarm.

Frank got up and hurried towards Clem.

Josh, still demanding tea, stooped and reinforced himself with more grass. Edmund, Alice, Edith, Emma and Hugh began to raise themselves from the ground. Nanny, hearing the noise, descended from the house upon Josh with a piece of bread and jam.

Through the lengthening sunbeams of earliest evening they came towards Juliet: the young faces alight with curiosity, the older ones anxious.

Clemence thrust the letter into Frank's outstretched hand.

He read it apparently with one glance, then lifted his head and looked at Juliet's transformed face. He was too moved to speak. She had kept her gaze upon his, and now moved forward and clumsily put her arms about him and held him for a moment.

'Thanks for everything, all you done . . .' Her voice died and her arms dropped at her sides and she stood, staring, eyes bright behind the great lenses of her spectacles.

'For heaven's *sake*,' screamed Alice. 'What IS it?' and she darted at the letter, while the rest crowded over her shoulder, reading and muttering.

'Great God,' Edmund said mildly at last. 'Well, *what* a birthday present, eh? Hearty congratulations, Juliet.'

'I can't take it in – it's *too* wonderful – I'm *so glad*, Juliet,' Clemence babbled, and almost added, *So glad for Frank after years of disappointment.*

Juliet turned quickly and, darting at her, bestowed a smacking kiss. Then withdrew rapidly, like a retreating animal. 'And – and thank you, too, Clemence. Choosing me clothes and all that . . .'

'I want *more* cake.'

'Ssh, ssh, Josh – you shall have it. Pipe down,' soothed Nanny. 'Well, Juliet, ever so many congratulations, I'm sure. Will you be on television, do you think?'

'Oh God,' muttered Edmund, hastening up with the replenished kettle. 'Of course there will be interviews and all the other horrors.'

'Josh light cangles.'

'No he won't, he isn't old enough.' Nanny sat him down firmly at the edge of the display of pretty foods. 'But he may blow one out, if he asks Juliet nicely. It's her birthday, you know.'

'Josh's birthday.'

'No it isn't, Josh. I've told you, yours is—'

The argument was lost in the clamour of excited voices as they gathered around the cloth. Long greenish shadows from the great oak fell across the party.

Edmund instinctively responded to the idyllic circumstances, but even so he knew that he himself would have welcomed 'interviews and all the other horrors', while Hugh was thinking *Cripes! A hundred thousand. What I couldn't do with that – though of course, she's got a lot already, and after tax . . . Might marry her . . . no. On second thoughts. No.* And his long, thin, clever face smiled. His strong interest in the making of money, which was not encouraged in the family, sometimes took refuge in fantasy.

And Nanny's thoughts were pitying, rather than admiring. *Who wouldn't rather be twenty-four, and engaged, than win some old prize and be a dried-up old maid?*

Everyone was drinking tea and talking at once.

'Where *is* this place? I've never heard of it.'

'Oh miles from anywhere. Bang in the middle of the desert. The proper desert, not all touristy,' from Edith, with her mouth full. 'What's the UAR?'

'Where did it get a hundred thousand pounds from, if it's in the middle of a desert?' asked Clemence.

'Oil, of course—' began Hugh.

'Be quiet, everybody, please.' Frank turned to Juliet, who was sipping tea with eyes fixed on the distance. 'Juliet . . . won't you please – tell us about it?'

She turned away from the sunlit meadow.

'Not much to tell, really,' she said, in her usual flat tones. 'You know I've been working all this time on my thesis. And last year I thought, it's really finished, I can't do anything more to it. But I gave it a year . . . to kind of get . . . ripe . . . if you know what I mean. Errors to come up to the surface . . . like when Clemence makes soup. And meantime, I came across this book.'

She paused to light a cigarette. The eight faces around the picnic cloth were fixed in the same expression of eager attention, with the exception of Josh, who was drawing pictures on his plate in jam.

'Saw a copy when I was up at that library in London, so I wrote in and ordered it. Last year about this time, it was—'

'Was that the parcel all over gorgeous green squiggles and stamps? I wondered when it came,' said Alice.

'That'd be it. Then I got to thinking – it's *proved*. And I got wanting someone to *read* it and *see* it' – her voice rose – 'so I sent it to this here Arab journal.'

'What?' Clemence exclaimed before she could check herself.

STELLA GIBBONS

'I sent it to this book I got – it's a journal, really, a scientific journal that the Arabs publish. It's printed in that place – Qu'aid.'

'Ah – I begin to see. You knew about the journal before you decided to send your thesis there.'

'That's it.' She turned gratefully to Edmund. 'I kept it by me when I'd read it. Liked the smell of it, as a matter of fact.' A thin small laugh. 'It goes all over the world, so I thought that it'd be the best place. See, I sent two papers there before, not about coincidence, and they printed them.' A pause. 'I didn't show you all,' apologetically, 'because I wanted – when I did show you something – really true and big. And here' – she held up the parcel which she had kept jealously at her side – 'it is.'

'You mean your thesis is actually there, printed in . . . Is that a copy of the journal with your thing printed in it?' Frank demanded.

She nodded. 'Hope so, anyway. They sometimes give a whole number to one paper. That's why I sent it there.'

'Oh do let's see!' cried everybody, and Juliet slowly unwrapped the thick paper, tied with a heavy silvery-gold string.

A volume bound in heavy green material was revealed, neither hardback nor paper. Printed, in English, in a beautiful silver type was the word *Thought*.

Below the single, impressive word was a note in the same type, but smaller: 'This number of *Thought* is given entirely to *The Law of Coincidence: Some Investigations and a Conclusion*, by Juliet Slater of Great Britain.' A silver crescent – slender, graceful, yet conveying a remorseless hardness and strength – finished the square, ornate cover.

'What oil will do,' muttered Hugh. 'Shouldn't like to say how much *that* cost to produce.' He took it from his father's hands – almost reverently. It represented such limitless and casual wealth. 'How often does it come out, Juliet?'

'Only once a year. S'pose they can't get enough thought to make up any more copies,' and everybody laughed.

'Arabic – I suppose that's Arabic? – on one page, English on the other,' murmured Emma, as the journal went round the circle. 'How pretty it is . . .'

'Juliet!' burst out Alice, sitting back on her heels, head held high up on her swan's neck, eyes dancing. 'You're *going*, aren't you? Oh, *say* you are, sweet Juliet, dear Juliet! And can I come too, as your lady-in-waiting? Ma, you'll come, won't you?' to Clemence.

'If I'm asked, Alice. It's Juliet's party, you know,' Clemence said gently.

'Oh – the candles!' Emma exclaimed, and everyone turned to stare at the cake, except Frank, who was looking alternately at the journal he held open in his hands, and at Juliet.

Josh began to move towards the candles until Nanny, with firm clasp of one naked leg, brought him to a halt.

'No, Josh. Juliet must blow. It's her birthday. Quick, Juliet – that one's nearly out!' cried Edith.

Juliet leant across the cloth, pursed the lips from which youthful fullness had gone for ever, drew a breath into her thin chest, and blew.

It was not successful; five candles remained burning.

With the aid of Juliet's encouraging hand, Josh launched a breathy gasp. Nothing would have happened had not a skilfully directed gust from behind extinguished the remaining candles.

'Bravo!' 'Clever Josh!' everyone dutifully cried, and Emma murmured, 'Clever Nanny.'

'Practise, dear, just practise.' But Nanny looked gratified.

'Well, what will you do with your cool hundred thou?' Hugh asked, when everyone was lying back, replete with tea and excitement.

Juliet shrugged. The familiar, indifferent shrug. 'Don't know. S'pose they'll tell me all that when I get there.'

'You're going, then?' said Frank.

'Oh yes,' decidedly. 'Always did want to see the desert.' And she smiled at him, even with mischief.

'And I can come too?' from Alice once more, ignoring Hugh's sharp nudge.

'I want you all to come,' said Juliet, looking round the circle of sun-warmed, familiar faces. 'Frank and Clem and the girls and – oh – Piers'll be at school.'

'It'll be his half-term,' his mother said calmly. 'I just worked it out.'

'That's good, Piers then, and Nanny, you'll come? To look after old Josh?'

'Well, thank you, Juliet, I've always had a longing to see the mysterious East.'

'And Qu'aid is about the last chance you will have to see it,' Edmund put in, speaking with an anger and jealousy firmly controlled, because he knew that Maida was never going to allow him to go to Qu'aid with the Pennecuicks. That was why, with unusual tact, Juliet had not mentioned him. 'They're not technologized at all, took a referendum under the new young Emir five years ago, and came out ninety-three per cent for staying as they were.'

'I bet the other seven per cent were women,' Edith cried.

'I hope not,' Edmund answered amiably. 'He had them hanged.'

'It sounds the most charming place,' Hugh said, with something of Alice's drawl.

'And I'd like old Artie to come,' Juliet went on, 'but we'll have to see about that.'

'That' was generally known to be Mrs Arthur, who shared Maida's implacable jealousy and suspicion of their men's friendships with 'those people'.

'It'll be an *entourage*,' exulted Alice, doing a half roll sideways in her flowing skirts: her affectation of general ignorance did not include French, which she considered elegant.

Juliet sank the knife into the rich round cake, and for a moment, while it was tasted and criticized, the Avicenna Award was forgotten. Then Frank said suddenly: 'You do all know what the award's given for, don't you?'

Murmurs of ignorance, from mouths full of cake.

'"For an outstanding contribution to the sum of human knowledge" – *that's* what it's given for. My God – Juliet – I'm – I'm so proud of you I could burst.' He leant over and gently pressed her hand. 'And something else – *Thought*, it says here, is dedicated "To the glory of Allah the All-Powerful, the All-Wise, the All-Merciful". So you see, your coincidences arrived at an unpredictable destination. Tell me – when you first began to see – what you were after – did you ever think of that?'

'Never had the faintest,' was the answer.

## 27

This was in early September. There was much to be done before the fifteenth of November.

First, there were the reporters. It was a story that could be described as 'a lulu': hundred thousand pound prize as prestigious as the Nobel, remote desert city, mysterious young Emir, unintelligible new Law, a female discoverer of working-class origin. The press hardly knew where to start.

Frank, always aware of the value of publicity to the AIEG, kept an open drinks table and a loquacious welcome for the hordes, while seeing to it that Juliet gave a fifteen-minute press conference and thus did not become exhausted, during the exact seven days that the story lasted.

In a week it was off the front pages and onto the back; Juliet's abrupt manner and plainness had undoubtedly a damping effect, and her one appearance on television successfully revived the general public opinion that all scientists were dotty.

There was some patting on the back from some quarters for Qu'aid, because it had spent part of its oil revenues on the encouragement of science ('as if it needed encouraging,' groaned Edmund) instead of megalomanic building and Rolls-Royces;

and then the family at the House was left more or less in peace
to prepare for its journey; though almost every day someone
tapped at Juliet's door flourishing a superior magazine and
announcing, 'Juliet, here's a bit about you – want to see it?'

She would rouse herself slowly from the long chair where
she had been lying, and come to the door. But her answer was
always the same: 'No thanks. What's all the fuss about?'

But on one of these occasions, Emma replied, 'They rang up;
they want to interview you. What shall I tell them?'

Juliet glanced at the article – on the women's page of the
*Custodian* – which took umbrage at someone saying that her
thesis 'was of interest, unlike most scientific theories, to the
woman in the street'.

'Oh hell – I don't know – yes, I s'pose so, Emma.'

The dedicated youthful feminist who arrived the next
day (Edith having been sent in ignorance, by her mother,
on an errand to St Alberics) was answered by Juliet mostly
in monosyllables, and when, almost in despair, the reporter
demanded: 'Miss Slater, I want your honest opinion of the
Women's Movement, as it stands today,' and received the reply,
'I never thought about it. What is it?' she left in cold annoy-
ance, believing that she was being mocked. The interview
never appeared.

Juliet continued to decline: in energy, in speech, in her interests.

'I told you, Frank. It's what the Victorians called "a general
break-up of the constitution",' Edmund said.

'But she's not forty! She's a genius, and established as one –
and she's at the beginning of her career! What's the *matter*
with her?'

Edmund only said: 'Well, Qu'aid may buck her up – I've heard the desert air's marvellous,' as a shadow of longing passed over his face, and Frank, cursing all loving, home-making, devoted and possessive women, said no more.

But early in November the story was on the front pages again: QU'AID ELITE OPPOSES JULIET'S AWARD, bellowed the *Daily People*, and the women's page of the *Custodian*, hardly able to believe its luck, rushed into the new angle with every feminist hackle on end. The free drinks and interviewing started all over again.

The heavier dailies explained in learned detail that the organizer of the opposition to Juliet was Khalid Lebardi, the powerful ninety-year-old principal of the university, who had been shocked to the recesses of his soul by the prize being bestowed upon a woman, and was even more troubled by the proposed award of the doctorate.

'I cannot die in peace while such an act is proposed,' he was reported to have said, and Alice Pennecuick said, 'How sweet,' and Edith Pennecuick, going scarlet, said, 'It's – it's unbelievable.'

But the ancient was held in such veneration by the young Emir, whose pupil he had been, and by his fellow members of the council, and indeed by the entire 900,000 who made up the population of the desert city, that for a few days it seemed possible that award and doctorate might be refused to Miss Slater. There was much regret, and feminist outrage, in the West.

Then the Emir, who fulfilled almost completely Plato's ideal of the Philosopher King, undertook to talk with his former tutor.

In the vast, cool room of the palace, where shadows tinted with rose fell from the steep, sun-hardened walls outside, the two – the ancient near his death and the young ruler – sat cross-legged throughout the long, silent day, talking.

The fading voice and the ringing one, the latter respectfully softened, went to and fro as if in some game of verbal tennis, the brief silences between their words filled by the silvery drippling of a little fountain, falling into a basin made from Qu'aid's rose-grey stone. The air was cool, and scented by spiced and dried rose leaves.

The Emir began with a strong advantage over one whom he would not think of as an adversary: a definite idea, to be inserted into the old man's mind. Khalid Lebardi also had an idea, but one so drenched in tradition and prejudice that it resembed an emotion. The idea upheld by the Emir was pure, uncoloured fact.

The Emir, who loved and impatiently venerated his former tutor, studied the face opposite him and remembered that, though in the real world of science there were envy and prejudice, the clash of theories, and manoeuvring for fame, in the pure world of ideas where Plato and Moore and Wittgenstein had lived their ideal lives, there was only truth.

And this was the Emir's truth: in that ideal world, as in the Christian heaven, was neither male nor female. The person they were discussing was the discoverer of the Law of Coincidence, given into her mind by Allah the All-Great and All-Merciful. She was the bestower, under His power, of a new Law, 'an outstanding contribution to human knowledge'.

The day waxed slowly, from the strengthening of the sun in early morning to the terrible fire of noon when all Qu'aid slept.

Servants came to the two when they awoke, with trays of iced water and peaches freshly peeled, and bathed the firm young hands, and the feeble, knotted old ones, with rosewater.

Then they resumed their talk, while the three journalists from the West who had been permitted to enter the city to learn the decision, yawned and drank iced tea and played poker in the one hotel, and tried not to notice the pale expanse of endlessness looking in, past them and their concerns, through the windows.

When the shadows began to stretch, and violet to flow upwards into the vast sky, Khalid Lebardi was very tired. Suddenly, the philosopher and sage deserted his spirit, and, even as the muezzin pealed out from the mosques and master and pupil prepared to kneel on the mats brought by attendants, he said in the peevish voice of a child:

'The words have convinced me, my son. Let the woman have it. Her Law is a Law, and true. Praise be to Allah, who hath in His wisdom bestowed the dim light of an intelligence even upon the worm of the earth, so that it knoweth at which end more easily to grasp the leaf. If worms have intelligence, shall not women? Yes, yes, let her have it – award and money and doctorate, all.'

'Shall I inform the Western journalists, my lord?' enquired Mark Audley, the Emir's secretary and aide, who had been hovering in the vicinity throughout the day-long argument, and now approached.

'Let the dogs wait,' said the Emir.

## 28

Clemence was wondering how to endure the next two days, which would bring them, they trusted but hardly dared to hope, to the city of Qu'aid.

Even the knowledge that Josh was safe in the care of Nanny and her young man, who, most fortunately, had ten days' leave at this time and was to stay at the House, could not banish the monotony of the desert stretching away on every side into hazy distance. *A likeable young man,* Clemence reflected. *Soon sat on Nanny's yearning for the mysterious East by reminding her that he had been stationed out there for three years, and that it was all dust, smells and flies.*

The huge open-top Rolls-Royce limousine which had been awaiting them at the airport must (Hugh and Frank decided) be at least twenty-five years old, and the road was so rutted and stony that it barely qualified as a road.

At least the cranking wheels and derricks, and the noisy lorries and squalid booths of the oilfield near the airport were left behind; and at the wheel sat a Qu'aidan, silent and mysterious enough, and wrapped from corded brow to sandalled feet in speckless white.

It was of course Edith who observed that the robes were darned and patched. And the Rolls, though gleaming as to its metal and arrogantly leaping mudguards, was undeniably shaky in its responses. This was disconcerting: discomfort they had anticipated, but not cheese-paring.

'Why doesn't the Emir buy a new one? He's got millions.'

'(Piers, *will* you keep your voice down.) I don't know. I expect he can't be bothered, and in this heat I'm not surprised.'

'I approve,' Frank said. 'It's just what I should do if I were an oil millionaire. Everything top quality and old and beautifully kept. Look at that robe,' in a whisper. 'It's the finest long-staple cotton – probably belonged to his grandfather.'

When they had been gasping and mopping for hours, too uncomfortable to notice the meagre green blurs that were acacias, the only colour in the universal blinding shimmer, the driver stopped in the middle of a landscape defined only by a range of remote, pale mountains.

'I knew it,' Hugh muttered. 'Back to town for spares, stored in Michigan.'

But the driver, with smiling eyes above the snowy material hiding his lips, adjusted some device, and out came an ample canopy, which shaded the limp occupants.

He resumed his seat, and they bumped on, passing through a minor sandstorm, which thinned away to reveal rolling dunes of a darker hue than the surrounding pallor. The Rolls did its honourable best to glide, but succeeded only in shaking and banging. The road wavered ahead in a blackish line, the acacias and, more surprisingly, the mountains, had vanished.

Again the car stopped.

'We'll sleep now,' the driver announced. 'Hottest hour of the day approaching. Too much sun to go on. I'll put up the tents. We eat and drink as well.' His hidden smile widened.

With the enthusiastic help of Piers, to whom all this was decidedly preferable to maths under old Scuggers, two large tents of thin black stuff were quickly slung up on poles; cool water and dryish food produced from the Rolls' boot; and everyone, after eating in almost complete silence, retired to the tents and slept for hours.

When they awoke, the sun was rushing down towards the line of the horizon, defined and sombre in the dying light, the air was noticeably cooler, and the sky above them a divine blue-violet.

'We drive until ten o'clock. Nice and cool now,' the driver said. 'Then we sleep. And at five o'clock we wake up and eat and drive on.'

'I say, are there any wild animals?' asked Piers, who had been reflecting that the black stuff of which the tents were made was on the thin side and that many carnivores are nocturnal.

'No. Nothing for them to eat. Rock doves in the mountains, scorpions, spiders in some places. Big ones starve. They wander out here, they starve. Soon learn.'

'You won't bother to cook, will you? If we're getting to Qu'aid in the afternoon, one doesn't want much in this heat,' Clemence said.

'Oh, I cook. You like to tell your friends you dine in the desert,' with the usual half-hidden smile, but different in quality. Could it be mocking?

*

Juliet was lying full length on the cooling sand, and staring up at the sky. She had been silent since they left Oued, and Frank wondered if the heat was making her feel ill. But her expression was serene and she glanced from side to side as if interested in the pallor and unending monotony. He wondered how she saw it; for so many years he had taught her to see detail, but here there was none.

He thought with satisfaction of the raven Hrothgar, generally regarded by the Pennecuicks as a menace because it bit. Juliet had announced her wish for a raven on a family visit to the Tower of London, where she had first seen Hrothgar's peers, and had exerted herself to find one, seeking out a London pet shop (she had ended, on recommendation, by going to Harrods) and insisting upon taking it back to Hertfordshire by hired car.

It had been the first time, in Frank's nearly twenty years' knowledge of her, that she had broken through her pattern of absorption in her work to go out after another living creature – except when she had rescued wounded birds or animals. From these exceptions had grown her interest in the menagerie which lived with her, together with their numerous smells, seeds, scraps and noises.

The sky quickly darkened. From dim argent points, the stars steadily enlarged until they were rounds of burning silvery gold, hanging in loops and clusters and sprays, or throbbing in solitary splendour: the travellers' eyes returned again and again to them, and when they spoke, their voices were hushed: and, now that the faint, pathetically hoarse sighing of the Rolls' engine had ceased, such a silence surrounded them as matched the overwhelming majesty above their heads.

'I feel as if I'd never seen them before,' Emma said at last, her lifted face illuminated by the mysterious light. 'If everybody could see them like this, surely they must believe in God.'

'Or not,' Hugh muttered. Excess in any shape embarrassed him.

Hugh and Piers helped the driver bring bundles of chopped wood out of the Rolls' boot. The others lay about or roamed, between the dim, softly coloured endlessness and the throbbing splendour overhead. A fire was started, and soon an iron pot seated skilfully upon it was breathing out the smell of vegetables blended with tarragon, sage and what Alice described as 'nameless herbs'.

'They've got names, ass,' Edith corrected. '"Nameless" is sloppy and romantic. It's just that we don't know the names.'

'Oh do shut up. I wish there was someone to dance with,' and Alice whirled, as gracefully as was possible in khaki shorts. 'Isn't it all exciting? Bedouins, perhaps!'

'I do rather wonder he doesn't have a decent picnic kit; it's all part of the same stinginess,' Hugh grumbled as they sat cross-legged round the fire.

'Who? (I say, this is ravvy),' Emma said through her first mouthful.

'The Emir, of course.'

'Ne parlez pas de lui avant le domestique,' his mother warned.

'Non, ce n'est pas convenable ni prudent,' observed a calm, if muffled voice from where the domestic was seated at a respectful distance; the tone was full of laughter.

'I wish Edmund could have come,' Frank said presently. 'How he would have revelled in all this.'

'Well, it's his awful old Maida,' said Alice.

'I'd have liked Artie, too,' Juliet murmured, sounding half asleep.

'Well, *that* was *his* awful old Brenda. What ghastly females our male friends do take up with,' said Alice.

'Any man who has the arrogance to assume the responsibility for a woman's life and self-fulfilment must be prepared to give up his own petty inclinations.'

'Edith, dear,' Clemence said, 'I hope this is only a phase. It really does rather dampen ordinary conversation.'

Frank slowly lifted his head and took a long stare at the heavens. Silence fell.

Presently Juliet raised herself from the sand and wandered off into the starlit dimness; but she had not gone fifty yards before the driver uncoiled himself.

'I'll go after her – that's dangerous,' he said, and quickly followed the slight, pale figure now hardly distinguishable in the bewildering hollows and shadows.

The others sat staring.

'Why? There aren't any animals or terrorists,' said Piers at last.

'I can see why it might be dangerous. It all looks alike. She could wander on and on—'

'She could always see our fire.'

'Not if she was thinking about something else, as she usually is.'

Frank was on his feet, and staring anxiously towards a towering dune beyond which the two had disappeared.

The driver caught up with Juliet. 'Miss Slater—' He put out a long slender hand and touched Juliet's shoulder, and she turned slowly. 'Come back, please. It's dangerous to wander off like that; you can become lost easily, so easily.'

She stood, looking at him absently. 'Sorry, I've never seen anything like this before. It's like – what's in my mind.'

'Yes, but we must not lose our award-winner. Come.' And keeping a slight touch upon her arm, he led her back to the camp.

'Oh there you are. We were getting worried,' said Clemence, hearty and relieved.

'Mum.' A head round the open flaps of the tent, silhouetted against paleness and blazing stars.

'Ssh, you'll wake Daddy. What is it?'

'Well, I know this seems a mad sort of question, and sorry to wake you up, and I know a lot of brainy chaps have been chewing it over for centuries,' the breathy whisper went on earnestly, 'so it's no use asking really, but . . . You believe in God, don't you?'

'Of course,' said Clemence, wondering if she did. But of course she did; hadn't He given her everything she wanted?

'And does Daddy?'

'Not churchily. You know he calls Him the Star Maker. But he does believe.'

'Oh. Well – thanks. Sorry, again.'

'Well, you'll be all right in the morning. Go to sleep now – night-night, love.'

A kiss, accomplished by much cautious crawling, was pressed rather wetly upon her, and with, 'Thanks, Mum, it was the stars, they're a bit much, you know,' Piers was gone.

The driver suddenly announced: 'Look – Qu'aid.'

They had seen it on the horizon for some moments before he spoke, but had supposed it to be an unusually high and dark-coloured dune; it was half veiled in a sandy haze.

Now, the road having become suddenly smoother and wider, they realized that it was a wall, at least a hundred feet high, and built of some material that was either rose-tinted with grey, or grey-tinted with rose; it was not easy to decide. It was circular; its great bulk curved away on either side into the sand-filled dimness; it looked like one of the Wonders of the World, and Frank muttered as much.

'It *is* one of the Wonders,' the driver said warmly. 'I'll drive slowly to the gate, so that you can see.'

## 29

The towering height consisted of bricks so small as to suggest that their origin might be Roman; their grey-rose hue suggested coolness, beneath the pale and glaring sky. Very ancient appeared the great wall of Qu'aid, and very forbidding; its majestic, stupendous curves were unbroken by tower or loophole. Perhaps for the first time, the party from the West realized how great and how strange was the honour that had been bestowed by this astounding place upon the engine-driver's daughter from North London.

'You're all frightened,' the driver suddenly announced, still smiling behind that veil.

Frank did not quite know how to answer.

They drove round a mighty curve, and stopped before a wooden gate reaching to the wall's summit, bleached to silver by the sun, and, even as they gaped again, the driver sent out a long, arrogant note on the Rolls' horn.

After a pause, there began a creaking sound which conveyed an impression of extreme age, and the gate split without haste down the middle, the crack widening to reveal a vision of tall, flat-roofed buildings made of that same rose-grey brick lining a narrow street, the windows framed in dazzling white stone, leading the eye away into a vista of booths draped in green and silver, piled with glowing fruits, and covered by canopies of the same dark blue as the sky.

'Those green and silver flags are in honour of you, Miss Slater,' the driver said, and when Clemence muttered 'Really?' because she could think of nothing else to say, he drawled, 'Yes, "really",' adding, 'Are you pleased, Miss Slater?'

Juliet only stared. 'I like the desert best,' she said at last. 'But it's nice of them.'

'Good, good,' he said oracularly, and turned to watch a tall, slack figure in white European dress who had emerged from a kind of porter's office attached to the wall like a swallow's nest, about halfway up the height of the gate. In leisurely fashion, the man descended a ladder.

'Hullo, Audley,' the driver said, and, turning to the English party, added: 'May I present Mr Mark Audley, His Highness the Emir's personal secretary and aide-de-camp,' and followed this with a run-through of their names. His eyes were mocking.

Mark Audley said, 'How do you do – I have the honour, on behalf of His Highness the Emir Abdul Ahmet, to welcome Miss Slater and her friends to the City of Qu'aid,' and suddenly, from the crowd of people who had been thrusting slowly forward, from booth and dark doorway, something flew across and struck Juliet's shoulder.

It was a rose, of so dark a red as to be almost black, and drenched in some spice-like scent. She deftly caught it, with something of the quickness of her youth. And then a soft, continuous striking together of dark palms began – the Qu'aidans were not precisely clapping, the gesture and sound were too languid to be expressed by the Western word. But undoubtedly it was an approving noise; undoubtedly it was admiring.

'Could anyone have had a lovelier welcome!' Emma exclaimed. 'Juliet, aren't you *thrilled*?'

Juliet breathed in the scent of her rose and did not reply.

'I hope we are to have the pleasure of meeting His Highness,' Frank was saying to Mr Audley. 'You must forgive us if we're rather overwhelmed – it's like walking into *The Arabian Nights*.'

Mr Audley, who seemed sleepy, said that the first sight of Qu'aid was apt to leave that effect upon the hundred tourists who were allowed, by ballot, into the city every year, and then suggested that they might like to go to their quarters.

'Should I not! I'm one mass of sand,' but Alice's smile glided off Mr Audley's somnolent features without return.

'Well, Audley, I'm off,' said the driver and, with a sweeping gesture that included the whole party, a pause, and a lower inclination to Juliet, his white robes vanished into the mass of green, blue and silver.

'Odd type,' observed Hugh.

'Mum, did you see the old man?'

'No.' They were following the aide down the curving narrow street lined by the softly clapping crowd. 'Was there one?'

'He put the Rolls away' (Piers' interest in the Rolls was decidedly anthropomorphic) 'in a sort of shed made in that wall. Cripes! He nipped down that ladder like a kid. I expect he looks after the Rolls and the gate. That's the kind of job I'd like – but fat chance,' he ended resignedly.

Juliet walked on, over cobblestones flattened to smoothness by a thousand years of footsteps. The smell of her rose pleased her, the subdued clapping flattered her, the heat warmed her cool blood, but she was wondering how Hrothgar fared, and thinking that in the hawthorn hedges of Leete the berries must be red. This place did not seem real to her.

'This is all jolly well' – as in a dream, she heard Edith's incisive voice behind her – 'but you just let one of their own women try it on, some piece of intellectual work I mean, and see what she gets.'

'Oh Edith, *do* shut up.'

The narrow lane was opening into a vast paved square under the full blaze of the open sky. The continuous soft clapping sounded like the beating of birds' wings in the dreaming, blazing air.

'What's that, in the middle there?' Hugh demanded of Mr Audley, pointing; he was anxious to stop Edith continuing her severe enquiries into the rules governing, and the privileges permitted to, unmarried young women. Mr Audley was looking faintly hunted.

'Those are the wells,' he said, turning to Hugh with an air of relief. 'It is His Highness's wish that all tourists – visitors to Qu'aid – should see the wells before going to their resting places, because without the wells, Qu'aid could not exist, would never have been built. But of course, in your case, if you are all very tired—'

'We are tired, but it's all so marvellous that we don't feel it,' Frank said.

In a few minutes they were peering wonderingly down into a hollow some forty feet deep; steps cut in the grey-rose rock led to a swiftly running stream, greenish and ice-clear, which sent up a fresh hissing sound. From a little platform cut in the stone above it, two women were lowering jars into the current.

'I suppose it's been there for hundreds of years.' Alice's voice echoed back from the cool, resonant pit.

'Thousands.' Mr Audley smiled down at her lifted face.

'Yes – Qu'aid was built in 950BC,' Edith cut in. 'Surely you know that – and Godfrey de Bouillion – only the Crusaders never got *here*—'

'Oh blow all that – I never thought I'd hear about him and his lot for the next ten days – cripes, what a ravvy camel,' said Piers.

Mr Audley turned towards a second well, resembling the first save that it was deeper; a superb white camel saddled in green and silver was tethered by a white cord to an iron ring sunk in the surrounding circular wall, moving its arrogant great head up and down, and implying, to the fanciful, a sulky contempt for everything in the universe.

'That's the leader of His Highness's herd,' Mr Audley said. 'They are brought down here to be watered every morning at this time. The people like to see them. Here come the rest.'

Juliet withdrew her head from a prolonged stare down into the cool shaft, where miniature green ferns sprang from the rocky sides, and gazed at the approaching camels.

The procession of twenty or so, some of the mares accompanied by high-stepping small clones of themselves, was advancing across the square. The clapping grew louder.

'This herd, too,' Mark Audley explained, 'has been in Qu'aid since "time immemorial". There are legends—'

'Oh do tell us!' from Emma.

But Mr Audley was, not effectually, concealing a yawn. 'The legends are long and complicated,' was all he said, adding more quickly, 'His Highness believes that the Qu'aidans draw a – a sense of their own history and importance from the wells, and also that they like to look at the camels. Which *are* very beautiful,' he added dreamily, staring at the ground.

'Yes,' Juliet said. 'I like them better than the wells,' she concluded, and Frank dared not glance at his wife.

When they had seen the third well, which was set between the others and had retained its original rim of uncarved rock, perhaps the remnant of prehistoric mountain rocks which had protected it when it lay in open desert, Mr Audley appeared to observe the general air of droop surrounding the party and said, with as much briskness as his languid voice could manage: 'Now you must want to rest; it's only fifty yards or so to the palace.'

'One camel—' began Piers with the suspicion of a whine, due, his mother thought, to lack of sleep, heat and over-excitement. 'One of those camels,' he repeated, 'looked at me as if he *meant* to be rude. Of course, I know he can't help it, his face is – is made like that – but some people – Mum, I'm *so thirsty*.'

'Ssh, love – in a minute.'

Clemence was relieved at this point to enter the shadow of a building which filled one entire side of the square.

It was a palace of dark-rose rock, its myriad windows veiled in lacy white stone, its roofs, placed at differing heights, crowned by white crenellations. Doves swooped and crooned, white as flour, against the rich warmth; every window was a gracious half circle. There were crenellations from which the summits had crumbled, broken fretwork, streaks of darkness from some unknown source down the walls. The place breathed a gentle, sensuous mystery.

'Seems in pretty bad shape,' said Hugh, as they drew near. 'Pity, it's a marvellous piece of architecture.'

In a moment two soldiers in worn, faded silver uniforms swung open a door of dark wood carved with every intricacy of loop, curve and triangle that geometry would permit, and the party entered a cool courtyard where tall dark green trees rustled and water fell into a wide basin.

'Your rooms are here,' Mr Audley said, pointing to a circular doorway leading to a stone passage pierced with rays of sunlight. 'I'll look in about seven – it's two now – and take you to dine with His Highness. That is, if you feel up to it.'

'We'd love to!' Alice exclaimed.

'You were an ass,' said Edith, when they had gone down the passage into a room whose walls were fretted with intricate patterns of blue, yellow and brown mosaic. 'It would have been more fun to explore the city. Who wants a sort of Lord Mayor's banquet?'

'*I* want something to drink,' announced Piers. 'Where's Mr Audley? Doesn't seem to be a bell or anything. I suppose we just clap our hands like they do in books—' and before anyone could stop him, he clapped.

'Piers!' exclaimed his mother. 'That may have been very rude.' But a green-robed figure was bowing before them and beaming and staring from one face to another with liveliest curiosity.

'Er – do you speak English?' Frank began. The general lack of conventional formality, mingled with dream-like beauty, was beginning both to irritate and confuse him.

'Surely, my lord.' Now the smile was undoubtedly mocking.

'We should like to bathe, please.'

'This way,' and he glided through a doorway at the other end of the room.

They followed him through a series of dim, cool, silent chambers, spread with carpets woven in red and turquoise, their walls hung with others in tints of ginger and apricot, to where the greenish water of a sunken bath glimmered.

'I say,' called Piers, who had darted ahead to explore, 'do you know what the loo is? You just—'

'Yes, we can imagine. That will do,' his father said. 'Thank you – er—' to the green-clad figure.

'Hassan, my lord.' A giggle.

'Thank you, Hassan. Er – where is our luggage – bags?'

Hassan clapped, and a boy not much older than Piers staggered in under the load of their possessions.

*If only they'd go away, I could get at the soap*, thought Clemence, as the man and boy remained, smiling, bowing, and frankly staring. She took a hold of herself and said, in a memsahib voice traceable to some far-off ancestress, 'Thank you, you may both go now. When we have bathed, we should like something to eat.'

'It will be ready, lady. In the room you saw the first time.'

'We will . . . er . . . clap when we want anything,' Clemence added, with some discomfort. She was being mocked, and did not know what the joke was.

'And I will come,' said Hassan, with a winning smile that was not in the least deferential and, with a gesture to the staring boy.

When they both departed, Clemence sighed, 'Thank God.'

'Very peculiar,' said Hugh. 'Mum, flip a coin for first bath?'

'Girls go in first. I'll collapse if I don't get this sand off me. What gorgeous towels,' as they rapidly undressed. 'They must be two inches thick. Juliet? Not coming in?'

There followed blissful shrieks and splashing.

'I'll wait till you've finished,' Juliet said. She took a walk round the edge of the pool, examining the wall tiles and avoiding glancing at the white shapes in the water.

'Where's Juliet?' asked Frank quickly, as his freshly washed females returned to what they already thought of as the living-room.

'Calm yourself, Pa, she's bathing. She didn't want to bathe with us,' said Alice.

'I'm not fussing,' Frank said irritably, as they arranged themselves upon cushioned divans, 'but she's hardly spoken since we left El Oued.'

'She's homesick,' Emma said.

'She's *what*?'

'Homesick? *Juliet*? How on earth do you know?'

'She told me.'

'*Told* you? Juliet?'

'Yes. When we were going across the courtyard to those wells. She said, "I wish I was back home, Emmie." I could smite anyone who calls me Emmie,' she added mildly.

'Well,' Clemence shook her head. 'How – very surprising.'

'But very satisfactory,' muttered Frank.

# 30

Juliet dressed slowly, enjoying the sensation of clean clothes against her de-sanded skin. She liked, too, listening to the silence, unbroken save for the far-off ripple of a fountain, and breathing the scent of dried flowers and spices and sun-warmed stone.

But she was thinking of her birds and animals at home; it was not anxiety, but an intent, hovering interest which made her present surroundings appear unreal.

She smoothed her greying hair into its accustomed knot; she felt very tired.

'You didn't mind our beginning, did you – we were all starving,' Clemence said, with a vague feeling that deference should be paid to the award-winner.

'I'm not hungry,' Juliet said, as she settled herself next to Emma and at the trays of food.

There were piles of thin pastry a foot wide, strips of what looked like cold roasted meat, delicate little bowls full of sugar-powdered sweetmeats, and the last tray was laden with peeled apricots and peaches. Dates there appeared to be none.

'You must eat something,' Clemence said. 'You'll need your strength.'

'I'm going to explore,' said Piers, and bounded away. In a few minutes, to the secret relief of his mother, he was back.

'I say, there are a lot of little rooms like cells in a nick, only they've got cushions on the floors. I've bagged mine; it's got a horse on the wall.' He stood on his head and waved his legs.

'Mum, can't we go to sleep until it's time for the Emir's "do"? I'm nearly asleep now,' Emma said.

'Yes, if you leave time to make yourselves look really nice – I don't want us to disgrace the occasion.'

Clemence was too full of food and too sleepy to heed Edith's mutter about 'sexist rubbish', and soon the silence in the guest chambers was complete, save for that far-off falling of water upon water that recalled all the music of Vivaldi and Couperin.

As they followed Mark Audley down the corridor some hours later, awe gradually checked all comment.

Darkness had fallen: through the half circles of the windows they could see a pale sky neither blue nor violet where the round stars burned; the rooms and corridors traversed were lit by single lamps in pottery containers of antique shapes, or left in deep shadow. Hassan followed at the end of the procession, in silence. They saw no other servants.

Juliet had, without persuasion, put on a long skirt, as had the other women. As usual, hers was 'sandy or tan or something', as Alice had resignedly muttered, but the stiff, full folds gave an amplitude to her narrow body, and the blouse was flecked with gold threads. Clemence, Alice, Emma and Edith had all hung over her while she screwed up her hair; not a wisp protruded.

Clemence, watching her hastily twist it up, thought rather sadly that no one, seeing the scanty handful, would guess at its beauty when Juliet was seventeen.

Mark Audley pushed open a door and they followed him, as he stood politely aside, into the most beautiful room they had yet seen.

Small, oval, yet lofty, its long windows opened on the darkening sky, in which the very crescent of Islam was now riding; the ceiling was intricately carved white woodwork and the walls of turquoise mosaic.

In this setting, the purple robes of eleven old men seated about a wide, low table glowed as if incandescent: six were on one side of a slight young man in fiery green, and five on the other, and all wore abundant or scanty white beards. Mr Audley wore a white suit which (thought Clemence, with satisfaction) needed pressing.

'Miss Slater and her family, Your Highness,' drawled the aide, and the young man slowly and deeply inclined his picturesque head, in such a manner as to convey the impression that he had risen to his feet.

The Emir spoke rapidly and smilingly, and Mark Audley turned to Frank.

'His Highness welcomes you to Qu'aid. He hopes that you are refreshed. He asks me to tell you that these – er – gentlemen are the learned doctors of the University of Qu'aid.'

He paused as the Emir paused, and there followed an exhaustive list of the doctors' full names and titles.

Clemence had been wondering where they were to sit.

At the conclusion of Mr Audley's recitation – 'and the most Venerable and Learned Ayatollah Khalid Lebardi, Ruler under Allah the All-Merciful of the University of Qu'aid' – she suddenly noticed a smaller table with attendant cushions at the side of the doctor on the extreme right.

His speech concluded, Mr Audley was silent, and she found servants – appearing as usual from nowhere – gently ushering mother and daughters towards it. Mr Audley had put two fingers under Frank's elbow, and was steering him towards the empty place beside the Emir.

'Tomorrow evening, when she has received her doctorate, Miss Slater will take the seat, now empty, at His Highness's right hand,' Mr Audley was murmuring as they went, and Frank, trying to avoid falling over numerous cushions, managed to mutter that it was a great honour.

'Mum! They've put us by ourselves at that little table because we're *women*! It's an *insult* – can't you tell that Audley—'

'Edith! Be quiet at once.' And Edith, who was (in spite of ardent feminism, and an unusually good brain, and an obstinacy amounting to a form of genius) only fifteen, was quiet.

And then, to Clemence's relief, they were comfortably seated and Frank was settled on the right of the Emir, with Hugh a few places away and Piers . . . why, Piers had been shown to a little table where sat a boy of his own age, all green robes and sparkling inquisitive eyes. Hands were before her own eyes, holding out food on trays which (and her eyes took nearly a minute to take in the fact and to believe it) were made of gold.

So was the fretted surface of the table. Clemence clawed a small handful of something exotic out of the great tray and put a piece of it into her mouth, and wished that she were at home, reading *Mrs Pepperpot* to Josh. The feast proceeded, for her, like a dream, beautiful to look at and disagreeable to experience. Edith muttered indignantly at intervals, Frank was conversing animatedly and apparently interestedly with the Emir, Piers and his bird-eyed companion were exchanging sentences and grins. Dish after dish appeared, was tasted, and vanished. The air remained cool; the stars burned larger, and the doctors continued to stare at Juliet, composedly eating, and she stared back.

Finally, sweetmeats and bowls of scented water appeared. When all had nibbled, and dried their fingers on fine linen napkins, the Emir rose, bowed to the party from the West, and left, followed by the doctors in a tottering procession with no signs of farewell to anyone.

They disappeared down a dimly lit corridor. Piers waved enthusiastically to his table companion, who replied with a gesture which caused them both much amusement, and which his mother resignedly supposed to be mildly obscene and native to the universal world of boyhood. The servants stood like statues in their green and silver, and the lamps flickered in the faint wind blowing from the desert.

Mark Audley lounged towards them.

'I expect you'd like to get to bed,' he suggested.

'Oh please!' Clemence's exclamation was irrepressible, though faces of dismay were exchanged among the young.

'I'll come back with you for twenty minutes, if that's all right? And put you in the picture for tomorrow.'

'We'd rather hoped we could wander round in the morning and sight-see,' Alice said, using her lovely eyes. 'What time is the – the ceremony?'

'At noon – after the muezzin.'

'Oh, then if we got up early?'

They were all straggling down the same corridor by which they had entered, now.

'The university is the thing to see; you shall be taken over that, if you like. The ordinary tourist isn't allowed inside,' Mr Audley went on.

'The Emir speaks excellent English, I greatly enjoyed our talk,' Frank said.

'I am certain that His Highness did too. Most of the VIPs who are allowed into Qu'aid are thundering bores and he just won't see them. That's my job.'

By now they were back in their living-room and feeling that Mr Audley, odd though he was in some ways, was an old friend.

'I'm sleepy,' announced Piers, and fell onto some cushions.

'Yes – off you come.' And Clemence, with an apologetic smile at Mr Audley, whisked him away.

'It's a short ceremony, but formal,' Mr Audley turned to Frank. 'It would be appreciated if your ladies wore long dresses and – er – jewellery . . . if they have brought any.'

'Oh – no – we were looking forward to buying—' Alice checked herself.

'The markets in Qu'aid do not sell to tourists.'

'Oh. Yes, of course.'

'Mr Audley, what else?' asked Frank.

'At half-past eleven a small guard will come to escort you to the university.'

'Is it those towers you can see from the windows, not exactly towers, round golden things – domes?' Edith asked.

'Yes, Miss Edith, that is the University of Qu'aid. The sands come up to its gate, which faces towards the desert. To get into it, you will have to walk round the wall – er – I'm afraid it may be rather hot, but sunshades will of course be provided—'

'Ravvy – I adore sunshades.'

'Alice, will you please be *quiet.*'

'—and we shall join the assembly in the great hall, the students will of course be present, all five hundred of them, from all over the Muslim world. There is great curiosity,' turning to Juliet, 'to see and hear Miss Slater.'

'*Hear* me? Have I got to say a speech or something?'

'It would be appreciated. I shall translate for you.'

'But what'll I say? I've never done a speech before.'

'Something, certainly, about the immense honour you are receiving,' said Frank. 'Because it *is* a great honour, you know – equal to the Nobel Prize.'

'S'pose so,' she said amiably.

## 31

The door leading into the University of Qu'aid was of cedar-wood, protected from the sun by a sloping hood of thin green marble in which was thinly incised a sentence in Arabic. The bronze tracery covering the wood was curved, flowing, intricate beyond the power of the eye to follow; the door was twenty feet high and it looked out at the shimmering, undulating desert.

The guard halted, dropping their rifle butts with imprecision on the sand. Their uniforms were not impeccable, and their demeanour far from alarming; there was the usual staring and smiling.

Mark Audley turned to the party beneath the sunshades.

'Miss Slater, will you pull that, please,' and he indicated a green silk rope hanging from the marble hood.

'I say, Mr Audley,' said Piers, 'will there be anything to drink? People *die* of thirst, don't they?'

'After the ceremony, old chap.'

'What does that say?' Piers went on, indicating the Arabic rune above their heads.

'Allah is Great, and Learning, beneath His Hand, is All. Miss Slater, please . . .' for Juliet was looking away into the desert.

'Learning damn well isn't, when you're thirsty . . .' Piers' mutter was checked by his father. who whipped out a flask and handed it to him.

'Miss Slater?'

Juliet turned slowly and looked at him.

'The bell, please. All right, guard. Er – dismiss.'

He nodded to the half-dozen, who slouched, rather than marched, away around the wall's vast curve and were at once lost to memory as they were to sight.

'Do I look all right?' Alice whispered to Hugh; her lacy white dress suggested a transparent cloud in the sunlight. Hugh took no notice.

'Emma! *Do I look all right?*'

'Yes, truly. It's one of your pretty mornings.'

'You are an angel. More than some people are.'

Juliet pulled the cord. There was silence. And then, far away, somewhere behind the door, a sweet and solemn tolling began – full, majestic, and suggesting the heaviness of years.

The door slowly swung wide, and revealed an old, old man with a broad snowy beard. Robed in flowing green sashed with purple, he bowed almost to the sand.

Their gaze travelled beyond him, across a vast courtyard, paved in white and purple mosaic, shining in the sun. All around stood buildings in the rose-grey rock of Qu'aid, towering into flat roofs or gold bubbles against the blue-black of the sky. There was no one in sight. The final echo of the bell died into silence.

The old man bowed again; three times; to Frank, to Hugh, and finally to Piers. One glance, faltering and guilty, went towards the women, then the wrinkled eyelids were lowered. He said something to Mark Audley.

'He is asking me to tell the visitors from the West that his father, grandfather and great-grandfather, as far back as the written records are preserved, were porters to the door,' the aide explained. 'The office is hereditary.'

Smiles of genuine wonder, admiration and kindness were bestowed upon the ancient, who, while continuing to bow deferentially, emanated a kind of modest pride.

'Where are all the students?' Edith demanded, in a voice less confident than usual, as they began to cross the great courtyard.

'In the Hall of Mathematics. They have a day without learning because of your visit, Miss Slater.'

'I bet they're pleased,' from Piers.

'Indeed, no. It is looked upon as a sacrifice, made in honour of the Law and its discoverer.'

'Yes,' Juliet said suddenly. 'The Law was here, you know. I only discovered it.'

'This is perhaps the one place in the world where that fact will be continually kept in mind,' Mr Audley said, with unaccustomed seriousness and an air of genuine admiration.

Edith, a little recovered from the unfamiliar awe imposed by respect for Juliet's Law, said, after a pause: 'No *girls* here, of course.'

'Oh no, Miss Edith. But you wouldn't expect that, would you?'

'No, I certainly shouldn't!' A mutter. 'And do the boys ever protest? Stage sit-ins? That kind of thing?'

Mr Audley uttered a slight laugh, and for a time there was silence. The shadow of a vast, gold-domed building began to creep over them.

The silence and the absence of human beings were beginning to irritate Clemence. She would have welcomed crowds and chatter, even television cameras. It was as if Qu'aid was deliberately demonstrating to them that here was the way for human beings to live: in remoteness, in simplicity, and slowly. *But it's only because the Emir owns an oilfield,* she thought, *and we couldn't live in the rather odd way we do if it weren't for Frank's money.*

She recalled the explanations, which she had by now reduced to a formula, that had to be made to new acquaintants, and sighed. Then she noticed the delicious delicacy of Alice's appearance, and saw Piers obviously resisting an impulse to do a handstand on the historic mosaic, and knowledge of her children rushed over her with grateful love.

Mr Audley was pulling another silk cord, and this time another and less impressive door opened into a smallish room brilliant with mosaic, and crowded with smiling, interested faces. Everyone broke at once into that soft clapping, and Clemence thought: *This is better.*

There followed many presentations of the smiling faces to Frank and Hugh, with benevolent nods to Piers.

Clemence and her daughters stood slightly apart, Alice and Emma respectively flirtatious and cheerful, and Edith more or less successfully concealing indignation. No one was introduced to them, but two or three of the students, and one elderly man of a distinguished appearance and manner, ventured to present themselves on the male side in admirable if formal English.

At length, Mr Audley inconspicuously gathered his party together, and led them, followed by the other guests, along another long, mosaic-lined corridor.

The oval tops of windows, the shafts of light, the soft slap of slippers on stone seemed to continue for an hour. The girls' slippers, silently handed to them on entering the reception room, were crimson, sewn with silver thread, but Alice regretted her pretty heels. It was the longest corridor yet.

*We must be going somewhere very important,* Clemence thought. She was prepared for the size of the hall into which the corridor at last opened: vast, rounded, where snow-white mosaic walls were traced with Arabic runes in purple and the dull gold dome high, high above their lifted heads shed a dim glow. And the hall was full of men; hundreds upon hundreds of white turbans bound with purple cords swayed towards the English party as they entered a small gallery set high in the wall, curtained and furnished with chairs.

But where was Juliet?

The Pennecuicks were glancing round, a little alarmed.

'Audley's taken her down to the platform,' soothed Hugh.

'God, what a place!' his father was saying without irreverence.

They arranged themselves on the ebony and mother-of-pearl chairs, Edith looking more and more critical as she realized that, except for her mother, her sisters and herself, there was not one woman present.

'There's Juliet!' Piers exclaimed. 'Gosh, she does look sandy!'

'She always does. Do be quiet. I want to look,' from Emma.

'Wouldn't it be ravvy if one of the old fogeys had a stroke at the sight of her?'

'Edith! That really is – not on, saying that sort of thing.'

'Well, I hate them, and when I get home I'll start my campaign.'

'When you get home, dear, if you like. But not here, please,' her mother said quellingly.

The cedarwood platform was paved with squares of white and purple mosaic, inlaid, as Frank pointed out, 'with mathematical symbols, and these are the mathematical colours'.

Six of the old doctors sat in a half circle on one side of an empty chair; five on the other; the last place on the right was empty. There was another empty seat, which Emma whispered was 'rather gorgeous', set slightly above the others and apart from them.

'I bet that's for the Emir – I bet he wishes it was on his state camel, I bet he rides splendidly,' said Piers.

'*I* bet you'll fall over, if you fidget like that . . .'

There was a stirring in the vast audience, and it swayed to stand as the Emir entered, wearing the plainest of white flowing robes. Clemence noticed how dark and slender his fingers looked, as, seating himself, he spread them delicately upon his knees, and turned his fierce young profile attentively to Mr Audley.

Standing beside the Emir, Mark Audley had begun to speak slowly in Arabic, with occasional pauses and glances towards the box where the Western visitors were sitting; his voice sounded indolent, low and very clear, as the perfect acoustics of the place wafted it to and fro. He ceased, then turned fully to the gallery, and began again, this time in English.

'We of the University of Qu'aid welcome the newest giver of knowledge to mankind, and her friends. Miss Juliet Slater was born of parents who had no veneration for learning.' (Five hundred faces were turned towards the box, as if hoping to detect these unworthy progenitors.) 'The friends accompanying her, and to some extent sharing her honour, adopted her as their own child, fostered her learning, gave her quiet places in which to study and to meditate. Under the hand of Allah the All-Merciful, the knowledge He had planted within her – er – within her . . .' ('Didn't want to say "brain",' whispered Edith fiercely.) 'It grew, as the watered seed grows in the rich earth. Let us praise these friends and thank them for their share in giving under Allah this new Law to mankind.' He raised one hand. 'These are the words of your Emir,' he called. Then he let it fall, and sat down.

The familiar soft clapping began, a sound in a dream, suggesting gaiety and joy; all the five hundred dark faces turning towards the gallery were alight and smiling. Juliet, who was sitting forward in her chair, looked bewildered and pale.

Frank, too, was leaning forward. He took in every detail of the astonishing scene. His mind's eye saw St Alberics high street on a spring morning twenty years ago, and a pale, sullen young face surrounded by beautiful hair lifting in the wind.

It had come true: his ludicrous dream, persisted in, followed steadily in spite of incomprehension and suspicion and disbelief on his own part, as well as that of others. Surely the Law itself had played its part in bringing itself to birth on the planet! Every incident had been drawn to work towards the one end.

Someone was speaking again. A thin, faint, shaking voice was wavering across the soft dimness of the air. The voice sounded very, very old indeed, and rather cross.

'Who's that?'

'Goodness knows. Do be quiet.'

The speech did not last long. Mr Audley was studying the toes of his sandals, with bent head. The cooing of doves could be heard beyond the windows.

The ancient voice ceased on a solemn, querulous note, and the doctor shakily reseated himself.

Mr Audley had taken a white object from his pocket and was studying it as if to convince himself that it was safely there.

'That's the cheque . . . gosh!' whispered Hugh.

'*Will you shut up.*'

Mr Audley had risen again, and was speaking in Arabic. When he ceased, there was an immense rustle through the audience, suggesting a sigh. The Emir was looking fiercer than usual, and Hugh observed gleefully that 'something was up'.

Mr Audley had begun again in English.

'The most learned Doctor Khalid Lebardi feels it his solemn duty, as Head, under Allah the All-Wise, of the university, to remind His Highness the Emir and the privileged students of the University of Qu'aid that this is the first time, in the thousand years of its history, that the Avicenna Award has been . . . bestowed upon a woman.'

He paused, moving his lips uncertainly and looked, as if for help, at Juliet, who was staring out unseeingly across the audience.

'The most learned doctor, as you have just heard, does not dispute the award, but he resents the fact that he, in his most honourable position as principal, is required to bestow this tremendous honour upon . . . upon an inferior – in short, upon a woman.' He paused, and the silence hung and quivered.

'Shame!'

Edith's cry rang like that of some young, furious wild bird, and every face in the vast hall swung round to stare upwards.

*If I could die or vanish*, thought her mother.

Mr Audley, having given Edith the satisfaction of seeing him give a noticeable start, addressed the audience again, briefly and in Arabic, then turned to Juliet and spoke to her in English.

'Will Miss Slater be so gracious as to express to the doctors of the University of Qu'aid her gratitude on receiving this great honour?'

Juliet stood up.

All the doctors instantly looked down at the floor, removing the glare of icy, incredulous amazement they had been directing upon the unrepentant Edith, who had folded her arms and was glaring back.

Piers and Alice were repressing giggles; Emma looked pale and awed, and Hugh disgusted, while their father was blessing the Emir's prohibition of the media being present.

Into the stillness came, thin and almost expressionless, Juliet's voice: 'Doctor Khalid Lebardi may feel a bit less upset about me having the doctorate if he remembers that it isn't me what – who – is having it. It's the *Law* that's having it. It's called Slater's Law because I discovered it. But it has . . . it's . . . the Law has its own honour. I shall use the title "Dr Slater" because I'm very, very pleased at having discovered the Law. I only wish my mum – mother – was here to see it. She wouldn't half – she would have been so proud of me. But not my father. He would agree with Doctor Khalid Lebardi, not believing in women having minds, he didn't. So – thank you, Emir, and the university – but thank you especially Dr Lebardi. It's *here*. The Law is here for ever. When I'm dead, and all the people I know are dead, the Law will still be here in Qu'aid. For ever.'

She stopped, looking helplessly around as if the effort of expressing so much had taken away her normal senses. Frank thought that she was going to faint. The old doctor in the seat nearest to her rose, tottered towards her, indicated with an outstretched claw the place where she was to sit; then, as she did not seem to understand but stood staring dazedly, he gingerly extended the claw, snatched at her hand, and guided her into the empty chair.

At the end of Mark Audley's translation of her speech the dream-clapping broke out again. This was the sound that, for the rest of their lives, would mean to the family from the West: Qu'aid.

## 32

To the dismay of the Pennecuicks, they were informed, after a peaceful family lunch in the privacy of their rooms, that the Emir and the doctors would have the honour of attending them at the Great Gate when they set out for El Oued at five that evening. Edith became slightly hysterical. 'I did think we'd seen the last of those old bores. I can't *stand* it. Can't I go and sit in the Rolls while they're rabbiting away?'

'And can I?'

'No, Piers, you can't – neither of you can. It would be dreadfully rude. You'll just have to stick it out.'

'It will be a very short ceremony,' soothed Mark Audley, who had come to break the news. 'Er – it's my fault, I'm afraid. After Miss Edith's interjection, I left a bit out of His Highness's speech this morning. I've got to put it in this evening.'

'Oh do tell us! Was it something rude?'

'(Alice, be quiet.) Oh, in that case, Mr Audley . . .'

'I say, I do wish you'd all call me Mark.'

'All right, Mark. Will the speech be long?'

Mr Audley laughed and ruffled Piers' hair. 'No – quite short – I promise you.'

The packing was done, the sun was beginning, under the mercy of Allah, perceptibly to decline.

They sat in the shadowy room, where red-gold light struck through the windows, in silence; very tired; half unwilling to leave this place that was a fairy tale, half longing to feel about them again the dear familiarities of home.

Half-past four. Here was Mark, accompanied by three servants, who took up the luggage and bore it away, silently as ghosts, along the long, sun-pierced corridor, down the winding staircase, out into the great market square where the booths glowed, and as they followed once again there broke out soft clapping.

The Great Gate stood wide, and beyond it the desert stared past Qu'aid in endless pale waves, and beside the gate were the twelve doctors, sheltered from the declining sun by a billowing purple canopy held aloft by six servants, and beside them – Piers gasped with delight – the Emir mounted on his white camel.

'Gosh! I believe he's going to ride with us. Oh, hurrah!'
'*Piers.*'

Mark had come to the side of the great kneeling beast, and was consulting a sheet of paper. A small crowd had collected and was watching every movement of the visitors.

'This concerns the people of Qu'aid,' Mr Audley said, after some sentences in Arabic which produced a ripple of laughter and nodding heads. 'Your Emir desires me to say to you what I – er – omitted to say this morning: it is this. Slater's Law' – here he turned and bowed to Juliet, standing beside him – 'is a law which injures no one. Marie Curie, daughter of Poland,

to whom the world owes, with her husband, the discovery
of radium, did not receive the honour that the University of
Qu'aid has bestowed upon Miss Slater and radium has not been
entirely beneficial to Man. But about Slater's Law there is an
aura both of pure knowledge and innocent magic belonging
to an earlier world. Slater's Law does not kill. All that can be
said about its destructive powers' – and here he looked towards
the Westerners and slyly smiled – 'is that it has destroyed,
once and for ever, one of your sayings. Never again will any
inhabitant of this most unhappy planet be able to say with
enjoyable astonishment, "What a coincidence!"'

The faint clapping began again. Clemence noticed, with
mixed feeling, that one of the servants was assisting Piers to
mount the Emir's camel. The little boy settled himself, his
face suggesting in glory the setting sun, in front of the rider,
whose fierce features were smiling.

'His Highness begs that you will allow your son to ride
with him,' Mr Audley said hastily. 'It is a great treat always
for his own sons.'

'Of course – how very kind. Please thank His Highness.'

And now – oh dear – the old doctors had somehow got hold
of Juliet and were talking to her. *If ever I get out of this place,
I'll never stir from Wanby again*, Clemence promised herself.

But they were moving at last. The doctors were making
stiff ceremonial bows, the camel had jerked itself to its feet in
three awkwardly graceful movements, the Rolls was bumping
towards them. Somehow they were all safely inside, and Mark
had climbed in with them, and the luggage was being stowed
in the boot, and the Great Gate of Qu'aid was slowly shutting

away the grey-rose and green-shaded booths and its smiling citizens.

Edith's sharp voice began: 'Mr Audley – Mark – it was funny. Some of the servants didn't behave like servants at all. Their manners were bad.'

(*And so are yours, my daughter. Must be taken in hand, and soon.*)

'Not really funny, Miss Edith. Some of those "servants" were the Emir's relations – cousins or nephews.'

'Oh, ravvy,' from Alice.

'There has been intense curiosity in Miss Slater and indeed in all your family,' Mark Audley said to Frank. 'But of course, to show it, especially towards the ladies of the party, would have been gravely discourteous. Barbaric. Unheard of. Western,' he ended smoothly. 'So, some of the younger ones, wild young men used to having their own way, had themselves dressed as servants, and waited on you.'

He shrugged. The car here ran into a stifling, stinging, miniature sandstorm, tinged scarlet by the falling sun, and the women wrapped their heads in scarves. The camel with its burden loped easily alongside, white and wraith-like in the haze. Piers was invisible, having huddled into the breast of the Emir's voluminous robes.

'How do wild young men let off steam, then?' Hugh demanded, as they emerged from the pallid cloud. 'It's a marvellously beautiful place, of course, but pretty boring, I imagine, stuck here year in and year out.'

'Camel-racing, gambling, hunting, mild drugs.' (A nudge from Hugh.) 'And of course they are always free at any time to leave Qu'aid.'

'Well, why don't they? I would,' said Edith.

'Because it would be for ever,' Mark Audley answered, after a pause. 'The law is: if you leave (unless of course you are a student) you may never return.'

The camel reluctantly ceased its long, swift pacing, rearing its sneering head back on the long, scarlet leather rein. Then it began, at a word from the Emir, slowly to kneel.

The Rolls slid to a stop on the road covered with sand from the recent storm, and Emma noticed how their shadows ran grotesquely away from them, dark on the pallor. Glancing behind her, she saw, against the setting sun, at a distance of perhaps half a mile, a number of soldiers mounted on white camels.

The Emir said, in English, lifting his right hand: 'Goodbye. May delights and good fortune go with you.'

Piers, disentangling himself from the protective draperies, paused to bestow a jerky bow, then raced towards the car and climbed in next to the driver. The Emir spoke in Arabic to Mark Audley, who replied. The camel rose; the hawkish face smiled above them for a moment. Then the great beast raced off into the red light, past the escort, and the Emir and his bodyguards vanished behind the dunes.

'Oh, are you coming on, Mark? Goody.'

This, of course, came from Alice.

'At His Highness's express wish, and at my request.'

'As far as that ghastly El Oued?'

'Yes. I shall see you safe aboard the Oil Plane.'

This was a very smart machine, nicknamed thus by the men of business who flew into El Oued.

Suddenly it was night, with soft eerie shadows in a cool wind. Edith let down the windows.

Juliet was seated beside Frank, her head turned to watch the soft pallor and the shapelessness going by; sometimes a gap between dunes revealed the Great Place itself, the endlessness, looking in at this moving dot, under a rising moon that had deepened in colour from water silver to a glowing gold.

Juliet's expression, Frank thought, was more serene than he had ever seen it, yet her face also looked noticeably older. He wondered what she felt about it all – the immense honour, the strangeness and the beauty.

Probably he would never know.

'When do we camp? I'm starving,' said Piers.

'In an hour – we'll go to bed early, then we can start at dawn.'

It seemed a long time before the black tents were up, the fire lit, and the servant, a smiling person, was boiling water, opening tins, and stealing glances at the girls – which Alice with flirtatiousness, Edith with indifference, and Emma with childish friendliness, returned.

## 33

Next day, when they had been driving along that familiar road for some hours, and were entering a region of low rock-strewn hills, Juliet suddenly exclaimed, 'Oh please slow down,' and pointed.

On a rocky ridge high above the nearest dune, the last outcrop of the vanishing heights, an ibex was standing, looking down at them. Its great curved horns glowed amber-white against the blue of the sky. Its large proud innocent eyes surveyed, without fear, the intruders below. For perhaps a moment it stood, then turned and sprang lightly over the rise of the rock, away into the desert.

Frank motioned the driver on.

'That was Qu'aid saying goodbye,' said Emma at last.

'And good riddance, judging by his expression,' said Hugh.

'Kind of scornful, like the camels,' Piers added.

'Oh no, Piers, not scornful,' said Emma. 'I don't know what he was saying, but I felt it was something.'

'"Instead", perhaps,' her father said.

'"Instead"?'

'It's from a poem by Auden. "Clear, unscalable, ahead/Rise the Mountains of Instead."'

'That's the way you've brought us up, isn't it, Daddy?' Emma said, in a moment.

'Tried to, darling.'

If he had a favourite among his horde of children, it was she.

'Oh,' Alice sighed suddenly. 'Won't it be lovely to be home.'

'You ought to apologize to Mark for that,' said Clemence. 'It's his country.'

'But I share your feelings, Miss Alice,' Mark said, fervently.

*Him and his Miss Alice*! thought Clemence. She turned to Juliet.

'Decided what you're going to do with your millions yet?'

'I hadn't thought – I was thinking about Hrothgar, wondering if he's been all right.'

'So long as no one teases him,' said Edith, who had, from her chosen study of Anglo-Saxon literature, named the interesting bird.

In another hour they were sitting in the shadow of the car and drinking scalding tea. The hills were low blue shades on the horizon; the black, ill-made road ran ahead through featureless flatness. Juliet said suddenly, staring out across its monotony:

'I'll be glad to be home.'

'Will you? Will you really, in spite of it all being so beautiful and strange here?' Frank asked, turning to her.

'Yes.' She nodded. 'That's why I said "no" when he asked me.'

'*Asked* you? Who did? What?' exclaimed Edith.

'The old doctor. Not the one who got uptight about me getting the award. The one what – who – showed me into the chair.'

'Well I never,' cooed Alice. 'I saw him rabbiting on, and I hoped he wasn't cursing you.'

'And he was asking you to stay on at Qu'aid?' Clemence marvelled.

'Oh yes, Mrs Pennecuick,' Mark Audley put in. 'I translated for him. "We, the doctors of the University of Qu'aid, invite you to remain here, within the university, as a doctor, to add to its honour and the richness of the learning—'

'I bet *that* nearly choked him,' from Edith.

'It's the formula they use when they invite anyone to join the faculty. About every fifty years or so,' Mark said.

'Wow!' exclaimed Emma. 'That's better.'

Juliet had taken out a crumpled piece of paper from an old notecase in her jacket pocket, and was inspecting it in a detached manner.

'Is that the cheque?' Hugh asked respectfully, and she nodded.

'I'll buy you all super presents, anyway,' she said at last, and put the cheque away.

But Frank was not satisfied.

'But why didn't you accept?' He leant forward, looking earnestly into the tired, sallow face from which all trace of youth had faded. 'I should have thought—'

'Oh, I couldn't. You're my family, like.'

She looked round on the listening circle of faces and slowly smiled. 'I couldn't leave you all now – you, and my animals. Oh no. I couldn't stay there. I told him so. Straight.'

And now time began to rush by like a rising wind; with Alice married to a rich, silly, likeable man thrice divorced; with Edith practising feminism and journalism, living with her small daughter in a cottage in Watford; with Emma a nurse; with Hugh finding a spiritual home in the City; with Piers working steadily through Hayleybury and Cambridge towards Medicine; and with Josh, unexpectedly, showing a talent for the piano that blossomed into modest but gratifying success. And Clemence and Frank were so occupied, with pain and joy in their children, with the ever-increasing growth, all over the world, of the AIEG, that their hair whitened and their bodies grew feebler without their taking much notice.

Juliet had settled into an early middle age, going about her daily routine of tending and observing the animals, that were replaced, as the years took them away, by others equally well cared for.

She smoked. She read: unusual books about mysteries at sea, and travel in the few remaining lonely places of the Earth. The oak tree beside her door, the 'green castle' beneath which old Hrothgar lay buried, was her reception salon, and there, in the months of summer, came grey-haired Edmund to sit opposite her (the little woman in the big cane chair who looked seventy but was in fact not yet fifty) and grumble to her about contemporary poetry; and here a bent, tired Arthur Robinson timidly brought his pert grandchildren. Her books of reference and her table were dusted meticulously, but never used; she worked no more.

Arthur once remarked to Edmund, after one of these visits, that whenever they saw Juliet nowadays she was lying back in that chair. And she had taken to employing a daily help.

'Burnt out at last,' was the glum answer, and Arthur, being on the whole a cheerful and contented man, changed the subject.

One summer morning of celestial beauty, her dog Young Robert, second successor to the first Robert, was heard barking urgently outside the door of her house. It was nearly breakfast-time; Clemence put aside the newspaper which she was reading in bed while awaiting her tray, got up with some difficulty, and went slowly to the open window.

'Robert – what is it, boy?'

More anxious barking and whining.

Clemence and Frank got there just as her eyes slowly opened. The yellowish face looked up at them from her narrow bed, and then the familiar ugly little hand crept out from beneath the coverlet towards them, and Frank clasped it, and held it fast in his own. The dog whined.

'Sorry – so tired. I can't get up,' she whispered. 'You can't imagine how tired I am . . .'

The whisper died away, and her eyes closed again. But her lips moved, and bending down to the worn, withered face, Frank thought that the words he just caught, as her breathing stopped, were: 'Love to all.'

# THE HISTORY OF VINTAGE

The famous American publisher Alfred A. Knopf (1892–1984) founded Vintage Books in the United States in 1954 as a paperback home for the authors published by his company. Vintage was launched in the United Kingdom in 1990 and works independently from the American imprint although both are part of the international publishing group, Random House.

Vintage in the United Kingdom was initially created to publish paperback editions of books bought by the prestigious literary hardback imprints in the Random House Group such as Jonathan Cape, Chatto & Windus, Hutchinson and later William Heinemann, Secker & Warburg and The Harvill Press. There are many Booker and Nobel Prize-winning authors on the Vintage list and the imprint publishes a huge variety of fiction and non-fiction. Over the years Vintage has expanded and the list now includes great authors of the past – who are published under the Vintage Classics imprint – as well as many of the most influential authors of the present. In 2012 Vintage Children's Classics was launched to include the much-loved authors of our youth.

For a full list of the books Vintage publishes,
please visit our website
www.vintage-books.co.uk

For book details and other information about the classic authors we publish, please visit the Vintage Classics website
www.vintage-classics.info

www.vintage-classics.info

Visit www.worldofstories.co.uk for all your
favourite children's classics